G000254932

THE WATCHER'S LULLABY

By Pippa Harvey

I

Cover design by: Andy Magee

This book is dedicated to my dad, Norman Smith,
who loved the Suffolk and Norfolk countryside.

PROLOGUE

The wind is constant, stirring the leaves and grasses into a dance that mimics the coastal breeze. Intermittently it roars against your ear drum, reminiscent of the surge of the tide or the echoes in a shell pressed to your ear.

Fragments of this countryside are near-exact replicas of the same spot years, decades and centuries before. This ancient earth clings to the past more than elsewhere. Holds secrets and grudges. Buries tales of folklore and tales of truth, so the thin line between them smudges and fades.

She is bound to this place, woven into the landscape, like the thread that pierces and binds patchwork together. She waits and she watches. Like the soil, she lies close to the living, entwined with roots, compounded by the footprints of those who came after her. But her interest is particular; the first to perceive the quickening, she is ignited by the sparks of new life.

She does not age, but the years are not kind to her: they bring no enlightenment, only the relentless pain of loss, overshadowed by unspoken accusation. The sharp sting of betrayal.

She will not fail those who follow; she is determined.

She waits and she watches.

Then she intervenes.

CHAPTER 1

Bea

"Ready?"

I struggle to twist my body and fasten the seat belt over my enormous belly. *If I'm this big at six months, how the hell will I manage in nine?*

"Guess so."

I have that nervous, giddy feeling like a child who's eaten too much sugar. The chill of the car is piercing, despite my human-incubator-temperature, and I'm glad of my coat and scarf. Scraped remnants of frost streak the windows and my breath steams in front of me.

We're parked a few doors down from our small Victorian terrace house. It feels strange looking at it from the outside, like departing visitors. Our home for the past five years, it's been the focal point of many ups and downs, and I'm not sure that I'm ready to leave it behind. A lump rises in my throat.

Seb catches my expression and places a hand on my knee. "I know. It'll be okay."

"We've so many memories here though. Parties and barbeques... when your mum met my parents... where you proposed," my voice quivers. In my head I also recalled the tensions. The bitter disappointments. Drips of blood on the bathroom floor.

As if reading my thoughts, Seb frowns.

He's so sure about this move. For him, relocating to Suffolk feels right, but I still have reservations. I gave in, eventually, but I'm still left with doubts. Now the moment has come for us to leave, and my stomach is tight.

The removal team stack the last of the boxes into the lorry. They were amazed at the paraphernalia that emerged from our two-up, two-down home, the music and book collection accounting for a fair percentage of it.

Seb mutters something about having one last check and struggles to unfold his lanky frame to clamber out of the car. He disappears behind the front door for a couple of minutes then hands over the keys to the buyer who is waiting outside, shaking her hand. I've met her before: she seems nice enough, enthusiastic and young. Her parents had clearly helped her take her first step on the property ladder. I wave to her and wind down the windscreen to call good luck.

Seb straps himself in. Before he turns on the ignition, he leans across and kisses my cheek. I inhale the woody aftershave I love and feel comforted.

"We'll be just fine."

I give him a small smile back then twist my head, checking for the third time that my hospital bag is within reach, perched on the rear seat.

He raises an eyebrow. "Not for a while yet, I hope."

"Yeah – you and me both." It seemed ridiculous having it ready so early, but one of the removal men was insistent we should keep it close, just in case.

As the car pulls away, I take a last glance at our home until it disappears from view.

It takes a while for the heater to outbattle the icy air of the car. Our journey begins slowly, every traffic light turning red. We take the lead, the removal van follows.

Trafalgar Road is decorated by the usual daytime bustle of traffic and pedestrians, unloading vans and lorries. This road is full of life: not just the bright signs of restaurants, independent shops and bars but the way it seems to evolve at every crossroad. Iron railings line its beginnings and every so often, between the hedges, you catch a glimpse of the pristine Queen Anne's House or the double-domed symmetry of the Old Royal Naval College. Then railings give way to a more urban feel, with shopfronts bordering pavements. The family run Turkish restaurant, teeming at night, sits opposite the Jamaican café, beats throbbing through the open door. The old-style Launderette, with 1950's signage, steamy warm in the winter or stifling hot in the summer, nestles between a bustling barbers and a Boots pharmacy. Weird to observe it all through the car window, when so often we'd be sauntering on foot, popping to the Italian deli for sandwiches or browsing the antiques and craft markets. Already I feel one step removed. Life will be a lot quieter from now on.

As usual, the queue for the Blackwall Tunnel is horrific, the lanes of traffic merging to funnel into the dimly lit tube. I'm not claustrophobic, but I've always felt wary of this antique structure, not helped by the droning sound of the cars pulsing through it and the knowledge of the weight of the Thames flowing above.

We break out into daylight and the hum ceases. From here on, our journey is less interrupted. I'm toasty now, and struggle to remove coat and scarf, wrestling with the seatbelt and my awkward shape. Once free, I rest my head and soon the soft purr of the engine and the monotony of the A12 send me to sleep.

Goodbye Greenwich. Time for our next chapter.

CHAPTER 2

Bea

I awake sometime later, as we turn off the main road, with a crick in my neck and a dry mouth.

"Welcome back. Could hardly hear the radio over your snoring." Seb briefly takes his eyes off the road to give me a lopsided grin.

"Sorry - haven't been much company. Guess the past few weeks are catching up with me."

"Not surprising, really. It'll be easier now you've left work."

I frown. "I haven't *left* work- it's maternity leave." We'd agreed to see how I felt about returning after the baby's arrival.

Seb's voice is cooler. "Okay. I didn't mean anything by it."

We both fall silent.

I turn my head away and take in the changing view. We're driving up a steep hill, barely wide enough for one car. Fortunately, there are no other vehicles: in fact, there is limited sign of any civilization. The hills and fields, punctuated by the odd farmhouse in the distance, are timeless. I imagine they've seen little change over passing centuries, the view only changing colour with the seasons.

Although it's only midday, it feels much later. Steel grey clouds bleed the colour from below, leaving the landscape cold and unwelcoming. Stark, bare trees, dark as ash, twist and stretch over each side of the road and grasp in the middle, like arches inside a church.

I catch a glimpse of movement from my left. Only a rabbit scampering, no doubt startled by the sound of the engine. I watch his tail bob as he darts then disappears into a hedgerow. How long will it take me to feel so at ease with these surroundings?

The first splodges of rain hit the windscreen and Seb flicks on the wipers.

"How are you feeling?"

"Ravenous. Think I'm going to have to make a start on that packed lunch otherwise I'll get nauseous again. This baby knows when a meal's due!".

"Sure. We'll be there in ten minutes, according to Sat-Nav. You tuck in, I'll have it later."

I'm not quite sure when the craving for cheese and tomato sandwiches kicked in, but it's still going strong. I devour my round and wish I'd prepared twice as many. I seriously contemplate tucking into Seb's too, but then I recognise where we are. The car slows down and we turn off the main road. Ahead is a steep pot-holed path, either side of which are bleak, muddy fields, with scarce patches of grass, the ground clawed and churned into ugly furrows. It's how I imagine the countryside in Belgium and France, at the beginning of the First World War. Barren and forbidding, this is not the view I remembered from recent visits, but I remind myself crops would have grown here in the summer. It's winter now: of course it will seem gaunt and lifeless.

The still bleakness of the fields ahead is interrupted by a slight movement. Through the murky drizzle there is a small

6

shape that appears to be a figure in the distance. It's hard to make out clearly, but the build suggests a female; she's moving away from the house with purpose, her drab coloured clothes blending into the surroundings.

"Who's that?" I glance towards Seb.

"Hmm?"

"Over on the left...someone in the field..."

But when I look again, I see nothing, only the landscape shrouded in rain.

"Can't see anyone," Seb says, his eyes returning to the track which is about to veer to the right.

"No, not now. It was too far away. Perhaps it was a piece of rubbish caught in the wind." I try to dispel the apprehension in my stomach.

We reach buildings and are confronted by the barn first, which shields the house from view. When we last visited, still blessed with hazy, sunny days, this building had seemed full of opportunities. We'd talked about converting it or using it for parties, where London friends could stay in the summer. Now, the broken panes of glass look like gaping mouths. The wood is clearly rotten, and parts have been patched up with rusty corrugated iron. The idea of it offering any kind of shelter or enjoyment is laughable. I resist the urge to share my thoughts with Seb. I don't want to appear negative. It will take time to adjust here, and maybe things will look different once spring arrives.

Around the corner, the back of the house comes into view. Oak Tree Farm. The former owners had a couple of temporary buildings here which I think they used for dogs. Since being removed they've left behind large, muddy spaces, as though part of the house has been ripped out and taken away. The rendering bears the scars: walls partially hidden from the sun are a dirty cream, like a nicotine stain. The overall effect is patchy, tatty, unloved.

We park and pause a moment to take in the outside of the building to be our new home. It was built around 1600, when the first Elizabeth was on the throne. With a thatched roof and thick stone walls, the farm was built with materials from the surrounding countryside and blends into it. Despite alterations and extensions over the years, the house still retained its character and historic roots.

Seb fell in love with its quirks straight away: the thatched roof; the high ceiling in one of the oldest parts of the house, with meat hooks suspended from it, currently used as the kitchen/diner; the low ceilings in other parts of the house, with original timbers requiring you to stoop or face being knocked-out; irregular walls and flooring; the latch-openings to heavy, wide, internal doors. He loved all of it and the potential it offered, with visions of expanding it to make a real family home. After all, the plot was huge, and we had plenty of scope. Importantly, it offered him a new way of living. An   opportunity to come home at the end of the day and put some distance between him and his work.

I needed more convincing. I loved the historic details and the size of the plot but was wary of the amount of work involved and the distance from...well, everything. It's so remote here, compared to what we're used to. Friends, family and work are a long car or train journey away. There are no local amenities – a "nip to the shops" will require a car. Neighbours are not even within sight of the property. But Seb's enthusiasm was infectious and eventually, after three viewings, I succumbed.

Returning to the house now, we see it stripped back, in the bleakest of months. From the outside, I'm already overwhelmed by what is required to restore it.

Seb catches the look on my face. "It's okay. Nothing a couple of tins of paint can't fix."

The seller, Mr Bryant, is standing outside his car, parked

opposite ours. He'd been easy enough to deal with during the house purchase, answering our many   questions and happy to let us visit three times, although he seemed to get impatient towards the end. He and his wife were obviously keen to sell.

The rain momentarily ceases. Seb gets out of the car first while it takes me time to unfasten my seatbelt and get my legs moving. My whole body feels tired and stiff.

Seb's already chatting away as Mr Bryant reaches into his pocket to explain the set of keys. He looks up with a smile as I approach, then his eyes catch sight of my bump and the smile fades. I've experienced some weird behaviours of people since I've been pregnant. Strangers have asked, "when's it due?", or have felt the need to reach out and touch my bump, as though pregnancy disentitles me to personal space. Odd as it seems, Mr Bryant looks ill at ease, a reaction I've not yet encountered.

Bemused, I strike up a conversation. "It's good to see you again, Mr Bryant." I rest my hands on my bump. "I'm sure I'm twice the size I was last time we met!"

He gives a pained smile then looks away from us, eyes darting back to the house. I'm not sure whether it's my imagination, but he seems drawn to the window of one of the bedrooms. He notices me looking at him, trying to work out to what's caught his attention. Embarrassed, he looks down, biting his lip.

"Didn't realise you were expecting, truth be told. We had high hopes of turning this place into a family home – having our own kids - didn't quite work out like that."

It's my turn to feel uncomfortable. Did my pregnancy bring back unhappy memories for him? He must have seen other expectant women. Why should I make him so awkward? We mumble our condolences, but Mr Bryant brushes them aside and continues discussing the keys.

"This is for the front door, these two are for the backdoor," he reaches into another pocket, "And this one's for the barn."

I smile to myself. A key for a building with so many holes seemed somewhat redundant.

"Right, I think that's all. I'm off now, before it gets dark. If you need anything…" Mr Bryant pauses.

"Just one thing… is there a right of way across the land?"

"No – why'd you ask?"

I shrug. "It's nothing - just that I thought I saw someone walking across the field as we drove past."

"No - no right of way." That strained look crosses his face again. "If you have any trouble, just give me a call. I'm only twenty minutes up the road. Mind, you'll be lucky to get mobile reception. Worth gettin' the landline sorted soon." He nods to us both and walks towards his car.

We smile and wave him off, just as the removal men finish their lunch and start noisily opening the van and setting up the ramps.

"That was awkward. How sad for the Bryants." I glance at Seb, as Mr Bryant raises a hand to us before his car turns the corner and out of sight.

"I know. Makes you realise just how lucky we are." He glances at me and quickly corrects himself. "Lucky now, I mean. Let's check where these boxes are going."

I follow him towards the house and hope he's right: that we're going to be lucky, from now on.

We open the back door, into the kitchen-diner. The opening is wider here and less of a struggle for the removal men to negotiate the furniture.

The inside of the house looks exactly as I remembered it, which is a huge relief. I hadn't much cared for the Bryants' furnishings and now they're gone, if anything, the property looks better. When we came to view the farm, it was clean and functional, but bare, lacking the finishing touches to make it warm and cosy. Now it feels like a blank canvas, ready for us to reinvent. Cheered by this thought, I lead the removal men upstairs with the boxes.

CHAPTER 3

Bea

Half-past ten. The alarm clock is one of the few items we've managed to locate, unpack and position, if only on a temporary basis, until we've figured out where everything fits.

I'm bushed. The removal company left just before seven o'clock. We ended up giving them a tip as they'd been so helpful; they insisted on building our iron-slatted bed before they went, not wanting me to struggle with a mattress on the floor. Since their departure, we've had dinner (a quick pizza) and set up the basics.

The bedroom to be ours is a decent size with small windows, typical for a cottage of this age. The walls are painted a cheerful peach colour. Not to my taste, but inoffensive. The floral curtains that hang on the two windows on adjacent walls go some way to keep out the draughts, although the room still feels cold. There are fitted wardrobes along one side of the room, ugly but useful.

Next to the wardrobes is a door leading to another room. To me, it seemed strange when I first saw it, but it's not unusual for an older property: according to the estate agent, it was once common to build houses where one bedroom would flow into another, without a hallway to connect them. The adjoining room is small and empty, with no curtain or fireplace. When we discussed our plans for the house, we'd agreed that it would make the obvious nursery. Now, with my due-date only three months away, the room is a reminder of what's to come and the fact that our lives are about to change drastically. Our lack of preparation for the baby's arrival is apparent by the absence of boxes for the room. For the time being, I move my hospital bag there. At least that was ready.

Another bedroom is situated on the other side of the staircase and landing. We have plans to use this as a combined guest room and study. It's larger than our bedroom but doesn't have the benefit of the nursery next door.

After such a long day, the bed looks inviting and I can't wait any longer. The panelled door of our bedroom rumbles as I slide it open and step onto the small landing. The steep staircase leading to the ground floor is directly below me. Not for the first time, I note the irregular shape and height of the stairs. Quaint and charming, they're also a carpet-fitter's nightmare and a potential death trap. I'm grateful for the sensible sturdy handrails fitted on both sides.

"Come on, Seb. Whatever it is you're doing can wait," I call.

No response. I sigh and make my way down to find him. He's in the kitchen, not the high-ceilinged kitchen/diner but the extension that was added much later,   containing the appliances. He's sitting on the floor, leaning against the 1980's formica kitchen units, clutching a sodden tea-towel to the top of his head. A drawer is open, and smashed crockery lies in pieces next to him, along with drips of blood.

"You okay? What happened?"

"I was reaching into the box to get more crockery - forgot I'd left the drawer open."

I peel away his fingers and the cloth covered icepack to assess the damage. A bump has formed, and the skin is broken, but thankfully stitches don't appear to be necessary. I stroke back his hair tenderly and kiss his forehead.

"This is what happens when we're tired. Let's leave the rest till morning."

Seb agrees and makes for the stairs, ice-pack held to his head.

I grab a dustpan and brush. The baby's first crockery set, a beautifully decorated matching egg cup, plate and bowl, the present from my team at work, is splintered into fragments on the floor. I'm disappointed that he or she will never get to use it, but porcelain crockery for children was not destined to survive long.

It's not long before we're both under the covers, appreciating the warmth of each other's bodies in the chill of the room.

"Shall we christen this home properly?" Seb's breath is on my neck, his arm encircling my large waist. I can feel him stir. Sex is not high my agenda tonight, but I agree. It's good to be physically close to him, even if I yearn for sleep.

He drifts off quickly afterwards. Typical. I, on the other hand, struggle to find a comfortable position. My natural inclination is to recline on my right, but I don't want to face the annex room. It sets my brain whirring. Thinking of the baby to come. Contemplating the babies that didn't quite arrive: the miscarriages, then the problems falling pregnant.

The pressure of wanting a family hovered over me, darkening my days, weighing me down. The more I wanted it, the further it seemed from my grasp. My body failed Seb, failed me.

After the last miscarriage, I found it harder to bounce back. Work was my saviour, both as a distraction and to provide a pattern to my days, but the rest of my life felt empty. I saw less and less of friends, particularly those with children. Eventually the doctor prescribed me with anti-depressants, but after almost a year of infertility, we started to consider the pills might be affecting our chances. With the doctor's advice, I gradually came off them, tried to use CBT to keep on top of things. I was open to trying anything.

As it happens, I'm not sure the absence of anti-depressants had any effect, other than on my mental state. Every month I took a pregnancy test, telling myself my period was late, rather than putting it down to an irregular cycle. My body played cruel tricks on me. It got to the point that I had to find different pharmacies to buy the test kits: I thought the staff were giving me pitying looks at the till, as though they knew what was going on and judged me for being obsessive. I probably was.

Eventually, we went for IVF. We confided in Seb's mum, Enid, who was brilliant and insisted on helping us out financially. My pregnancy was the product of our third cycle. I hadn't fully appreciated what was involved until I lived through it. Google and leaflets can tell you the physical demands IVF places on the body: the daily injected drugs to suppress your natural menstrual cycle; the chemicals and hormones to stimulate your egg production and maturity; endless scans, blood tests, cramps and discomfort. But nothing can ready you for the emotional demands. While hormones soar and plummet, you feel the wrench of each opportunity lost. Then you repeat the whole process, facing the disappointment in your partner's eyes, yet again.

So, this pregnancy is a miracle. Statistically, Seb and I are very fortunate: many people have travelled the same journey yet never conceive. But I don't feel lucky. Not yet. We've been through so much - physically, emotionally and financially. I'm bone china, just like the set I swept up this evening: fragile and easily shattered, too wary to feel hope and excitement yet. Maybe that will change over the next few months.

It's different for Seb, though. Sure, he experienced the blows, but it wasn't his body that was chemically altered, punctured, prodded, assessed. He wasn't coping with depression without the assistance of medication. He's ready. Like everything he ever does, he wants to apply maximum energy, control the situation, relish the joy of being a dad. His drive should encourage me, but instead it exhausts me, makes me hesitant about what comes next.

I must have eventually dozed off because suddenly I'm awake. It's pitch black. Something disturbed me. Unnerved, I try to take my bearings. It takes a few seconds to remember we've moved house. I struggle to prop myself up. The only light in the room is from my alarm clock. 00:29.

Shaken, I try to place the sound that woke me. Like a shriek. Animal or human? I can't recall it exactly but, in my half-awake state, it filled me with dread. I hold my breath and stay perfectly still, straining to listen. There is only the whispering of the trees outside, unsettled by the wind.

I turn towards Seb, but his place in the bed is empty. Could he have made the noise?

"Seb? SEB?!" No response. He hurt his head before we went to bed. Could he be concussed, lying confused somewhere in the house?

I must get to him. I stumble out of bed. The sliding door is already open, and I switch on the light above the stairs. As I make my way down, as fast as I dare, my heart leaps as Seb appears at the foot.

"Careful! What's up?"

I tell him about the strange noise and why I'd been concerned for him. Apparently, he'd heard nothing and had only got up to fetch some paracetamol for his sore head. He puts his arm on my back as we reach our room.

"It's going to take a while to get used to it here. Bound to be more wildlife at night. At least there are no drunks!" His voice turns more serious. "Look, if you need to get up in the night, wake me up first, yeah? I don't want you falling down those stairs."

I try to protest that he wasn't there, and that I don't need help to visit to the loo, but he's not listening.

It takes a while for the adrenalin to subside, but eventually I fall back to sleep. When I next open my eyes, sunlight is seeping under the curtains and I'm struck by the sound of birdsong. It's loud enough to wake Seb too. He mutters something about infernal dawn chorus, but rolls over, pulling the cover with him so that it slides off my body. The cool air is a shock to my exposed feet. I consider reclaiming the duvet but think better of it. I'm awake, so I may as well get up. Besides, I'm ravenous.

Settling down on the sofa with my bowl of cereal and coffee, I reach for journal and pen. It's a task I do at the beginning of every weekend – reflect on the past week, think about the week ahead. Since I stopped taking the medication, I find it really helps. I can off-load my brain, rationalise my thoughts and plan ahead to ease my anxiety. The only difference this time is that there will be no work on the agenda. *Paid work,* I correct myself. Still plenty to do here. I start to think about which room to tackle first when Seb saunters in. I tell him the kettle's just boiled and he returns to join me on the sofa, hoody over his pyjamas, warming his hands around a mug.

"How's the head?"

"Fine thanks. What's the plan for the weekend?"

I laugh and waft my hands in the direction of the boxes stacked around the room.

"I know we'll have to do a few of those…" he said, "but I was thinking, now we've finally arrived, wouldn't it be great to get things sorted? We could go into Ipswich, buy the cot, car-seat… you know, the basics. And if we pick up paint too, we could make a start on the nursery?"

I can see he's been plotting this idea: his eyes are bright and look expectantly into mine for a reaction. I start to protest, argue there's too much unpacking, and I see the light fade and a frown form on his brow.

"Look, I know you've been putting off doing stuff for the baby. I get it. But you need to start believing it's happening this time." He takes my hand in his. "Start to enjoy it."

I feel my shoulders rise. "What's the rush? We've been in the house for all of five minutes." Slyly, I add, "You were only saying yesterday I should be taking it easy. Plus, we desperately need groceries."

What follows is a debate about the pros and cons of Seb's plan. Eventually, I give in. It was either that or endure him sulking. As a compromise, he agrees we'll limit shopping to two stores for baby gear and the collection of paint from a DIY store, and he would collect some groceries the following day.

It's so typical of Seb. He wants to share the experience, enjoy the preparation. While he's kept track of the baby's size and milestones, week by week, I've gone through the motions of a pregnant woman without really believing it. When I catch myself in a mirror, it feels like the reflection belongs to someone else. I find it hard to take comfort from the internal flutters of the baby's movement, still fearful that my body's playing tricks. Even the scans, showing the image of its curved form, nestling in my womb, feel detached as though I'm watching film footage of a child in another woman's abdomen. My brain struggles to accept that a baby is alive inside me and will soon be born. But I need to try harder.

It takes forty-five minutes to get to Ipswich. At least we now know we're within reach of a city! The next four hours are spent assessing the various merits and features of every piece of baby equipment in store: sterilizers, cot, car-seat, pram, baby-monitors, bedding. The glare from the shop's lighting and the piped music grate on me. Who knew every item would be so complicated? We feel torn between not wishing to spend a fortune on things that would shortly be redundant and not wanting to invest in poorer substitutes that may be inadequate. The choice of baby monitor was mind-boggling, weighing up all the various features. Did we want a motion detector? Was a camera required to watch our baby's movements, every minute of every hour? Who knows how paranoid we'll feel when the time comes?

Do I need a steriliser if I intend to breast feed? And that leads me into another minefield of new bras, pads, breast shields, nipple cream...Would I really need to pump my breasts, and if so, would I do one at a time, or both simultaneously?? I wince just thinking about it.

Thankfully, Seb seems more decisive, so we emerge with all the necessary equipment. So much so, it requires two trips from the checkout to the car to stow it all. After the first drop off, I take a rest in the car. When Seb returns with the second trolley load, I notice in the wing mirror him removing a box from the top of the trolley that I don't recognise. He fills the car and joins me.

"What was that other package?"

"What?"

"There was a medium sized box with a cellophane front – looked like a toy or something?"

He winces. "Sorry, I couldn't resist. It's a Record-a-Bear. I read about them: they play a sound similar to the noise babies hear in the womb. Soothing, apparently," he buckles up. "Also plays songs and you can record voices."

The side of my mouth creases, infuriated. "But we agreed no toys! Just the essentials!"

"I know..." his voice is sing-song, playfully persuasive. "But I can have a little fun, can't I? He has a very sweet face..."

I laugh, despite myself. "You sure it's the baby you've bought it for?"

Seb smiles and starts the car. "Right, just the trip to B & Q now. With all this stuff, I reckon the baby will need our room and we'll be crammed in the annex!"

The DIY store is far less stressful, and we agree on a colour easily. Lemon Spirt. It feels bright, hopeful, like a ray of sunshine. As we drive back to our new home, I feel exhausted but also a glimmer of optimism, like I've turned a corner. There's a lot to take in, but we've made a start. Making decisions and spending a small fortune on baby-kit makes this baby seem more real. Perhaps he or she senses it too: this afternoon I feel a stronger kick, like the beat of an irregular drum and I trace the movement with the palm of my hand.

CHAPTER 4

Maud

I have been sitting in the rocking chair, by the window, for the past hour, watching the wind dance through the leaves on the oak tree outside and whisper through the fields. It is a welcome distraction from the small, screaming body in my arms. Nathaniel cannot be comforted. I have tried my breast, but his little fist slapped it away, the tiny fingernails catching on my pale skin and scratching angry red lines across it. I fetched an extra blanket, but it was kicked in fury, his legs stomping against his swaddling clothes in rage. I moved away from the range, in case he was too warm. All to no avail.

It was the same last night. And the night before that. And almost all of the other nights of his life, which so far stretches to three months.

It's strange how you can long for something, and yet when it arrives, it confounds you: alters the rhythm of your daily existence to such an extent you hardly recognise it as your own. Everyone assumes you are content. How could you be otherwise, when the Lord has answered your prayers, blessed you with the baby for whom you yearned? Surely every woman in my position would feel lucky, fulfilled, complete in her purpose. Yet I feel numb, ill-equipped, ill-prepared.

Struggling in my arms, his dark hair is more unruly than ever, curls clinging to his neck and sticking out at odd angles like a thistle. He and I could not be more different: my skin pale, where the folds of his skin are often flecked with pinkish red; my hair glints dark gold in the sun, or a light, dull brown in the current winter months.

I must put him down, begin making lunch. I lie him on another blanket, on the floor, close enough to the range to feel some benefit but not too close. Relieved to have use of my arms again, I slice the bread and cheese, ready to be toasted. William will be hungry after a long morning sawing logs with Thomas, the farmhand. They are building a new pen gate, ready for the sow that we've agree to buy from a farmer five miles north of here. Much of this time of year is spent repairing and improving the farm. Putting right the ravaging effects of storms and frosts. We've been told the pig is in farrow; hopefully the piglets will provide a new source of food and income.

Thankfully, Nathaniel has exhausted himself. His cries are broken now as he soothes himself into a slumber. As though in tune to his son's movements, I detect William's footfall outside, pausing at the privy before he joins us.

The door opens and a gust of cold air shoots ahead of him while he struggles to take off his boots, making the flames of the range dance and hiss and causing Nathaniel to stir and wriggle.

"Close the door!" I whisper. "He's been a beggar to settle this morning. I don't need you waking 'im up!"

"What's 'e doing on the floor then, poor mite? Surely you could have laid him up in his crib?" William looks at me darkly. He doesn't mince his words, my William. His bulky frame seems to fill the parlour, shoulders hunched after a morning of sawing, the sweat of his labours making his dark hair clump to his head, wild dark curls like his son, only thicker.

He brushes down his clothing and rubs his hands over his breeches to remove any wooden splinters, then stoops and tenderly scoops up Nathaniel, like a gentle giant. His face, ruddy and creased, softens as he looks into that of his sleeping son's, and he carefully carries him through the doorway. I hear the tread of his footsteps up the stairs and to our bedroom overhead.

My chest is hollow. I should be grateful for the love William shows for our son; many women complain their men show little or no interest. But instead, it makes me feel worse. Where love and affection should be, there is only emptiness and shame. William is bestowed with the patience that I lack. His energy is like a river, constantly bubbling and gurgling, whereas mine seems to dwindle and diminish in the early hours of the day, as I nurse our son in the darkness. Alone.

He returns and sinks into a chair by the range, avoiding my eyes.

"I tried to settle him for hours. I think it's the milk he can smell - it distracts him." Even to my own ears, I sound apologetic and guilty.

William grunts in response and I pass him his toast, cheese and beer.

"We'll be seeing your family in a couple of months, for Easter. Maybe you could ask your mother for advice?" His eyes search mine while he attacks his lunch.

I wince. If only it were that simple. I tried speaking to my mother and sister at Christmastide, but they could offer no advice that made any difference. My sister, Charlotte, has a brood of her own; although motherhood seems to come naturally to her, my nieces and nephews give her little time to share words of wisdom with me. As for Mother, her words still echo in my head: "The bond between mother and child is a divine blessing, Maud. You should be offering prayers of thanks, particularly at your age. You've a healthy boy, a good husband and a roof over your head. What more could you want?"

Unlike them, it took a long time for me to be with child.

The tenancy for Oak Tree Farm became available not long after we were wed. Fifteen miles away from where we were raised, it had been leased to an older cousin of William's who had just died. Although it seemed too far from my family, we could not turn it down. It was everything we dreamed of, and we had plans to fill it with children of our own.

For over six years the babies never came. Each month, the blood would appear, like a stain to mock me, an unwelcome signal that our attempts at coupling had been fruitless. It was hard to keep the bowl of monthly rags hidden in the farmhouse. Wherever I put it, it registered in William's eyes, and I dreaded the flicker of disappointment that would darken his face.

Barren. It is a stigma that hangs heavy. At that time, I was conscious of the looks from my mother, on the rare occasions I saw her. *"How tired you look Maud!"* or *"I swear you look more like the branch of a willow tree each time I see you!"* She may have commented out of love and concern, but in my ears I heard only blame. How could a woman in her twenties be unable to conceive? Motherhood, deemed to be so natural and instinctive, seemed beyond my reach.

A farm such as ours, with hens, two dozen sheep, a couple of pigs and three cows, revolves around fertility, new life and death. The harsh realities of nature are no stranger to me and perhaps helped me come to terms with my own difficulties. Before Nathaniel, I helped with more tasks about the farm, like wattle work and tending the animals. I was there for the lambing: keeping awake all hours to make sure they were safely delivered; supporting the weaker ones who struggled to take milk from their mother; removing the runts who were unable to survive or the mothers who died from complications. At the end of each day, I enjoyed the ache in my body from physical labour, to feel it had been useful, exerted, productive. It numbed the pain from my failure to make children.

Eventually, one month the bleeding didn't come. I hardly

believed it at first and was fearful of raising William's hopes. Then the nausea came, and there was no hiding my condition. We were both delighted, excited about the prospect of becoming a real family.

Many girls fret about the birth, but it was of little concern to me. I knew there were risks. All women understand the beginning of their baby's life can mark the end of their own, none more so than a farmer's wife. But I was lucky. The labour was painful but short, the baby was healthy, and it didn't take me long to recover, physically.

It was after the birth that I felt it. Or rather, it never came. That joy you expect to feel, the burst of love you assume will course through your veins as soon as you set sight on your little one. All I felt was relief that it was over, and wariness about what lay ahead. It was something I couldn't discuss with William. But I could tell by his glances and comments that he had his suspicions, like a dark cloud hovering over us.

William finishes his lunch quickly and I refill his tankard for the afternoon. He is always keen to get back, only resting on a Sunday. I am lucky he works hard and is keen to provide for his family, not like some I could mention. But I miss his company and being close to his body, working alongside him.

His hand briefly touches mine before he takes his leave. I enjoy his touch, albeit fleeting. It's as much affection as I can hope for these days.

CHAPTER 5

Bea

T hree weeks have passed since we moved, but in some ways it seems longer. On the plus side, I'm more in tune with my pregnancy. With each day that passes, I'm growing more confident in my body and the baby growing inside it: more aware of the baby's movements, the subtle flutters of a hand, the sweep of a kick. On the downside, I'm more out of breath, large and unwieldy, but that might also have something to do with the volume of biscuits consumed. Unfortunately, the loose hours and quiet days provide too much time for snacking.

It's the massive difference in lifestyle that I'm still struggling to accept. I don't think Seb fully understands the adjustment it requires from me. It's like I've temporarily swapped my life for someone else's, like some awful reality TV show. There are no scheduled meetings, planned phone-calls and deadlines to structure my time: unless I'm disciplined, the day can just drift.

While I'm floating in a limbo between my old life as a full-time lawyer and my future lifestyle as a mum, Seb still has his job, of course - a constant that centres him, a part of him that bridged our old life in Greenwich to our new life here. By contrast, very little of my old life remains. I'm slightly resentful of him, having a career and only being required to dip his toe into this new existence, leaving me isolated and misplaced.

For the first time in my life, there is silence. I've always lived in towns or cities, worked in busy offices with colleagues, phone-calls and interruptions. Noise is my norm. The quiet of the countryside is oppressive. Every creak, strain and rustle that breaks the silence of the house seems magnified.

Moving here was bound to feel odd and unnatural but on top of this there have been unexplained occurrences; strange happenings that have started to make me feel uncomfortable.

At first I assumed it was me. Most women at this stage feel emotional and apprehensive about what lies ahead, as well as experiencing physical problems. But it's not my pregnancy that's making me feel unnerved. It's the irregularities in this house, a house that doesn't yet feel like home. Individually they don't sound much, but together they put me on edge.

I've tried to explain it to Seb. He listens but he thinks there are innocent explanations and I just need to get used to spending time on my own. I can tell he's worried that I'm falling into a pattern of behaviour that he's seen before: he's encouraged me to write things down in my journal, challenge my thoughts. I acknowledge that my solitude and thought processes may be part of the problem, but there's more to it than that.

I remember my first day alone in the house clearly. It was the day after Seb had begun painting the annex-come-nursery. I'd intended to get stuck in too, but he insisted on doing it: he was worried about me continually bending over and hurting the baby. I kept him company in our bedroom next door, unpacking clothes from the storage boxes and making frequent cups of tea and coffee. The weekend passed pleasantly, working alongside each other, so I begrudged the arrival of Monday morning arrived when he had to leave for work.

I had plenty to keep me busy but found it hard to settle. Out of habit, I logged on to email first. Nothing of interest apart from a weekly missive from my sister, Harriet. She's been sending round robins ever since she left for South America, two months ago. Currently in Peru, she was about to catch a train to Cusco, to begin the Inca Trail, having just survived a nasty bout of food poisoning. Logging out, I smiled to think how our parents would react when reading it. Roughing it wasn't their style.

The first couple of tasks on the to-do list took an age. Mr Bryant wasn't joking about the lack of mobile reception; I couldn't make a call inside. My phone showed a couple of bars outside so, wrapped up in my coat, I walked around the perimeter of the farm while I registered the landline in our names, contacted an internet service provider and enrolled us with a new doctor and the midwifery service.

Next on the list was unpacking. Every room still contained unopened boxes and the question was where to start. I picked the lounge, mainly because everything was accessible at a height that didn't require much bending. The first boxes contained books. I enjoyed finding new homes for them on the shelves; each was like an old friend, reminding me of a time in my life we'd shared. *The cases of Sherlock Holme* - Seb and I read it travelling around India in our early twenties, swapping books to save space in our rucksacks. *Tess of the D'Urbervilles* I started reading when I was inter-railing around Europe, after my first year at university. Never did finish it.

I was about to open the third box, scanning the room to find the stanley knife, when I had the sensation that someone was watching, behind me. I can't explain the feeling; it's like being aware of someone's stillness, the focus of their energy, even though they're out of sight. I spun round but obviously there was no-one there, and no-one outside the window. I poked my head into the hallway and even checked outdoors, feeling foolish as I did. Who would watch me, here? Nevertheless, it left me feeling tense and alert.

I mentioned it to Seb. He thought I'd probably imagined it but recognised how remote we are here and consequently installed motion monitors near the front and back doors, which send messages to our mobiles if triggered. I felt a bit silly, given we're unlikely to get many visitors or burglars trying their luck, but Seb said he felt more at ease, knowing I was home alone most of the time.

After that first day, my daily timetable began to fall into a rhythm. Empty a box or two in the morning, have lunch, attempt to do something productive in the afternoon but eventually give in to my increasing   tiredness and have an afternoon snooze. By the time I woke, the house had normally fallen into semi-darkness, and it would be time for me to start preparing dinner.

One morning, the following week, rain was teeming down. Droplets dripped from the thatched roof too, making a beat out of kilter with those which fell from the sky - a slower, steady cascade. The thatch absorbed much of the sound, but, I hoped, not too much of the water.

I was working in our second reception room that day. We hadn't yet figured out a use for it, but had vague ideas of a playroom in future. For the time being, we referred to it as the music room because it housed Seb's vinyl collection and our amassed CDs. That day's task was to order them and find storage places.

Seb and I are both collectors. As I ordered the CD's alphabetically, I came across albums I hadn't listened to for years and now and then I couldn't resist popping one in the CD player and rediscovering the tracks I had once listened to on repeat, transporting me to my past. Unlike our home in Greenwich, I could sing along at the top of my lungs here with no risk of disturbing the neighbours.

The last track on an album had just finished. I'd got as far as *H,* searching for a hidden PJ Harvey album to group with her others, when I heard a sound. It seemed to be coming from directly above my head, our bedroom. It was deep and heavy, like something rolling or being dragged across the wooden floor. It only lasted a few seconds, stopping as quickly as it began. Curious, I left my classifying to investigate.

The staircase was unnaturally dark for that time of the day. Looking up ahead, I found the reason: our bedroom door was shut, the key source of light for the   stairwell. Strange, I never left it closed. It couldn't have been Seb - he always leaves before I rise. The door, in common with many in the house, is large and heavy, but unlike the others, it slides open and shut on wheels that run along a track above it. It's old, but not an original feature.

I reached for the handle. The door rolled open, making a sound like the one I'd heard when I was downstairs in the music room, the same rumble and roll. But how could it have rolled shut by itself? A breeze could not have buffeted its weight across the opening. Perhaps there was a mechanical fault? There are few straight lines in this place - the track may have bent, encouraging the wheels to roll with gravity. However, to my eyes it appeared to be working fine, all fittings looking horizontal and correct. I spent a while playing with it at various points of opening, to see whether it would roll close by itself. Each time it stayed put, obediently.

I scanned the rest of our room. Everything looked normal: slightly messy, with a few unfinished projects on the go. As I left, I made a point of pushing the door open as far as it would go, and returned downstairs to my CD sorting, slightly puzzled.

It wasn't long before the sound occurred again. This time it was louder, faster, as though the door had been pushed with force and aggression. Shaking, I moved as fast as I could to the foot of the stairs. Sure enough, the landing was dim, as before, and the bedroom door shut.

Looking back on it now, I'm not sure how I had the courage

to stay in the house that day. I guess there were limited options open to me. But for some reason, I felt safer downstairs. So long as I stayed there, I managed to get on with chores, and put the experience to the back of my mind. I distracted myself by continuing to listen to music and logging on to emails, reading Harriet's latest message about Machu Pichu and the Inca Trail. But despite my distractions, I was shaken and longed for Seb's return.

By the time evening arrived, I sat in the kitchen diner area waiting for him, trying to read a book. I suppose at one time it would have been the main room of the house, the rear parlour, and it had become central to our homelife too, a place where we ate, chatted and dumped stuff. The range still stood along one wall which may have once heated the house, although for us it serves as decoration and a place for gathering dust, not having plucked the courage to try it out. We had stuck to central heating and thick jumpers for warmth.

Eventually, I heard Seb's key in the lock at around 7.30pm. I flung my arms around him as soon as he'd crossed the threshold, almost knocking him off his feet. The chill evening air seeped in with him. I nuzzled into his neck and breathed him in, a mixture of his skin, faded aftershave and the faint tang of London transport. He rested his chin on my head, then dropped his head lower to find my lips.

"That was some welcome! Is everything okay? How was your day?"

I told him what had happened, how I'd investigated the sliding door system and deliberately left it open, only for it to mysteriously slam shut again. He sat down to listen, but it seemed to make little impression on him.

"Sweetheart, you can't let yourself be spooked by noises and creaks in this house. Older properties come with their imperfections. The door probably has a temperamental running track, perhaps needs re-aligning. Nothing to worry about – I'll look into it at the weekend." He walked away, coat in hand, trailing off to hang it in the hall.

Frowning, I went to the kitchen. I carelessly sloshed the braised roasted vegetables and pearl barley onto the lipped plates. It wouldn't hurt for him to be a bit more empathetic. He'd be spooked if he witnessed it. And given his lack of practical skills, I wasn't comforted by his diagnosis of the problem, nor his offer to resolve it. The more I thought about it, the more frustrated I felt.

I returned to find him seated at the table, looking at his phone. He looked up as I slammed the plate in front of him.

"What?"

"What? *What?* You've no idea what it's like, stuck here all day, conscious of every noise." Despite myself, angry tears fill my eyes. "It's easy for you. You get to see everyone – chat, interact - then come home."

His mouth dropped open. "Where's this come from?"

"I'm lonely here," my voice cracks.

"I know…" his hand sought mine across the table. "But you'll get used to it in time. It's not so easy for me: getting up at the crack of dawn; de-icing the car; driving to Ipswich in the dark. Then over an hour and a half's commute. That's before my working day's even begun!" He sighed. "It's worth it, being here with you, but there are sacrifices. For both of us.""I know… but I feel vulnerable here, on my own. I don't even know when you're coming home, half the time."

"Yeah…I've tried texting - I can't help the poor reception, and you know what the internet's like. You could always use the landline if you're worried."

"I need a car, Seb. I'm literally stranded." I toyed with the food on my plate.

"Let's look at how we're fixed. Money's a bit tight after the move, but we can consider some options and work something out. We're going to need a bigger car at some point anyway."

Pleased he supported me, I broached my other concern. "I'm also feeling cut off from people locally - we don't even know where our neighbours are, yet alone their names! Can we introduce ourselves at the weekend?"

"Good idea. I'd feel better too, if you knew a few people nearby."

I felt more content that evening, knowing we had a plan to help me feel less cut off from the world. I tried to ignore the unease triggered earlier by the sliding door.

The next few days passed without incident. On Friday, I awoke later than usual. Normally I'd stir as Seb got ready for work, but that day I slept in. As I stretched, I remembered that I was going to bake that day, for the neighbours we planned to visit the next day. I looked forward to it, a welcome change from unpacking.

Washing and dressing quickly, I pondered what to make. I settled on a Victoria sponge and a carrot cake, given I'd baked them many times before and they were likely to turn out okay. The kitchen and the attached diner were the coldest rooms of the house, designed as they were to be reliant on the range. I was glad when the heat of the oven generated some warmth for my fingers as I worked.

I was just stacking the ingredients ready on the work-surface when my phone pinged. Fishing it from my back pocket, I had an automatic message that someone had been detected at the front door.

Curious, I crossed through the diner and opened the door to see if anyone was there or if we'd been left a package. No-one. I took a set of keys with me, in case the door slammed behind me, and ventured outside in my slippers. Hunching my shoulder and wrapping my arms across my chest against the cold wind,

I looked around the side of the house and as far as I could see down the driveway. It was clear.

Returning to the front door, I couldn't see a stray branch that might have triggered the motion detector. It was strange – perhaps a bird had ventured nearby?

I was glad to be back in the kitchen, where it was comparatively warmer, and to return to my task. Baking has always brought me pleasure. It was the whole process: wading through recipe books, full of tempting ideas and pictures, deciding which to make; the exacting process of measuring ingredients and following directions; the achievement of creating something from scratch, and enjoying it with others. It reminded me of spending time with my mum and my nan, in the holidays away from boarding school.

The sponge mix consistency was looking good and I was scraping it into the twin tins when I heard a sound. I held the bowl aloft, allowing the last splodges to drop soundlessly into the tins beneath, while I strained my ears. It was a soft noise, hard to detect over the low hum of the oven, and it came from somewhere outside the kitchen. I crossed into the diner. The noise was slightly clearer here - a scratching noise, as though something was taking short, repetitive strokes, like a rake scraping leaves. I tried to dismiss it and went back to my baking. After all, it was the kind of noise animals could make. Who knew what wildlife was lurking in that thatch? We could be co-habiting with squirrels, mice or nesting birds, any one of whom could be sharpening beaks or claws on rafters and beams.

Popping the tins in the oven, I began grating carrot for the next cake. But the noise continued, persistent. Despite my best efforts to ignore it, I found myself grating in rhythm to the sound. Exasperated, I dropped carrot and grater to find out where it was coming from.

I searched the hallway, lounge and music room. It was no louder there than in the diner. However, when I entered the bathroom, the sound seemed closer. I put my ear to the wall - not easy, with a bathtub, wash basin and an enormous belly in the way. In the end, I climbed into the bath. It seemed to emanate from directly above. I felt dread in my stomach - not our bedroom again. But then I remembered the room above was not our bedroom – it was the spare room, the bathroom being situated on the opposite side of the stairwell.

I never thought I'd find myself wanting a squirrel infestation, but I really hoped I'd discover wildlife as the source of the noise. It was better than another unexplained incident. But as I climbed the stairs, the scratching stopped. I searched the spare bedroom thoroughly, looking for any sign of damage or droppings and placed my ear against floorboards and walls. Nothing: no ripped materials for bedding or tell-tale droppings.

While I found the noise unsettling, initially I saw it more as an annoyance rather than something to fear. Even though I'd found no traces or trails, I still suspected wildlife. I mentioned it to Seb when he came home from work that evening. We agreed that I'd contact pest control on Monday, to avert any future disasters, like chewed cabling or contamination of our water supply.

Saturday came. We had a leisurely breakfast then set off at ten to try the closest neighbours either side of us, along Hill Road.

"Which way first, left or right?" Seb had driven to the end of our lane.

"Let's take right."

I watched the mileometer. It registered an additional 1.4 miles by the time we reached the driveway of our neighbour. The house was redbrick, newer than ours – possibly Victorian? It was clearly a working farm, surrounded by modernised barns. A still-shiny, green Claas tractor was parked close to a barn full of hay bales, packed tightly and wrapped in black polythene, like giant sized liquorice. There was the unmistakeable smell of pig in the air and as we approached the front door and you could hear the sounds of cockerel and cows nearby.

There was no doorbell, so we rapped awkwardly on the door, not knowing whether we'd be heard. Young, animated voices seemed to come from inside, yet we waited a couple of minutes with the door unanswered.

"Did you hear children or was it just me?" Seb said, face puzzled. I nodded and shrugged back.

"Come on. Let's try to find someone on the farm."

Seb held the cake box and we walked around the side of the house, towards the barns. There, at the back of the house, we found a woman, probably ten years older than me, feeding chickens that clucked and pecked around her feet. She saw us and twitched her head back, by way of gruff greeting. Her brows raised and she tilted her chin, seeking an explanation.

"Hi, we just tried your front door. I'm Bea and this is Seb – we recently moved in Oak Tree Farm." I raised my voice to make it carry across the yard and gave a broad smile.

The woman made no attempt to move closer but continued to stare questioningly.

"We just wanted to introduce ourselves, really, and say hello to you and your family," Seb added. He held the cake box above the top of the fence. "And Bea made you a carrot cake."

The woman moved forwards and accepted the cake, awkwardly. "No need for that, but ta anyway. Didn't realise the Bryants were selling the place. Haven't had much to do with 'em, truth be told. Seems like they were only 'ere five minutes."

"I see. Have you lived here long?"

It was clear she had no intention of inviting us inside, so we remained on the other side of the fence.

"All my life. My mum and da bought it when I was a little 'un. They still live 'ere with us but Pete took over the farm." She nodded her head towards the barn, from which we could hear clattering noises. Presumably Pete was a reference to her partner or husband. She then looked pointedly at my bump. "See you're due soon. Twenty-nine/thirty weeks, I'll be guessing?"

I'm taken aback. "How did you know? It was twenty-nine earlier this week!"

The woman (she had not divulged her name) looked pleased with herself. "That's what comes from being a farmer. It's the same with the cows. I can tell at a glance when it's gonna calve. And I reckon she's going to be ginger, like her Da!"

Seb's mouth twitched and I had to look away from him to swallow a laugh.

"I've got three – two girls and a boy. You may have heard 'em bickering in the 'ouse. They're right little buggers this time of year. Not much chance to get outside to let off a bit of steam. Cheerio then, hope you settle in alright. Oh, I'm Josie, by the way." With that, Josie raised a hand in farewell and turned towards her back door.

We walked back to the car. As soon as we were out of ear shot, Seb said, "Well, that was an experience. Don't think we'll be asked over for dinner any time soon."

"Nope. Didn't even make it over the threshold! Hopefully we'll have more joy with the ones on the other side." I couldn't help but feel disappointed. "Do you think Josie's right?"

Seb laughed. "There was always a risk of a ginger! Let's hope he or she inherits your ravishing, dark beauty."

I smiled back. "Perhaps not the curls ...I wouldn't mind him or her having your hair colour, though. Could look stunning on a girl. Now, your ears...they're a different matter..."

"Oi!!"

I laughed and softly tweaked his left lobe. "It's weird how

some people say they can tell the baby's gender. Do you reckon there's any truth in it?"

"Nah. I'm happy whatever this baby turns out to be."

We drove past our lane, and I watched the mileometer again. By the time we reached our other neighbour, it clocked an extra two miles. An attractive metal sign with a cut-out design of a tractor in fields displayed the name, "Tanner's Farm".

It was another Victorian working farm, although the welcome from its owners couldn't have been more different. As we turned in from the main road, a portly man came out of one of the buildings.

We parked the car and Seb whispered, "This seems more hopeful."

"Hello there, can I help you?"

The man held onto his hat as the wind whipped across the farm. His trousers were tucked into stout labouring boots, and he wore a waxed jacket with snags and marks. He smiled, warm and confident.

We explained we'd just moved in. He beamed when he saw the cake.

"That looks delicious, we'll make short work of that. I'm John, John Tanner. Come in for a cuppa – meet Kath."

He took us into the house via the backdoor and we came into a utility room. He pulled off his mucky boots, but as we started to remove our shoes, he beckoned us through.

"Leave 'em on! They look clean enough, I can tell you've not been mucking out pigs! So, where're you from?"

We told him our potted history as he led us into a large farmhouse kitchen. The room radiated warmth from a huge range cooker. To one side of the room, there was a large pine table, and next to it stood a Welsh dresser, stacked with vintage plates and tea-set. A cloud of flour puffed from the island opposite the cooker, where a woman stood kneading bread. She looked up and smiled as we entered. Of a similar age to my own mother, early sixties, she had a face full of soft creases, the kind caused by a readiness to smile. Her eyes were twinkly and her salt and pepper hair was casually pulled back in a wavey pony tail.

"Kath, this is Seb and Bea. Moved into Oak Tree Farm from London! They've made us a cake."

"How kind! Good of you to stop by. Excuse me a tick, I just want to prove this bread."

She dropped the dough into a bowl and slotted it into a drawer of the range oven. Wiping her floury hands on her apron, she came towards us enthusiastically, ushering us to take seats at the table.

"There now, tea? Coffee?" She nodded towards my bump. "Something caffeine-free?" She busied herself making drinks while Seb and John talked about their respective jobs.

"So, what brings you to this part of the world? Must seem a bit different to London." Kath placed the steaming mugs in front of us and offered us slices of the Victoria sponge.

I took a piece. "Thanks - yes, it is different - but we wanted a bit more space as a family."

"So, you're a lawyer too?"

I swallowed my mouthful while nodding. "Just started maternity leave."

"That's a lot of changes at the same time!"

I nodded slowly, giving her a crooked smile.

She met my eyes. "How you finding it, so far?"

Something about her gentle concern unbalanced me. "Not so easy – Seb's in London – it's hard in the day." I shake my head. "So different to what I'm used to."

She nods and looks at my bump. "And you're keeping well?"

I rested the plate on the table and placed a hand on my bump. "Yeah – it's all starting to feel more real. Took a while for us to get here."

Her forehead creased and she spoke more softly. "Well, if you ever need anything, don't be shy to ask."

"Thank you," I pressed my lips. Although Seb was still talking to John, I could tell he was keeping an ear on our conversation too. He frowned. Changing the subject, I looked towards the range. "It's the little things, you know? Take that, for example. We've got one – it terrifies me – haven't even plucked up the courage to use it!"

"They're fine once you get the hang of them. I can show you…"

"Don't worry now. Actually, there's something slightly more urgent …"

I told Kath about the scraping sound coming from somewhere near our spare bedroom. For a brief moment, I thought I saw a wave of concern pass over her face. Whatever it was, it was fleeting and she was quick to give advice.

"We've the number for a good pest control service, if you need it. We tend to put up with a bit of unwanted wildlife here. Had a wasp nest in our loft for four years until the ceiling started to bow!" She chuckles as my eyes widen. "Have to be careful of rats and squirrels with electrical wires, though - you're sensible not to ignore it."

She left the table and returned with a phone number on a post-it note. She also gave me her landline and mobile number.

"If ever you need anything, don't hesitate to call. We've got two daughters and five grandchildren now. Had a bit of experience with young ones!" She pointed proudly to a large photograph hanging opposite the dresser. It was a lovely informal shot of the whole family, eleven members in total. She proudly told me their names and interests, all living nearby, then she turned her head to face me. "I know what it's like, with your first child. We're here if you need us."

I swallowed hard, tears threatening again. Something about Kath was comforting and reassuring. She was one of those people who you instinctively felt you could trust. I suddenly felt that everything would be alright, and my concerns over strange noises and occurrences in the house now seemed ridiculous.

I managed to avoid crying as I rose to say goodbye, and no-one but Seb seemed to notice my reaction.

"What upset you, back there?" he asked, as we drove away.

"It was nothing... relief to have found nice, normal neighbours possibly."

"Probably hormones too. I really wish you hadn't told them private stuff, Bea – we hardly know them."

I felt myself bristle, like a cat stroked the wrong way.

"What harm did it do? There's no shame in it. It hasn't been easy - not just the falling pregnant part but work stresses ...how it affects us both. And don't blame everything on my hormones."

Silence. Seb is generally guarded but is even more so about his own difficulties. It's like the projection of himself to the outside world must be flawless. Few are allowed to peek beneath the surface.

Of course, I wasn't the only one affected by the miscarriages and the struggle to fall pregnant. We couldn't experience something like that without it having an impact on us and our relationship. But Seb never talked about it, throwing himself further into work and anything to preoccupy him - sports, hobbies, interests. He dealt with it by taking charge of the rest of his life - the parts he could control.

I changed the subject. "Well, I'm glad to have met Kath and John. At least I know I've got someone to call upon if I suddenly go into labour while you're in London. It's been playing on my mind, if I'm honest."

Seb humphs in agreement as we turned off to our house. I knew it worried him too - when I would go into labour and how quickly he'd be able to return. We had limited people to call upon. My sister would be the obvious choice: she'd be back from her travels soon, and could perhaps stay with us around the due date. However, I was reluctant to ask as in case she would feel under pressure.

My parents lived in Chelmsford, a good couple of hours away, so I couldn't rely on them in an emergency. My father still worked as a GP and, unlike my sister, my mum was considerably less flexible and would never agree to stay with us for any length of time.

Seb's mum lived closer, in Norfolk. She'd come and stay with us if we asked, but she was currently abroad, having recently retired and lost her husband, and we didn't want to curb this happiness.

No, Kath and John seemed a safe, local option. When we reached home, we added Kath's phone numbers to both of our mobiles.

During the rest of the weekend, Seb investigated the noises that had disturbed me over the previous couple of weeks. He tightened a few screws on the track for the door in our bedroom. He wanted to inspect the loft for the source of the scratching sounds, but although he found the hatch door, we didn't have a ladder to reach it. Given the loft wasn't boarded, he didn't fancy hoisting himself up and risk putting his foot through the ceiling.

It was strange, but when Seb was in the house, I never noticed the sounds that had put me on edge. I assumed that the bustle of us both in the house scared the culpable animal and made it retreat further into the roof. That was my only explanation because, sure enough, when Monday came around and Seb had left for work, the scratching resumed.

That time it started when I was upstairs, getting dressed. I tiptoed across the landing to the spare room. It seemed to be coming from the back wall. I tried knocking, to see if it would scare the animal – rat, mouse, squirrel, whatever it was. There was a brief pause, but then it resumed, faster if anything. Perhaps I scared it? I listened intently, but it was hard to distinguish whether the sound was made by claws, teeth or beak. After a minute or so it stopped.

At least I had a plan. The phone was downstairs, and I found the number for the pest control company Kath had recommended: *Houseguest Removal.* Luckily, the company could visit on Wednesday. In the meantime, I decided to use music to distract myself and cover up the sound, should it return.

When Wednesday arrived, a red van pulled up outside the house. The two men were surprised when I opened the door before they'd had a chance to knock.

"You're keen – or desperate! Where are you having the trouble?"

I led them through the house to the bathroom, where the noises were usually most audible downstairs, then showed them the back of the spare bedroom. Naturally, not a whisper could be heard in their presence.

One of the men went to get a ladder from the van while the other chatted to me. He was admiring the old features of the property, the original timbers and the irregularity of the rooms. He tapped and stroked the surface of the back wall, the one where I had heard the scraping.

"Course, that one's not original. You can feel the difference, eh? That's different material. Can you hear the hollow sound?"

Sure enough, although all the walls of the room were

painted the same clotted cream colour, the back wall felt slightly rougher. Why was it different to the others? When I asked him, he just shrugged, and suggested maybe there had been damage at some point.

His mate returned with the ladder. He held the bottom while the guy I'd spoken to climbed up into the roof through the hatch, armed with a flashlight. I stood nearby, eager to hear what he could see.

The streak of light from the torch danced into view every now and again and you could hear the beams   overhead creak as he progressed across the loft. He returned towards the hatch, head popping into view.

"Well, I've found evidence of birds helping themselves to straw; there are a few holes near the top, on the frontside of the house. They use it for their nests. It's often sparrows that do it around springtime, so these holes are old ones. Crows, magpies and jackdaws may also be culprits. You're best off contacting a thatch company to deal with that, particularly before spring's upon us again. Doesn't explain your scratching though. Other than that, there's plenty of spiders, some real big'uns."

He grinned as I shuddered, and he made his way back down the ladder.

"So as far as I could see, no sign of vermin."

He knocked on the back wall of the room again and listened. "I can't hear anything now. My only suggestion is that something's got behind this wall. It's possible mice or rats could be getting in and out of the roof through the holes made by the birds, to collect food and water. They could then be nesting behind this wall." He taps it again with his knuckles. "Unfortunately, you'd have to remove it to see what's going on."

A mystery wall, with space behind it. This was news to me. I was keen to find out why it had been built and if there was anything living behind it. However, I knew Seb would be reluctant to knock down a stud wall in an otherwise perfectly usable room, particularly when we had more pressing projects to complete, like finishing off the nursery. I paid the men their call-out fee, and they agreed to offer a discount if they were called back, should we knock down the wall and find any four-legged intruders.

After they left, I was curious about the stud wall and the amount of space beyond it. It took me a while to locate a tape measure, but when I eventually found one, I measured the combined length of our bedroom and the annex nursery. This came to 8.54m. As these rooms were directly opposite the spare room, on the opposite side of the stairwell, together they should be roughly the same length as it. However, when I measured the length of the spare room, it was only 7.2m. Obviously, a house of this age was unlikely to have uniform measurements, but such a difference seemed extreme. It meant the stud wall blocked over a metre of the spare room's length.

The space was sufficient for a large cupboard. Surely Seb and I would have remembered this information in the survey? We'd kept a folder of documents relating to the house purchase. I fetched it from the lounge, found the survey and scanned the section relating to the first floor of the house. It made no mention of any stud wall. I called the telephone number of the surveyor printed on the form, but the guy I spoke to couldn't shed any light on the situation. He fobbed me off with waffle about old buildings having irregular measurements and some caveat in his terms and conditions about not investigating anything in the survey which could damage the structure.

After hanging up, I went back upstairs to the spare room. This time I felt all the walls. The stud wall was warmer than the other walls, confirming there was space behind it that acted as insulation. I lowered myself to the ground and put my ear against it.

My proximity seemed to trigger a response. Scrape, scrape,

scrape. It made me start. More deliberate this time, like fingernails clawing a blackboard. I flinched, clasping my ears, edging away from the wall. The atmosphere seemed to change; the air felt thicker, oxygen thinner, but perhaps I was breathing faster. My skin prickled with the sense of being watched, observed, similar to the sensation I'd felt before. Looking back, I can't rationalise the feeling but I knew I had to get away.

Staggering to raise myself from my knees, I backed out of the room, pulling the door closed behind me. Shaking, I made my way downstairs, as fast as I dared, gripping the handrail tightly. I needed to be outside, far from that wall. I grabbed my coat and mobile and hurried through the music room into the garden.

I pressed digit one, the speed dial for Seb. Thankfully the spot outside still had reception.

"Hello? What's wrong?"

His voice was abrupt, concerned. I never rang for a chat in the day. He didn't like to be interrupted at work.

"Is it the baby?"

"No."

By this point, the adrenalin had subsided, but I found it hard to speak, words catching in my throat as I tried to hold back sobs.

"Bea, whatever's wrong? You're worrying me."

"It's the - " The line beeped, reception poor.

"Hello? Hello? Can you hear me?"

"Yeah, reception's bad but I can hear you now. The pest control people came..."

"Hello? It's gone again. Just caught the bit about pest control coming. It doesn't matter about the squirrels, rats... whatever. We'll get it sorted."

"No, it isn't that. They couldn't find anything...the pest

46

control company. But they showed me part of the spare room has been blocked off, boarded up. The scraping noise's coming from there. I just touched it, and it started up again. It only makes the noise when I'm alone. I don't like it, Seb! I feel like it's watching me... taunting me."

I heard him take a breath. "Look, you're overreacting Bea. You just notice it more when you're on your own. If there's a blocked-off space, maybe the vermin are using it for a nest. We'll have to investigate when we decorate." His tone changes, like he was talking to a child. "Please don't get yourself worked up over it...it's nothing. The extra space might even be useful for storage – maybe we could make a cupboard, once we've reclaimed it from the wildlife! Go and make yourself a cup of herbal tea and have a biscuit."

"I don't want a bloody biscuit! I want to know what's going on now, not wait till we decorate!"

He continued to talk to me with controlled patience. "There's nothing going on. It's just a noise that will have some logical explanation. Getting yourself upset like this... it's no good for the baby."

"For Christ's sake, Seb, I'm not just a baby-carrier! Please come home. I really need you and I don't want to be on my own here!"

"Look, I can't talk to you when you're like this. I'm up to my eyeballs, Bea, working to a deadline. Disclosure is by close of play tomorrow, and we're less than half-way through three files of documents. I'll see you later. Put a film on or something to take your mind off it. Or call Kath. Please. I've got to hang up."

"Thanks!"

I pressed the red button hard and shoved the phone into my pocket. My free hand was clenched so hard, it's made fingernail marks on my palm. I snatched a tissue from my other pocket and wiped away frustrated, angry tears.

I took some deep breaths of the frosty air and looked across the fields. The colours were muted and cool. A kite circled above the field: prey had obviously attracted his attention and he was biding his time before swooping for the kill. In the distance, trees stood stark, stripped of leaves, like distant watchers.

It wasn't a bad idea to call Kath. But what would I say? I didn't want to come across as loony or clingy, particularly as I hardly knew her. And without a car I'd have to ask her to come over here or pick me up. No, it was too much to ask.

More than anything, I wanted to speak to my sister, but I didn't want to worry her so far from home, when she was busy on her adventures.

The chill of the concrete slabs beneath my slippers made my toes curl and numb. I couldn't spend the rest of the day outside on the footpath, freezing to death. Eventually I plucked up the courage to go back inside, intending to linger near the door of the music room in case I needed to make a quick exit.

Entering the house, but leaving the door open, I listened cautiously for the scraping sound. Nothing. Only the solitary song of a bird outside. I waited a few minutes, rigid and alert. Silence, apart from the click of the door as I cautiously pulled it shut. I couldn't spend the rest of the day waiting, ears straining. Taking the opposite approach, I chose a CD to drown out the noise in case it returned. I slipped *The Killers* out of its case, slid it into the cd player and set the volume high.

Sitting on the edge of a seat with the lap-top, I wrote a long overdue email to Harriet, updating her on my life over the past weeks: leaving work, maternity leave, our move, the strange occurrences in the house.

All the while praying for Seb's swift return.

CHAPTER 6

Maud

I was the first to leave the church, not even waiting for the end of the Easter sermon.

Never have I been so thankful to be outside, away from the staring eyes. The wind pulls at my skirts and an April shower peppers my skin, but I care not. At least the rain soothes my reddened face, goes some way to bring calm.

It may seem blasphemous, to seek to escape a church rather than find sanctuary within, but it is the truth, may the Lord forgive me. Nathaniel was beside himself during the sermon. He took exception to the Pastor's words about the resurrection of Christ, as though possessed by the anti-Christ himself! It was all I could do to keep hold of him. No amount of rocking and cuddling brought comfort. His arms and legs flailed, his cry angry and inconsolable.

I felt shame that he behaved in such a way in a place of God and that I was unable to control him. Either side of me, eyes flickered, and heads twitched from the pews in front. All strained to see the source of the disturbance, their foreheads creased in disapproval.

My mother is staying with us over Easter and she sat on

the pew next to William. She glanced towards Nathaniel and me several times. No doubt I have embarrassed her too, drawing unnecessary attention to the family. She cannot think much of me as a mother.

Despite the weather, Nathaniel also seems relieved to be outside the church. *Could this mean...* No, Maud. Do not make that connection. Plenty of children struggle to keep still and quiet during a service, there is no reason to think about it too deeply. Perhaps it is exhaustion that brings him calm: certainly; his limbs are less tense and his cries are no more than a whimper.

Why is it so hard for me to comfort him? Does he sense my unease in my new role as mother? Or is there a deeper problem that lies beneath the surface of his skin, darker than its soft, peach, innocent appearance? A problem that disturbs him - simmers until it boils over into a rage that cannot be quelled. In the dark hours of the morning, he is unrecognisable, like an animal. At those times, he bewilders me such that I can only wait and watch for the fury to pass.

I round the corner of St Margaret's, hoping its aged walls will shield me from the majority of the parishioners now snaking out of the entrance. I do not wish to encounter their judgmental faces. I clutch Nathaniel tighter to me, use my body to protect him from the worst of the elements.

William joins me but avoids my eyes, arms folded, shoulders hunched. He transfers his weight from one foot to the other, impatiently. I wish he would speak to me, offer his suggestions of how to soothe Nathaniel. Recently he seems to have given up, as though we are both beyond help.

A dozen or so parishioners have trickled outside within our view, but so far not my mother.

"What's she doing? Don't she realise we need to get going, bring Nathaniel home to the warm?" William scowls. He hates to be kept waiting, or any waste of time for that matter, particularly on the one day he had a chance to rest his weary body and read by the range.

I sigh. "No doubt she'll be talking to the Pastor. She won't be hurried William, you know what she's like."

He grunts in reply, just before my mother emerges.

"There you are! I've just been talking to the Pastor. He's a nice young gentleman, but I favour the sermons at All Saints," she comments.

Mother is a regular churchgoer in her parish of Wickham Market, where I grew up. A much larger village than Ubbeston, she is very proud of the beautiful church of All Saints, with its octagonal tower and spire, but she tolerates St Mary's on the odd occasions she comes to visit.

We walk towards the cart, William up ahead. When she thinks he is out of earshot, Mother turns to me.

"Why on earth didn't you put Nathaniel to the breast?" she hisses. "That was how I settled you and your sister in church."

I was hoping to delay the discussion about my milk drying up until later, presenting, as it did, an opportunity to pass judgment.

"I can't Ma. It just stopped – the milk."

"What do you mean? He's not yet four months and a slip of a thing. A strapping girl like you should have no problem sustaining 'im."

Whether he heard, I know not, but for once, William turns and saves me from further explanation.

"Let's be going. There's no sign of the rain easing up and we should get Nathaniel home in the warm," he calls.

Mother sniffs as we follow William in the direction of the trap. "At least one of you has got your 'ead screwed on."

She holds Nathaniel as I climb into the back then passes him back to me before climbing in next to William.

I am grateful to be rattling along the road back-to-back, a few moments peace without scrutiny or comment. My milk stopped flowing a couple of weeks back, but truth be told, I have never had confidence in my supply, nor Nathaniel's ability to suckle. I remember my sister's children at his age. They seemed to thrive and grow chubby after the first couple of months; the fat around their little limbs curved and pinched in at dimpled knees, elbows and wrists. Nathaniel could not be more different. His skinny limbs have scarce enough fat to feed a ferret, his clothes not yet filled.

My supply trickled to a stop around the time the sow came to farrow. She is a good mother. When her time was near, she gathered hay and made a nest for herself. William was up all night, making sure each piglet arrived and that she did not accidentally squash them under her enormous weight. She had twelve in the end, with three hours of labour. It seemed so easy for her, giving new life.

Right from the start, the piglets had a sixth sense for her milk; sucked her poor teats with a ferocity and vigour that made me wince. It was like her whole existence was for their benefit, and they greedily took without a second thought. Watching them made me think we're no different: the mother is a source of sustenance, her pain of no consequence. It doesn't matter what she wants or needs.

Shortly after that, when Nathaniel cried for his feed, I placed him next to my breast as normal. But his rooting for my nipple made me feel sick, bringing to mind the piglets with the sow. With me distracted, he latched on poorly, shooting pain from my cracked nipple. I had to stop, break the latch, making him scream in rage. No matter how many times we tried, it failed. In the end, I sated his hunger with cow's milk, warmed on the range, spooned into his mouth drop by drop. I have fed him that way ever since, adding a little porridge once a day. At least he is starting to put on weight; I can feel it in my arms.

When we reach the cottage, William helps Mother down and she reaches up for Nathaniel again, freeing my hands to clamber to the ground. Returned to my arms, he wakens and cries. Always the same near me.

Without a word, William walks into the rear parlour and adds some coal to the range. Taking a seat by the fire, he reaches for Henry Stephen's Book of the Farm. It's always beside his chair and, apart from the newspaper, the only reading he ever does, usually on a Sunday afternoon. Not only does it guide him on the animals and crops, but it also means he can avoid conversation.

I see Mother's lips purse as her eyes scour the room. My cheeks flush. The cottage, as familiar to me as my own arm, looks shabby through her eyes: pots tarnished by coal smoke sit forlorn at the range; air sour from the cloth pail in one corner, the bucket of bones in the other; every surface under a shadow of soot. Since Nathaniel's birth, chores that were once woven into my life have been neglected or poorly done. Sleep deprived, hours of the day are taken over by soiled cloths, washing and feeding, crammed into the short gaps between his cries.

Looking around, I am shamed by oil lamps so dark they would smother the light from any flame. Our windows, once carefully polished with vinegar and newspaper, are clouded with grime, a shield keeping out the rays from the weak winter sun.

I cannot remember the last time I scourged the beds with turpentine and salt to remove any bugs, or when I last prepared a camphor solution to ease the chilblains on William's hands and feet. These are the visible signs of me letting things slip. Others are more hidden.

But no-one can argue I have neglected the house in favour of myself. I avoid the mirror in our bedroom, not wanting to witness the mess I've become. My skin has turned sallow, my hair duller and thinner. The lack of sleep leaves dark rings around my eyes. My mother always told me I was the fairer of her two daughters, and my golden hair and clear skin turned heads in our village. Now I am less visible.

"I see you need help, my girl."

I brush a tear away with my hand, and she notices it is cracked and bleeding.

"Do you have no salve for your skin?"

I shake my head. "I have the fat left over from the mutton and some wax and alkanet root from a while back, but not the time to make it."

"Fine. I'll tackle the cleaning in a while, but first I'll make it for you."

William looks up from his book but his expression is inscrutable. I wonder whether he has noticed me slipping and fading? In times past, I was proud and took care with my appearance – how my mother's comments would have prickled me then! Now I let the words wash over me.

Mother busies herself in the parlour, tutting as she finds the ingredients and discovers my other lapses. I focus instead on heating the milk in the jug for Nathaniel's next feed.

When the pan starts to warm, I test a spoonful then pour it into a bowl. I take a seat at the table, rest Nathaniel on my lap, and he immediately fusses and fidgets.

"Leave the salve a day to cool and thicken. I have left it in the larder."

"Thank you, Ma."

She joins me at the table, vinegar and cloth in hand, reaching for the oil lamp to polish. She rubs the cloth over the glass as she watches me tip the spoon of milk into Nathaniel's mouth. Before she has the chance to comment, I steer the subject elsewhere.

"I have made brawn for lunch, with potatoes and carrots, your favourite. William slaughtered one of the old pigs last week, to make room for the piglets."

My mother sniffs in acknowledgment.

"I'll put the potatoes on the range as soon as Nathaniel is finished."

I don't even get a sniff this time. She carries on polishing, holding the lamp to the light to check for smears.

Given how little advice I was granted last time I sought help, I suspect it will be fruitless asking now, but I'm conscious that William is here and I want to show willing. Now is as good a time as any. As Nathaniel gulps down another spoonful, I brace myself.

"I've had such trouble settlin' 'im, Ma. He gets in such a rage – draws up his legs and balls his hands into fists. I hoped it was a problem he'd grow out of, but there's been no improvement. What would you do?"

William looks up briefly. At least he heard me try.

Mother pauses rubbing to look at me. "Well, you've created your own problem, Maud. Why'd you stop feeding him yourself? One of the best ways to settle a babe is on the breast."

"Like I say, the milk dried up. I tried, but he was not getting bigger or stronger on it. And his cloths were as often dry as they were wet, which showed 'e weren't takin' much."

"I never heard of that. Well, you're stuck with spoon feeding now. You could try Godfrey's to settle 'im – some mothers swear by it. Of course, I just used a drop o' gin when you were gripin," Ma sniffs.

At this, William forgets to conceal the fact that he's listening to our conversation. "He won't be having any of that infernal cordial! It was in the paper a couple of weeks back. One of the doctors said any so-called medicine that contains

Laudanum could harm babies. Evil stuff! And gin's no better!" Waiting for a reaction from my mother that is not forthcoming, his head tilts back to his book.

Her face turns sulky. It was rare to hear William openly disagree with her. But she would not retaliate. Mother would never argue with a man.

"Well, you will just 'ave to keep tryin' Maud. No-one ever said it was easy." With that, the conversation was closed.

As if sensing he had been discussed, Nathaniel squawks in rage and knocks the spoon from my hands and across the room. Tutting, my mother finds a clean one and takes him from me. She holds his arms firmly against his sides and the crying stops.

"None of that nonsense with me. Finish your milk." She tips the spoon and he sips obediently. She humphs with satisfaction.

I move away to prepare the vegetables, feeling worse than ever.

CHAPTER 7

Bea

I wake to find myself alone.

I didn't hear Seb come home last night. You'd have thought after what happened yesterday, the culmination of several weeks of strange incidents taking their toll, he'd have made an effort to be home early. Yet when I went to bed at half ten, there was no sign of him.

Don't get me wrong. I understand what it's like when you're working on a case. I'm not one of those who soon forgets what life was like at the coalface five minutes after taking a step back. In litigation, nothing short of death or near death will shift a deadline. But at the very least, he could have phoned me on the way home.

I get out of bed feeling crotchety. I hate beginning a day like this. I wish I coult call Harriet. She gets me, without explanations or justifications. Her opinion can be different without irritating me.

On the kitchen dinner table, I find a note.

Bea,

Sorry we didn't get a chance to talk last night. The firm sent me home by cab –got in at 1am! Back at it again today. I'm hoping to be home for 8 – let's catch up then.
Hate to hear you upset.
Love Seb x

It's something, I guess. God knows what the cab would have cost from London to here, but no doubt the client would pick up the tab.

As I make a coffee, I glance at the calendar. Shit, midwife today! I'd completely forgotten. Luckily, I've just enough time to shower and tidy the place up a bit.

She arrives promptly at 9am.

"Mrs Haddon?"

Standing on the front doorstep is a frizzy-haired woman, in her mid-fifties, I'd guess, in nursing uniform with chunky cardigan, clutching a medical bag and clipboard. She has a stern look about her which reminds me of a schoolteacher. I beckon her in and try to steer her to the lounge, but she has other ideas.

"I'm Maureen. I think it's best that we go to your bedroom, so you can lie down comfortably, and I can take measurements. I'll just pop my shoes off."

She declines a drink, so I lead her upstairs. I see her eyes surveying the untidy state of the room; half-emptied boxes, clothes spilling out of holdalls, a laundry   basket full of dirty washing. I explain we recently moved in, but she still looks unimpressed.

"Yes, I can see. Well, you'll need to sort it out soon if you're planning for a home birth. Maternity notes?"

"We'd like a hospital birth, actually. The notes are in my bag through here."

She peeks her head into the annex, her eyes taking in the half-finished paint job and the bags of baby related items, dumped there after shopping and not touched since. The cot, having been delivered last week in its flat-pack box, is propped up against them.

"I can see you have your work cut out for you. Don't leave things too late. First-time mums have a tendency to think babies will arrive like clockwork, but it doesn't always go to plan! Here, I'll read through those while you give me a urine sample. No doubt you've done a few before?" She reaches for the notes and hands me the pot.

I head downstairs, irritated. I had high hopes for a warm and friendly midwife, not this curt woman who so far had only made me feel ill-prepared. When I return, self-consciously handing her the warm pot, her voice is softer as she unscrews the lid ready to test for sugars and proteins.

"I can see you've had quite a time of it, bless you. How many times did you miscarry, my love?"

She must have read the summary in my notes.

"Twice."

My fingers rub the duvet cover. Both times within the space of a year. I hate the word miscarriage. It sounds so innocuous, as though you absentmindedly let something slip through your fingers. A mistake that could have been rectified, if only you'd held on properly. I've lost many hours thinking about what I could have done differently. Did I spend too long in the office? Was it my stress levels? Seb never blamed my workload directly, but sometimes the way he fusses over me, his insistence that I take things easy, makes me feel like maybe he did and still does. Or perhaps I'm just being paranoid.

Both "misses" were early so we kept it to ourselves. They were painful secrets to keep. Sometimes they would sear like a fresh wound , at christenings or when we found out Seb's sister was expecting. But to the outside world I kept the smile on my face and hid the tears.

"Judging by the handwriting, you've also seen a fair few mid-wives, which isn't ideal. Never mind; you'll have me now for the rest of your pregnancy. I won't be in the hospital at the delivery, but I'll meet him or her at home and help settle you in as a mum. Now, let's get you comfy on the bed and I'll listen for baby. Do you feel much movement each day?"

"Yes, some... "

She fluffs up the pillow and I lie back, pulling my leggings down over my bump. We stop talking as she moves the cold stethoscope over my belly. I always find this part stressful: the silence while you wait for that heartbeat to be detected. Maureen looks at me and nods.

"Baby's heart sounds fine. Now we need to work out the position. I'll try to warm my hands a bit."

She puts her stethoscope down and rubs her hands together vigorously. Laying them gently on my tummy, she sweeps over the bump. Her eyes look towards the wall above my head as she lets her fingertips read and assess. It reminds me of that party game I used to play as a child, where you try to guess what's inside the sack without looking. Satisfied, she stops and signals for me to pull up my leggings and roll up the sleeve of my top.

"I believe he or she is currently in breech, but I'm not worried at this stage. You're 30 weeks so there can be a lot of movement in that time, and if you stay active that will help. Now, let's check your blood pressure."

She concentrates on the numbers as my arm is squeezed and then released. She frowns.

"It's slightly higher than your previous readings. It's something to keep an eye on. I'll just check that urine sample." She nods with approval, confirming all's well on that front. "I'll come back in two weeks. As I say, keep active – light housework and walks are good - but make sure you take plenty of rest too.

Try to avoid anything stressful. We want to keep that blood pressure in check."

I think back to my recent experiences here. Could they have caused the surge in my blood pressure? I'll try to follow her advice, but not everything is within my control. Of course, I say none of this to Maureen, who is packing up in readiness to leave and see her next patient.

As I close the door behind her, I stroke my bump: "Don't worry: I'll do my best to keep my cool."

I busy myself with more tidying and unpacking and then treat myself to a check of my emails.

Fantastic! Harriet's replied.

Bea,

So pleased to hear from you. I don't often get a chance to check emails (I've visited places that don't have running hot water, yet alone broadband!), but I've returned to Cusco before I fly to Lima. You just caught me!

Are the group emails a bit much? I worry I'm annoying people and maybe no-one's reading them, but I'm pleased you are. Would be great to keep up the one-to-one chat, but no pressure. Sounds like you're busy.

Not had much response from M&D (surprise, surprise) but I'm trying to call every couple of weeks from payphones. Hard to find!

I've had a few nice messages from friends at work and elsewhere. Not homesick yet... but fed up with searching for decent veggie food! I've met some great people here too, but I'll save that for another time...

Pleased your pregnancy is still going well. Can't believe I'm soon going to be an auntie! Very excited. Auntie Harry or Auntie Harriet? The former, I think. Auntie Harriet sounds ancient, like a

Miss Marple sidekick.

House situation sounds mysterious. I'm not surprised you're on edge! As you say, could be logical explanations, but you should trust your instincts. I don't want to spook you, but who knows what it could be? I've always been open minded about spiritual stuff - find it comforting in a way.

Seb's reaction is unsurprising. It's just his character: he's not comfortable with anything outside his experience. M and D would be the same!

Keep me posted. Can you send a few pics of the house?
Can't wait to see you (and the baby) in person.

Lots of love, H xxx

I smile. Trust Harriet to say the right thing at the right time.

With only two years between us, she's always been a close friend as well as a sister. We look so different: her willowy figure and auburn straight hair, me shorter and curvier, with dark chestnut curls. But in personality we're very similar. She's also a lawyer, but after a horrible break up with her long-term partner, she took a sabbatical and went travelling. More champagne back-packing than roughing it, judging by some of the hotels she'd described in her emails.

Until recently, we've followed similar paths: boarding school, university, law school and fast paced life in London. Now our journeys have forked in different directions - she pursuing adventure and new experiences, me laying down roots and starting a family. Despite our choices, it's a comfort to have her support, even from afar.

I check the time – 4pm. I guess I should follow Maureen's advice and do a bit of hoovering to keep active. Before I get stuck in, my phone pings. It tells me someone has been detected near the front door. As the internet connection is still good, I play back the video footage. The front of the house looks normal, no visitors in shot, but the scene suddenly blacks out before returning. I check the signal but the connection symbol still displays full bars. I play it back again, frowning. There it is again – blacking out the screen - but this time I notice movement, like something close to the lens, a flicker from right to left.

My shoulders tense. I slip my phone in my pocket, shove my feet into shoes and grab my coat, making my way through the house to the front door.

I turn the lock and survey the view from the doorway before stepping outside. The light is fading but there is nothing unusual. I retrace the steps I took on the previous occasion when the monitor had sensed movement, walking around both sides of the house and scanning the field and driveway. Nothing – no clue as to what could have made the flash of black across the screen.

"Aaaagghh!"

A sudden crash from behind makes me scream. The shrill sound cuts through the silence. Spinning around, I see straightaway that it was the door slamming shut. *Shit.* I don't have much choice but to ring Seb.

"Hello?"

"Seb, I'm sorry – I've locked myself out the house."

He sighs. "Right, well I guess I'll have to come home early then. How did you manage that?"

"It was the door monitor. It's triggered a couple of times now – I went outside to have a look. Did you see the black thing cross the screen?" The system sent messages to both of our phones.

There's a pause. "I don't know what you mean, Bea. I've got nothing from today."

"Maybe it hasn't reached you yet – anyway, I'll see you in a bit."

"Are you warm enough? Should you call Kath in the meantime?"

"No, I'm fine – I've got my coat. Sorry again."

I hang up. Standing in the cold, I try to replay the video clip on my phone, but the recording is no longer there. *That's odd. Perhaps they delete after you've watched them several times?*

It's an age waiting for Seb outside, in the diminishing light. As if I didn't need reminding, it emphasises how stranded we are, and the distance between home and Seb's place of work. Another job for the to-do list; have a set of keys made for Kath and John in case of similar mishaps.

Killing time, I amuse myself by walking around the house and the barn, making notes on my phone of all the things we need to fix, paint or change. It's a relief when eventually a set of headlights swings off the road and bobs up our bumpy driveway.

Seb's more concerned for my health than irritated. "Your hands are like ice! Come on, let's get you inside."

"Sorry again. We'll have to heat something from the freezer for tea – it will take too long to make a curry now."

He nods. "By the way, I checked the app for the door. Still no message or recording on my phone," he raises his eyebrows to me.

"That's weird. I definitely saw something." I put a Tupperware in the microwave and while it whirrs, I tentatively broach the subject of the scratching sounds again. "Have you thought anymore about the wall   upstairs?"

"Look, I don't want to go knocking it down at this stage. We need to get the annex straight, for a start." Seb opens the drawer for the cutlery. "But I don't want you to worry though, so I've ordered a ladder and some mousetraps. They should arrive in a couple of days." His voice trails after him as he walks through to the diner, "I'll put some traps in the loft at the weekend, particularly over the area where you say the scratching could be heard. Seems cruel, but it's the only way we're going to stop it."

Mousetraps don't sit well with me either, but I can't see any alternative. At least it feels like we're doing something. At least he's listened.

He emerges back through the doorway. "Mind you, I'm irritated the cavity wasn't picked up in the survey! We'll have to knock it through when we decorate the spare room. Might as well make use of any extra space!"

Over dinner, I tell him about Maureen's visit, although I keep quiet about my blood pressure. I don't want to worry him. Besides, if he knew, he'd be questioning what I do each day and lecturing me to take it easy.

There's only so much cosseting and protection I can handle.

CHAPTER 8

Maud

I pinch the skin on my arm to stay awake. The swaying motion of the cart and the unexpected warmth of the sun on my cheek lure me to sleep but I do not want to seem rude. Emily is one of the few women around my age who lives nearby, married to the tenant at Tanner's farm, and I would hate to offend her.

"Pleasant day for it. Scarcely need a shawl! So, what is on your list?"

William arranged for our trip to Halesworth. I think he thought it would help me, a trip out. Six miles away, it is a rare visit, with the promise of small treats from the haberdashers or the bakers. Today I am less enthusiastic, visiting for the first time with Nathaniel strapped to me, likely to erupt at any moment. For the time being, he is peaceful, and I am thankful for it.

"Not a lot. Some linen for Nathaniel's clothes, to replace those he's outgrown – yarn and buttons too. I would like some new ribbon for the May Day celebrations … and perhaps some buns. And you?"

Emily looks at me knowingly, resting a hand on her small

bump, now visible under her apron. "I have let my clothes out as much as I can. Time to make new ones, and some for the baby." She smiles, the image of a glowing, expectant mother.

I smile back but my mouth is taut and unnatural.

For the past week, Nathaniel has cried through the middle of the night without pause. I am too agitated to sleep, his voice echoing in my head long after he finally drifts off. In the day, I am half-present, finishing essential chores, but little else. Hours drift into days, days drift into weeks. And all the while the bond between him and me, the one I assumed would grow automatically, fails to appear. I go through the motions of motherhood, numb and fearful.

Does he hate me, or is he scared? When his eyes meet mine, they're shiny and dark like coal, searing into me as he howls. *Is there something wrong with him? Something that makes him burn with rage?* Sometimes it seems he belongs to another, not me.

I spare Emily these feelings, not wishing to taint her happiness. I smile and nod in the right places as she chatters about her hopes for the baby, her family, the things she needs to buy and do. I keep my fears locked inside.

Before long, the fields give way to clusters of buildings. Roads widen, branch off and multiply and the spire looms in the distance. Tanner's farmhand, Joseph, pulls the cart to a standstill just a few yards from the market square. He hops down and reaches up to help Emily. Once her feet hit the cobbles she takes Nathaniel, and Joseph looks up at me, hand outstretched, smiling at me. I accept his hand. After I land, his fingers continue to hold mine for the briefest of seconds, the smile still playing on his lips. I feel myself colour. His behaviour is forward, but I would be lying if I said it did not lift my spirits. After weeks trapped indoors with Nathaniel and an increasingly distant husband, I enjoy feeling attractive, to be appreciated, like I am visible again.

If Emily had noticed his attentions, she gives no sign of it.

"Meet us back here at half past one, please, Joseph."

He passes us our baskets, doffs his cap with another smile, then hops onto the carriage and away.

Halesworth is busy, the town centre noisy with traders calling from the stalls. Fish, fruit, vegetables and cheese are temptingly displayed. We try to be self-sufficient on the farm, mainly eating produce that we have reared, made or grown, but I make a mental note to buy some fresh haddock before we leave for home, a rare treat.

Watkins' haberdasher is our first stop. Emily's purse is clearly plentiful, choosing a blue floral cloth for the May Day celebrations, and yards of soft woollen cloth for the new baby's clothes.

I choose some white cotton, linen and thread to make outfits for Nathaniel, and yellow and green ribbon. Refashioning my hat for the celebrations with ties and bows is the best I can do with our budget.

Tempting displays draw our attention at the confectioners. A three-tiered wedding cake is in the centre, the palest of pinks with white scrolls. Whether it is actually a cake or iced tins, it is impossible to tell. There are rows of pink and white sugar mice, shortbreads, fancy cakes. I cannot resist buying two Madeleines. Emily takes a box of marzipan fruits, so bright and realistic they look like the real versions on the market stalls, shrank to miniatures.

"Ironmongers next?"

I hesitate. I planned to visit the apothecary and would rather go alone. This could be the opportunity to separate from Emily.

"I don't need to him today and you know how noisy and hot it is in there! I fear it will wake Nathaniel. You go, I'll be in the apothecary. Come find me when you're done."

Emily nods and disappears up the road.

Two streets away is Bishop's Apothecary. Huge glass vials, filled with jewel coloured liquid – ruby, emerald, sapphire - stand in the glass fronted window display. Fingers on the handle, I pause for a quick breath to steady my nerves.

The bell rings as I enter, and the gentleman at the counter looks up without a smile. His eyes, behind half-moon glasses, look stern and add to my agitation. Inside the shop is stacked with dozens, if not hundreds, of dark wooden drawers and shelves, each one neatly labelled.

"Can I help you, madam?"

"Yes please. I would like something to soothe my son. I have terrible trouble settlin' 'im, both night and day."

He looks at the peaceful Nathaniel, swaddled against me, and raises his eyebrows.

I bluster. "Well, clearly he is sleeping now, but this is irregular. He is often red with anger… refuses to be comforted. Keeps me awake most of the night."

With finger and thumb, he pushes his glasses further up his nose. "Has madam tried Godfrey's Cordial? I am assured it has a very calming effect on babies and toddlers."

From behind the counter, he reaches for liquid in a thin, tall bottle. I remember William's reaction, when my mother suggested it. His feelings were clear – he was dead set against it. Sitting on the counter, with a jolly picture of a baby on the label, it seems so harmless. *Imagine if it worked! Just a few drops could soothe him, give me time to clear my head, find my strength. Did William need to know? If other mothers use it…*

The apothecarist is staring at me strangely. I have to decide quickly, one way or the other.

"No - no thank you. My husband does not agree with it. I was thinking of a herbal remedy, perhaps? And something for my headaches."

He reaches behind him and produces a bottle.

"This should help with the headaches and to improve the quality of your sleep."

He hands it to me. Laudanum. No doubt William would have an opinion on this too, but I feel too embarrassed to decline the apothecarist's suggestion again.

"Lavender is very good for cleansing and soothing. You could try hanging some in the house to purify the air."

"Thank you, yes please."

We have lavender aplenty at the farm in the summer, but it is too early for it now. As he fetches dried sprigs of the flower from the drawers behind him, I think how to broach my next question: one that has been troubling me for some time, but I have kept to myself.

"And what if the child was deeply troubled? What if that was the reason he rages and cannot sleep?" My face flushes and I feel moisture on my skin. He frowns at me, as if I am the one who is troubled, or simple of mind.

"I am not sure I follow, madam. He is a child - he cannot have melancholia."

My face burns. "No, no, I did not mean that. I mean ... what if he was possessed by somethin'... a demon or spirit?" The words trip out of my mouth, fast and clumsy. I have had difficulty piecing together fears in my own head, yet alone air them to someone else. Now they jump out like a jack-in-a-box.

He frowns. "I am a man of science; I cannot advise on spiritual matters. If you have concerns of that nature, I suggest you speak to your parson who would be best placed to advise you." He surveys me with a long, steady look. "Of course, historically sage has always been used to ward off evil spirits. It would not do any harm to hang a sprig on his crib."

I thank him and ask for some sprigs. I cannot wait to leave

the shop. He wraps the herbs and flowers in paper, and I place them in my basket, tucking the bottle of laudanum underneath, away from curious eyes. Emily is unlikely to think anything of it, but I would rather not take any chances.

As I step out of the door, she nearly bumps into me.

"Do you have everything you need?" she asks, eyes drifting over my basket.

"Yes, I think so. Now, I just want to purchase a couple of haddock. Shall we set off back to market before we meet Joseph?"

CHAPTER 9

Bea

A week has passed without further unexplained noises in the house. You'd think I'd take comfort from this and start to relax, but I'm finding it impossible. I'm holding my breath, waiting for something else to happen. All day I carry the tension, jumping at the slightest murmur.

Disrupted sleep doesn't help. I go to bed each night feeling exhausted and yet the rest for which I yearn is beyond reach. Whichever way I lie in bed, I can't find a comfortable position and my brain won't switch off.

Seb installed the traps last weekend, as planned. We assumed they had worked – that was the logical explanation for the sounds disappearing. He was apprehensive about checking the loft this weekend, anticipating ensnared rotting animals, but when he shone his torch above the hatch, he found none. There was no sign that wildlife had been near the traps. I had mixed feelings about this. On the one hand, I hated the thought of an animal feeling terrified and in pain, so I was partially relieved. On the other hand, if there were no pests, what had made the noises?

We don't have much time to discuss next steps as Seb is

swamped by work. He only seems to emerge from the spare room, his office from home, at mealtimes. Even then, he's quiet and distracted, his mind elsewhere. I try to engage him in conversation, but his responses are mostly monosyllabic. By Sunday lunch, I've had enough.

"I thought the whole point of moving out of London was to give you some perspective, a chance to leave work in the office?"

His body is rigid, shoulders hunched over. I've half-caught his attention. He looks up from his pasta, but his eyes are elsewhere. It was unlikely to be a productive conversation.

"Not now, Bea, okay?"

It's like unpeeling a plaster from a cut, cautiously teasing it away. Now that I've started, I've got to keep going.

"Well, when is a good time to talk? You've got to break the habit at some point, Seb. Your workload wasn't going to miraculously change just because you moved to the country. You need to take control."

"I just said, leave it please!" His voice is frosty, closed. He takes his last mouthful, pushes the plate aside and makes to leave the table.

"You could at least say thank you for lunch – and I assume I'm washing up too?"

"Alright, sorry, thank you," he emphasises each word deliberately. "A bit of support wouldn't hurt at the moment."

"Likewise," I snap.

He disappears upstairs while I buzz with frustration.

I know he has a lot on his plate. He and the rest of his team are in the middle of preparing draft witness statements for his big case and they had worked long hours this week. Seb's been an employment lawyer for as long as I have, but it's his first court hearing where he's in charge: no supervising partner to confirm his approach and next steps. Part of me understands, having been in similar situations of pressure and responsibility myself, but it does little to alleviate my loneliness.

He moved to his current firm in the spring, last year. It was all part of his plan to improve his life, our lives: join a smaller firm, where the culture is less driven by billable hours, in the hope of becoming a partner and having more control over his schedule. By moving to the country, he thought he'd have more separation between home and work environments. At the moment, none of it's working. The commute tires him and makes him late home, and work continues to dominate our home life.

"Shit, shit, shit!"

He's cursing from upstairs.

"What's wrong?" I call up.

"I don't understand it... half of the work I did on the witness statement this morning's disappeared! How?!"

"Perhaps you amended a different version?"

"No! I've checked. It's just vanished. That's another two hours I've lost!"

I leave him to it, but his sullen mood permeates the walls. I can't escape stress in this house, whether alone or with him. My nerves are stretched to their limit, and it won't take much for them to snap.

At dinner he apologises, making an effort to sit and watch a film with me in the evening. I appreciate the gesture, but he's only partially there; his body is sitting next to me, but his brain drifts back to his case, constantly scrolling his phone for messages and news.

For once, I'm not disheartened when Monday morning arrives and I can have the house to myself. I may be uncomfortable here on my own but it's preferable to toiling under Seb's gloomy shadow.

Given how busy he's been, we've had little time to sort out the house. I've got to the point that there are so many half-finished projects, I just need to crack on by myself. First on my list is the nursery. Seb didn't want me to paint a couple of weeks ago, but beggars can't be choosers. And I've found a large box that's been emptied which I can turn upside down to make a supporting table for the paint can. This avoids too much bending.

I climb into my overalls. Catching my reflection in the mirror, I smile. It's been a long time since I've worn them, when we decorated the lounge in   Greenwich, shortly after our wedding. I remember it well. It was exhausting, after a long week at work, but we had the energy and enjoyed working together. The overalls covered more of me then. Now, I just about manage to hook in my arms and shoulders. The buttons have no hope of meeting their matching holes, the bump forming a peak between them. I hunt for an old, oversized T-shirt of Seb's to wear over the top. It's uncomfortable but will have to do.

The room is still set up for painting. I turn on the radio and stir the yellow paint with a stick, swirling together the parts that have separated. Of all DIY tasks, painting is the best. There's something satisfying about dipping in the bristles, loading them up with smooth, gloopy colour, making a vibrant mark on the wall; the gratification of a clear before and after.

Seb had given three of the walls their first coat, so I begin with the remaining fourth. The first splash of yellow against the dull peach is egg-yolk bright, but the other walls reassure me it will mute on drying.

I hate to admit it, but I find it harder than I thought. Even though my make-shift table is helpful, I feel it in my back, the constant dipping and stretching. Even my wrist aches from holding the brush. I push up the overalls to check my watch. 5pm. I've been painting since 10am, with only a brief break for lunch. The evening's drawing in and I switch on the light.

The instant the room illuminates, a sound makes me freeze. It's music. Tinny and quiet, but unmistakeable. I turn down the radio to listen more closely. The notes are chilling, and after a few bars I recognise the melody: Rockabye Baby. *Where is it coming from?* It sounds close.

Breathing fast, I scan the room and tilt my head, trying to place the location. It's coming from under the dust sheet, where the baby things are stacked. It doesn't take long to find the culprit: luckily the box is the second one my fingers find under the cover. It's that bloody bear Seb bought. I press the glowing button on its tummy and the music stops.

I give the bear a wry smile, relieved to find an easy answer to at least one problem. "I've got enough mysteries here without listening to you." I place his box back on the pile of baby paraphernalia under the cover and return to my painting.

Picking up the brush, I survey what I've achieved. The first wall is complete, and I've given the others a second coat. The last job, where wall meets ceiling, requires a finer brush and the support of a sturdy chair. Heavily pregnant, my centre of balance is different. I carefully step up with one foot, then the other, clinging to the back of the chair. I get to the point where I've reached as far as I can with the paintbrush from that spot when I hear Seb's car pull up.

I climb down and move the chair along for the next section, expecting Seb to come through the door at any minute. Not until it's necessary to move the chair for another section of the wall, I realise that he's still outside. I go to the window. Headlights are off. He's invisible, the interior of the car in darkness, but the glowing slit of his mobile phone hovers and sways mid-air, indicating he's talking. *Why would he choose to speak in the dark when he could come inside?* I turn away, rattled, continue painting.

Twenty minutes or so later I start as I hear a noise behind

me.

"Jesus, Bea, what were you thinking?" He wraps his arms under my ribs and helps me off the chair. "I said I'd finish the painting. You shouldn't be climbing on furniture or breathing in paint fumes!"

He rolls up his sleeves in irritation as he replaces the lid on the pot and takes the brush from my hand.

My hands are on my hips. "I'm fine. In fact, I've made good progress. I just need to see if any parts need touching up tomorrow after it's dried."

"I'd rather you left the rest for me. I can finish it one weekend or evening."

"You say that, but work always gets in the way. I was surprised when I heard your car pull up - bit earlier than it has been," I look at him pointedly, expecting an explanation for his delay in coming inside.

"Steve agreed to look at final versions of the witness statements, so I was able to get away on-time tonight... at least, I hope they're the final version. I've seen so many, I've become word blind."

He offers no explanation for staying outside and looks ghoulish in this light, dark rings circling his eyes.

"I'll fix dinner if you want – you go take a shower. You've got splatters in your hair."

The right side of his mouth twitches up in a tired smile, and he teases paint off a strand of hair then kisses my forehead. I'm itching to ask about his call, but I don't want to start an argument when he's making an effort to be nice.

I follow him downstairs and run myself a bath, my first in this house. It's not until I'm immersed in the warm, soapy water that I realise just how stiff and achy I feel. As I lean back, raking my fingers through my billowing hair under the surface,

I look up at the ceiling. It reminds me of when I climbed in here a few weeks ago, following the trail of scraping sounds. *What caused them? And why have they stopped?* Whatever the reason, I'm grateful. I've achieved something positive today, only marginally spooked by a teddy bear. Perhaps I've just got more used to the house and the sounds within it?

Dinner feels like an event. Not that we eat anything fancy – just pie, mash and greens. It's the fact we're actually eating together, talking. It hasn't been fun recently, cooking meals for two but eating alone, rarely knowing what time he's coming home.

I don't want to spoil things, but his mysterious call is still niggling away at me. It's odd that he hasn't mentioned anything about it since he's been home. Despite myself, I can't let it lie.

"So, who were you chatting to, outside?" My voice is calm, but I watch his face for a response.

He holds his forkful of pie mid-air and raises an eyebrow quizzically.

My face flushes. "I heard you draw up almost half an hour before you came in tonight. Why didn't you come in?"

He puts down his fork and looks at me. "It's not a big deal, Bea. I was just finishing a work call I'd started over blue tooth on the drive back. You know what reception's like here."

"But who were you talking to?"

He frowns. "Does it matter?"

I bristle. "Yes, if you're avoid answering the question". *Stay calm.*

"Jeez, I speak to people on the phone all the time, do you want a list?" Seb's face is pained. He sighs. "If you must know, it was Jessica, one of the assistants on the team. She's adding Steve's amendments to the statements this evening. Happy?"

I'm a mixture of annoyed and embarrassed. "Perhaps if

you just communicated with me, I wouldn't feel the need to question."

Seb leans into the table, eyes fixed on me.

"What's going on with you, at the moment? First, it's doors moving by themselves... strange noises only you can hear... then messages from the door camera that only you receive. And now you're implying I'm having secret conversations. Sound familiar, Bea? Are you keeping up with the CBT?"

So, he's playing that card. Using my past mental health problems against me. Next, he'll argue I'm unstable, undermine my credibility.

I'm determined to keep control this time.

Take a deep breath. "I'm not obsessing, and I never said you were having secret calls. I just wondered why you needed to sit in the dark on your phone."

He pauses and when he replies, the edge to his voice has disappeared. He stretches across the table for my hands. "And now I've told you. Look, I think we just need to be aware of the bigger picture here. You're acting a bit how you used to... after the miscarriages..."

Mentioning the miscarriages is a low blow. I snatch my hands away but he continues.

"Bea, don't you remember how you questioned everything then...mainly me? I see similar patterns now. You've no reason to distrust me. Maybe it's time to revisit the strategies you learnt before? Use your journal more?"

I've heard enough. My chair shoots noisily behind me as I stand. I scoop up the plates and take myself away from him and into the kitchen. As I run the hot water, angry tears prick my eyes. It's one thing to experience depression and anxiety, triggered by grief. It's another to feel like it can never be left in the past. Like a vulnerability that forever makes others doubt you, makes you doubt yourself.

It's a blur to me, the time when things were really bad.

I lost interest in most things.   I had no stomach for socialising: it required too much effort. On the odd occasions I went out, conversations felt stilted. Relationships with friends felt fake when so much was going on below the surface, kept hidden: nights out were pointless charades. I started to refuse invitations and eventually they dried up completely. Work kept me going - got me out of the house, gave me a routine and a sense of purpose. That, and Harriet, who was the only member of my family who knew what was going on.

I may have maintained my professional life, but I lost confidence elsewhere. I began to wonder what Seb saw in me; in my eyes, every female acquaintance seemed more attractive, voluptuous, fertile. That's when suspicions took hold. I know I gave him a rough time. It strained a relationship that was already fragile and bruised. I understand that it's hard for him to put that episode behind him, but that's exactly what I want him to do. Need him to do.

I immerse my hands in the warm water, close my eyes and take deep breaths. This was supposed to be a new start for both of us. Time to take responsibility for our behaviour and recognise the impact it has on each other.

Stop letting the past haunt us.

CHAPTER 10

Maud

I am sitting beside William in the cart, Nathaniel in my arms. It is one of those days where the sun shines one minute then hides behind clouds the next. The occasional gust of wind taunts and snatches at my hat and would make it dance over the fields were it not for the ribbon fastened under my chin. But I shan't complain. We have had far worse weather for May Day.

This will be our eighth since we took the tenancy of the farm. It is a highlight of the year, marking the end of the hard winter months and a chance to relax and enjoy the longer daylight hours, before harvest begins. The landowner, Lord Huntingfield, will provide the cider, made from his apples picked last September, and the rest of us will bring food of some sort. This year I have made ginger beer and an almond pudding, still warm in the dish at the back of the cart.

Last year was memorable. Nathaniel had begun to grow inside me, but it was early on: too soon to share with my neighbours or even William. I hugged the secret close to me, precious and hopeful. I took care not to dance too enthusiastically, tried to hide the nausea that seemed almost constant. All my senses were alive: the smell of the beer and cider mixed with grass was overpowering; the sour sweat of the dancers repellent, cutting through the air with every twirl and fling.

No sickness today, thank goodness. William is dressed smart in his tweed trousers and waistcoat. Already his forearms are golden, stretched out before us holding the reins. I have made an effort too. The green and yellow ribbon, stitched around the crown of my hat and attached in a bow, adds some cheer to the pale green dress I have worn for many such occasions. I had to take it in a little; my appetite has dwindled over the past months. Without the extra weight, my face looks pinched; nose, chin and cheekbones are more pronounced. But William gave a rare nod of approval this afternoon when he saw the effort I had made with my hair, having teased the wiry curls into ringlets pinned up behind my ears.

Even Nathaniel seems in better spirits. I expected the motion of the cart to send him to sleep, but he is alert, taking in the colours of the countryside as we trot past. He is probably enjoying being next to his father, rather than being stuck at home with me.

My last trip in the trap was to Halesworth with Emily. William did not ask too many questions when I came home with the sage and lavender. I explained to him that I had bought them to soothe the baby to sleep. After all, it was not too far from the truth. He does not need to know my suspicions about Nathaniel and why he behaves the way he does. So far, the herbs seem to have made little impression. His cries still fill the hours alone with me, whether during the night or the day. At least the sprigs bring a pleasant fragrance to our home.

As for the vial of laudanum, I have kept it hidden at the back of my drawer, beneath my undergarments. When the night has been particularly long and hard, and Nathaniel has just settled, I sometimes take a secret swig to ease me to sleep. It works, and William is none the wiser, being fast asleep. I soon drift off, although my dreams are warped and vivid. Rising in the morning is more difficult on those occasions; I find the light too bright, my eyelids and limbs heavy.

As we round the bend, the white tent and maypole come into view.

I will myself to stay light and content today. "Are you looking forward to a dance and a song, William?"

He nods and glances sideways at me. "It'll be good for us both. This winter's been as long as ever I have known."

He draws the horse to a stand-still under the shade of an oak tree, next to the stream that feeds into the Blyth. He takes Nathaniel from my arms so I can drop to the ground. Once returned to me, he fidgets. Increasingly he wants space to wriggle his limbs, hates to be confined in my arms for too long. After William has tended to the horse, we make our way towards the tent, where many others crowd. Drawing closer, the light-hearted hum of the accordion can be heard amidst laughter and chatter.

"Maud and William! Lovely to see you. My, Nathaniel looks well! Come, put your food in the tent."

We weave our way through animated friends and neighbours to the tent entrance. There, trestle tables have been laid out, covered with plates of sandwiches, pies, boiled eggs, celery, pound cakes and buns. William adds our offerings, and we make our way back to the throng.

Emily and her husband Matthew are the first we meet. She has bloomed since we met several weeks back, looking pretty in a dress made from the floral fabric she purchased that day. Her palm rests on her bump, satisfied and serene. His hand strays protectively to the back of her waist, eyes drawn to her face, like a plant leaning towards the sun. I feel a pang of envy, then shame. It's been a long time since William has looked at me that way. Before I dwell on this, Nathaniel makes a squawking noise and starts raising his legs, exasperated at being carried for too long.

"Maud?"

I look up. I've missed the question. Emily, Matthew and William stare at me expectantly.

"Sorry, I was elsewhere. Too many sleepless nights!"

Emily laughs. "I think there is our answer! I asked how Nathaniel was faring."

William looks uncomfortable, no doubt worried how I will respond. He would rather I kept my struggles to myself.

"The nights are sometimes hard. But he feeds well now and enjoys bein' outside," I smile thinly. By now, Nathaniel's limited patience has worn thin and William sweeps him from my arms. Instantly his cry stops.

Emily allows him to curl his small hand around her fingertip and she coos at him. Matthew smiles, watching her. "Well, he's a fine boy and hopefully soon to be a fine playmate for our son or daughter! You are without a drink, Maud. The cider is good this year!"

I nod and make my way to the table of beverages, pouring two glasses of cider. On my way back, I catch sight of Joseph, Emily and Matthew's farmhand. He's entertaining a group of young men with some tale that has set them all laughing. As I pass, his eyes meet mine. He doffs his hat slowly again, as he did that day in Halesworth, his smile slightly lopsided. I blush and take a sip from my glass, self-conscious as I return to my husband and neighbours.

The cider is heady, crisp and cool, a delicious combination that slides down all too easily. We find a spot in the shade of the tent to lie Nathaniel on a shawl. He seems to enjoy the music and chatter from his spot on the ground, watching the shadows of people moving on the walls of the tent. I return to the table to fetch more cider. By chance or design, Joseph approaches just as

I arrive, our hands both reaching for the open bottle.

He laughs. "Ladies first."

"Thank you." I curse myself as I feel my cheeks flush again and hope he doesn't notice. His eyes are on me as I pour the amber liquid, making my hands clumsy. When he takes the bottle, his hand brushes against mine.

"Thanking you. The landlord's brewed a good one this year. Perhaps I'll see you later for a dance?"

I smile and move away quickly, neither accepting nor declining. It's not unusual to dance with everyone on May Day. Most will be merry by the end, enjoying a good sing-song. But it's unusual to request a dance in this way, to single out a married woman. Despite the improper request, I cannot help but feel flattered.

Thomas, our farmhand, and his sweetheart Celia have joined William. We all help ourselves to cheese and potato pie, pour cider and enjoy the sunshine. When the landlord is nearby, William takes his leave to express our thanks and exchange pleasantries. He is good that way: keen to make a positive impression. Shortly afterwards, Thomas and Celia move away, making their excuses, seeking others for conversation.

Finding myself alone, I sink to the floor next to Nathaniel, who by now has fallen asleep. More people are dancing, clasping hands and skipping in formation, a fiddle and a banjo joining the accordion. I close my eyes, let the music and voices wash over me. The cider is taking effect: my head is woozy and buzzing, like a spinning top running out of momentum, swaying and rotating on the spot.

A song ends, signalled by cheers and clapping. A few have begun to call for the maypole. More join in, until it becomes a compelling chant.

"Are you joining us for the maypole?"

I open my eyes. Joseph's face hovers over me, smiling again, slightly blurred. I sit up, embarrassed.

"What about Nathaniel?" I stammer, turning to see him still fast asleep on the shawl. I have no idea where William is, but I can see he is no longer talking to the landlord, who is currently deep in conversation with someone else.

Joseph shrugs. "He seems pretty content to me."

What harm can it do? It is only a dance. And as Joseph says, Nathaniel is calm on the blanket, away from drunken footsteps. I try to stand up, swaying a little, and Joseph offers a hand. He keeps hold of it, hidden from view in the crowd making for the maypole.

Women form the outer ring, facing clockwise, men on the inside, facing the opposite direction. The music begins and we keep to our circles. As we dance, the colours of the spectators seem to form patterns and merge like a kaleidoscope. The accordion plays faster and our feet pick up pace to keep to the rhythm, the women weaving in and out of the men. I am giddy but laughing and breathing noisily at the same time.

In the next song we change direction, this time the men turning around the women. Each time Joseph passes me, he grins and I smile back. The fiddler plays the last bars of the song. We bow to each other and release the ribbons, ready for the next dancers.

Stepping away from the maypole, blood rushes around my body. I cannot remember when I last felt so light and airy, when I have smiled and laughed so freely. But a strong grip on my arm brings me back to earth.

"What the hell were you doing, leaving Nathaniel on his own while you moon over some farm'and?"

William hisses through his teeth as he propels me forward, away from the crowds. He stops when he feels we are far enough away from others so as not to be heard, releasing my arm so I can turn to face him. His eyes are blazing and droplets of sweat speckle his forehead. Nathaniel is tucked into his other arm: he isn't crying but recent tears have left streaks on his face, a trail crusting from his nose.

"He was fine...I would not have left him if he was awake. He was fast asleep and safe from harm's way."

This seems to anger him more. "Clearly not, as he was bawling his 'ead off when I found 'im! Of course, you would not have noticed - dancing and flirting. Shame on you, Maud Catchpole."

"I wasn't...it was just dancing," but I could feel my cheeks burn, remembering how I enjoyed Joseph's attention. How my spirits soared.

William's eyes narrowed. "I saw how you smiled at him. I am no idiot. You know Maud, I think I have been patient with you, where other men would be less so." He shakes his head at me. "I know you've struggled, becomin' a mother. You've let the house slide. You forget to milk the cows. You forget to collect the eggs. I've stepped in to fill the gaps, so has Thomas. But this... this is a step too far. You are a mother, Maud. Behave like one. We're goin' home." He storms out the tent. I follow, struggling to keep up.

We journey home in silence. The sunset would have been beautiful in other circumstances, the clouds streak the sky a golden pink, the colour of ripe peach. Only this evening, the colour feels fierce and lurid, like the light that fired in William's eyes. The taste of the cider still lingers in my mouth; delicious earlier, now sickly and acidic.

Marriages have their ups and downs, God only knows, but today I feel a line has been crossed. I have lost William's trust, as a wife and as a mother.

He won't see the part he has played in us getting to this place: his cool distance and judgmental remarks; his eyes closed to Nathaniel's difficulties. He just sees a woman who is struggling and who has allowed herself to stray off the straight and narrow.

What happens to us now?

CHAPTER 11

Bea

My arms hold a bundle close to my body. I move awkwardly, weighed down, pushing to go faster. My chest is tight, but the rising panic is quashed by something more urgent. I must stay focused.

I'm alone with just the sound of my breath, fast and laboured, heart thudding. Beneath my bare feet, the dry, crumbling earth seems to move at a different speed. Newly cut crops are dry and sharp and the odd stone sends pain from my soles and up my leg, but I don't care. I keep going. I must keep going.

It feels like early morning, summertime. The landscape is flat and branches, laden with leaves, beckon in the breeze. My head twists -left, right, behind - desperate for someone.

I look down at the bundle. It's a baby wrapped tightly in a blanket. He's solid, heavy next to my chest. But something feels strange. His body is unyielding. There's no movement, not even the twitch of a toe, no whisper of a breath on my skin. No sound except my own ragged breathing.

The dread inside takes control. It's hopeless, too late. My feet accept the awful truth and stop moving, knees sinking to the ground. It takes all my strength to look down at the bundle, to confirm my worst fear.

A scream roars through me, tearing out of my lungs, throwing back my shoulders, piercing the air. Blackness descends.

I wake with a start. Hair is plastered to my head and beads of sweat chill my skin. With difficulty, I untangle myself from the duvet wrapped around my body. I heave myself up to sitting position and take a few sips of water as I try to recall the details. I rarely remember dreams, yet alone nightmares. This one was so real it was tangible, yet I'd never experienced anything similar in real life.

The location felt familiar. I guess fields and countryside are much the same everywhere in the UK, but it reminded me of here.

It's only a dream.

That's what happens when you go to bed on an argument. By the time I'd finished the washing-up last night, Seb had returned to the spare room, presumably to work, door closed. I found it hard to settle, his words still stinging. *You're acting a bit how you used to...after the miscarriages.*

I dipped in and out of TV programmes, picked up my novel, but whatever I tried, I couldn't focus. I ended up making notes in my journal. Not because Seb had suggested it, or because I doubted myself, just because I needed to let off steam.

I tried to sleep without him but was restless till he came to bed. When he eventually joined me, we exchanged goodnights but didn't talk. The rest of the night I grasped fragments of sleep until I fell into my bizarre dream.

I'm starving. Not surprising, given it's 11am! *Was an empty stomach another explanation for my brain's strange wanderings?*

Before I go downstairs to fix breakfast, I check on the paintwork from yesterday. It's not bad, but my first wall yesterday could do with another coat.

After eating, I spend the next couple of hours on admin, calling companies for cost estimates to render and paint the exterior walls. I tell myself it's time well spent, but really, I'm delaying my painting task – I'm still a little achy from yesterday.

Come on Bea, get stuck in.

It's 2pm by the time I put on my overalls. In the afternoon light I can see a few areas where the stubborn peach colour peeps through the yellow. It will take a few hours to cover them and to complete the fine brushwork to sharpen where yellow meets white skirting. I need to work fast if I'm to make the most of the natural light.

I put the radio on. The first couple of hours pass quickly as I listen to Radio 6. Soon after the show ends, I hear a noise other than music. It's faint and I turn down the volume on the radio. There it is again, the scratching.

Shit.

My skin turns clammy and muscles stiffen. Why should that noise grate on me so? The baby kicks hard on my left as if he or she also senses something is wrong.

Scratch, scratch, scratch.

I try to ignore it, dip the brush into the tin and raise it with shaking hand, causing drips of paint to fall to the dust sheet and spatter my overalls. One stroke of paint across the wall, then another. But try as I might to focus on the painting, I can't block it out.

Checking the soles of my feet for stray splodges, I tread softly over our bedroom carpet and flick the switch as I cross the landing to the spare room.

As before, near the back wall the sound is louder. I rap the surface with my knuckles. *Surely that would be enough to frighten any animal?* Yet it has no effect. Persistant. Insidious. Demanding my attention.

"What's wrong? What do you want?" I yell in frustration.

I must look ridiculous, talking to thin air. I don't expect a response, but when the scraping abruptly stops, a chill runs through me.

Was it was listening to me?

I freeze. Wait.

The room remains silent, but I'm suddenly hit by a different sensation: an intense smell. I can't believe how quickly it fills the room - lavender and some kind of herb. It's oppressive, invasive, greedy for the space in my lungs.

Coughing, I lean across the desk and open one of the windows, sticking my head outside. A few gulps of cool air clear the taste from my throat and steady me. *Where did it come from? And why so suddenly?* I leave the window open in the hope of diffusing the invisible, fragrant cloud and close the door of the spare room behind me.

I need a break to calm myself and I go downstairs to put the kettle on. *Was the sound linked to the smell? If so, how? Could there be a logical explanation?* I dislike lavender so none of my perfumes and beauty products contain it. There were no room sprays or plug in air fresheners left by the Bryants, to my knowledge, at least none that were visible. It seems unlikely that the smell came from the fields or garden outside; no windows were open at the time, and the lavender blooms of June are yet to come. It didn't add up: another odd, unexplained occurrence that leaves me feeling baffled and jumpy.

Draining the dregs of my tea, I pluck up the courage to return upstairs. Listening and sniffing intently, the sensations seem to have passed. I carry on painting, but with one ear pricked, like a dog ready to run.

"Dum-de-di-dah-dah,

Dum-de di daah..."

Rockabye-Baby. Record-a-bear's at it again. I put down the paint brush and pull him out from the dust cover. I press the glowing belly, but in my haste, I must have pressed twice, because instead of stopping, it changes to a different function: a strange swishing sound, deep and repetitive. That must be the sound of the womb Seb was going on about. I press again, trying to make it stop, but this time it makes a different noise, a faint crackle. Over the muffle, I hear something else. My eyes widen. It sounds like sobbing. Then a voice, faint but wrought with emotion.

Shush now, shush – I am coming.

Shaking, I press the button again and the sound cuts out.

I skim read the box, head buzzing. No information there, I break open the packaging, impatiently untwisting the wires that hold the bear in place. I find the instructions in the concealed space underneath him, and flick to the section on recording sounds.

'Maintain pressure for more than five seconds to record a message, keeping your finger depressed throughout. Hold down for more than five seconds to delete and record over a former message.'

I look up. So, who recorded this message? It's the kind of thing you'd say to comfort a child – *shush now, shush – I'm coming.* Maybe a customer recorded it, trying out the toy in the shop? But that doesn't explain the sobbing in the background.

I don't want to think about it anymore and throw the bear on our bed to take downstairs later on. I'll show Seb when he gets home – see what he makes of it.

I push the nagging fear to the back of the mind and focus on finishing the room. The rest of the afternoon passes without event. I finally add the last stroke of paint and check the time: 6.30pm. Just enough time to have a shower before Seb comes home, while the jacket potatoes bake in the oven. Clearing up can wait until tomorrow.

He turns up at 9pm to find me in the lounge, feet up and half watching some TV show. I've eaten dinner and am trying to keep my eyes open. The combination of painting and this afternoon's incidents have left me physically and mentally exhausted.

The door creaks behind the sofa so I lean back and swivel my head to see him. "Hello, you must be tired – another late one. Your dinner will need reheating."

"Sorry. Had to run through Steve's comments on the statements. I'll just pop this stuff upstairs and get changed."

"Just before you do, can you listen to this?" I pick up the bear and press the button several times until it plays the recorded message.

Shush now, shush – I'm coming.

His face is tired but impassive. "What? Did you record that?"

"No – the bear's gone off by itself a couple of times now – I came across this voice when I tried to switch it off."

He shrugs. "Probably someone trying it out in the shop." His body turns to leave.

"But what about the sobbing sound?" Agitated, I press the button repeatedly, perhaps too hard as it sticks, staying depresssed. I press harder again to release it and flick through the functions. On rotation, the bear sings a lullaby and swishes, but at the point when the message should play, there is only silence.

"Shit, why isn't it working?"

Seb takes it from me and tries. "You must have just deleted it. Hey – maybe if the button was sticking, it would explain why the bear made noises out of the blue." He hands it back. "It's obviously faulty so I'll return it to the shop. Did you keep the packaging?"

I nod, frustrated and perplexed. "Didn't you hear it, though? The sobbing?"

His voice is strained. "No, Bea, sorry. Just the words. You might want to remove the batteries so it doesn't make you jump again." He leaves the room, keen to get settled, not linger in conversation. His footsteps climb the stairs. Seconds later I hear him swearing loudly. Sighing, I swing my legs to the floor and follow him to find out what's wrong.

He's in our bedroom, half-undressed, inspecting a pair of his work shoes.

"For fuck's sake, Bea, could you have made any more mess?"

He's livid and thrusts the shoes towards me. They're covered in splatters of yellow paint. He beckons me over to the wardrobe. I shake my head, baffled.

"Oh, it doesn't end there!"

He points with the shoes, impatiently. My eyes follow. With horror, I see larger splashes on the bottom of the mirrored wardrobe and the carpet.

"But I was so careful...I didn't bring any paint through here!" My mind races as I try to work out what happened.

"It should come off the wardrobe, it's only emulsion. We'll replace the carpet eventually. But my shoes are completely buggered." He looks at them again, angrily.

Seb invests in expensive work shoes and wears two pairs on rotation. This pair of brogues, black with suede inserts, had been left by the wardrobe. I take a closer look.

"How could it have happened? They look like splatters from a tin or brush, but I left both in the annex. If I had any paint on my clothing or feet when I passed, it wouldn't have made marks like this...and besides, I checked my feet."

Seb cuts in, "So you walked through here in your paint

stuff? Where did you go?"

"Just the spare room…"

"Fantastic. Shall we check whether there's a mess in there too?" He is cold and patronising as he dumps the shoes on the floor, and in a few strides crosses the landing to open the door.

Angered by his tone, I still find myself following him.

"I don't believe it!"

He's standing in front of the desk, his body blocking whatever it is that's caught his attention. I peer round him. More spatters of paint litter the surface of the desk and everything on it. The fine paintbrush, which I'd been using earlier, lies discarded on the top.

"You've covered the computer, the desk, the witness statements drafts…what were you thinking?" he seethes in disbelief.

I'm dumbstruck. *How did it get here?* It wasn't me.

A gust of dark, wet night shoots through the open window. Seb reaches across the desk to close it and wrenches the curtains together.

"And the fabric's sodden too. Why did you leave the window open? In fact, why open it at all?"

"I… I opened it to let the smell out."

"Smell? You weren't painting in *here*. It would make more sense if you opened the windows in the annex, to let the fumes escape!"

"No, not paint smells. Just listen to me for a minute." I close my eyes, gather my thoughts and try to remember. *None of this is my fault.* "There was this strange lavender, herby smell – it was so strong and sudden, it came on just after the scratching started up again…"

"*Seriously?* You're still obsessing about noises?" Seb

interrupts, incredulous, shaking his head.

I ignore him, try to finish my explanation, close my eyes and speak louder over him.

"Yes, the noises returned. I traced the sound, and it led me here. It was coming from behind that wall again. I shouted at it, and the scratching stopped, but then this strong smell came from nowhere – like lavender and some kind of herb. It was overpowering and... smothering. I had to get rid of it, whatever it was, so I opened the window to let in some air. Then I left and closed the door behind me."

I open my eyes and he looks down, avoiding me. In this light he looks older, worries forming ridges and furrows on his forehead. He's silent for what seems like an age. When he speaks, he's controlled but unnatural, as though censoring his words before releasing them from his lips.

"Bea, this has to stop. The obsessions have to stop. We spoke about it last night and I'm asking you again. Use the journal to challenge your thoughts. If you're still feeling anxious and concerned by the end of next week, we need to find someone locally who can help. I don't want this to escalate."

"I'm not being irrational, Seb. Something's going on here; I wish you'd believe me! How can you explain all this paint?" my voice rises as my brain spins.

He shrugs. "I don't know... but perhaps you were so caught up in noises and smells, what with the bear going off, you weren't thinking what you were doing."

"No! I remember checking...I was careful...something else did this!"

Tears run down my face thick and fast in hurt, angry streaks and I start to shake.

He puts his arm around my shoulder, leans his head on the top of mine, but his movements are automatic, mechanical. Instead of bringing us closer, I feel we're miles apart.

After a minute or so I pull away, mutter my intentions to clean up our bedroom. He nods, agreeing to tackle the other room, but I still feel the weight of his eyes on me.

It doesn't seem possible that half an hour ago I was downstairs, feeling relaxed and ready for bed. Now my blood is racing and mind whirring, churning over the mess we discovered and Seb's reaction, trying to make sense of it all.

I switch on the light in the annex and survey the painting equipment from today, retracing my steps. The larger brush is just as I left it, wrapped in a plastic bag so the bristles don't harden. The lid on the tin is slightly misaligned. *Did I leave it like that?* Normally I'd click it into place. Perhaps I forgot? *What other explanation can there be?*

Unable to remember, I throw myself into removing the paint marks. Kneeling on the floor of our bedroom, the yellow splodges are easily wiped away from the mirrored surface of the wardrobe with soapy water. I rub the fibres of the terracotta carpet with a dry cloth and some of the paint transfers as a sticky yellow dust, like pollen.

Seb's shoes are a different story. The stain clings tight to the suede but I scrape it away from the leather with my fingernails and remove the rings with black polish.

I wrack my brain, replaying my steps this afternoon.

Could I have left this room with the fine brush between my fingers?

I don't think so, but my attention was on the sound. It's possible it may have remained in my hand, my mind elsewhere.

No, wait! I rapped my knuckles on the wall! If the brush was in my hands, that wouldn't have been possible.

But if I'm not the culprit, who was?

I exhale slowly, try to take stock. Up till now, I've been able to find ordinary explanations for some of the whispers and oddities in the house: faulty door tracks, animals nesting, birds triggering the door monitor. But there's no logical, ordinary explanation for the paint. Either I'm going mad, moving objects without any recollection, or that paintbrush was moved by something else.

And if it was something else, it has implications.

We're not alone in this house.

It's extraordinary and terrifying in equal measure. As I try to get my head around it, another thought hits me: so far as help is concerned, I'm on my own. Seb won't want to hear this explanation: he already thinks I should be seeking professional help, as he made abundantly clear last night. If I tell him, I'd be adding fuel to the flames, further undermine my credibility in his eyes.

No, he couldn't countenance a presence in the house, particularly as it hadn't manifested to him. Or had it? I think back to his injured head on our first day here. *Was that just an accident?*

His shoes I can tackle again tomorrow with a little white vinegar. I've no idea how to deal with the rest.

I've never felt so scared and alone.

CHAPTER 12

Maud

"**M**aud!"

I wake with a start. I have no idea how long I have slept, but it is bright and my chin feels stiff with spittle.

"For God's sake, Maud!" William shouts from outside.

His voice carries an anger and fear I have never heard before. It jolts me into motion. I try to move quickly but my limbs feel detached from my body, heavy and cumbersome. Reaching the backdoor, I shield my eyes, like a mole sensitive to the sun.

"Look at him!" William bellows in disbelief.

Nathaniel is quiet, which would normally be a blessing, but now I see why. His breath is shallow, his skin very red. Trails of salt crust his face, the ghosts of tears.

William lifts him from his cot, blows air on his face. " How long has he been left out here, in the sun?"

"Not long... I only closed my eyes for a minute."

Is that true? I cannot be sure. I cannot even remember

leaving him outside. All I remember is a blinding headache and taking a sip from my vial. It is not the first time I have succumbed to it in the afternoons, to take the edge off and dull the pain in my head. Perhaps I had a drop more than usual. I know I had to sit down but clearly it led to me falling asleep.

I look around, trying to piece together what happened. The crib is next to the washing line, our white undergarments and the baby clothes dance side by side in the June breeze. I must have taken him outside when he was crying, while I hung the washing out to dry, and accidentally left him there. But when that was, I have no idea.

William storms inside with him and I follow. Out of the sun's glare, Nathaniel's skin is tomato red.

"You were outside for a minute? That's a lie, Maud! With this colour, the boy's been out for hours! Get some water and a sponge, quickly!"

My movements are leaden and clumsy as I fetch a sponge and pump water into a dish from the well. My heart thuds against my chest. *What if he's come to harm? How could I have let this happen?*

Without a word, William snatches the dish from me. He squeezes the sponge and gently dabs it on Nathaniel's skin. It leaves droplets like beads, makes him stir.

"Get some milk for him. No, there is no point trying to heat it – we need to get liquid in him, but I want to keep his temperature down."

Silently, I say a prayer of thanks for William's knowledge and experience on the farm. He has dealt with pigs who have suffered too much heat, sprayed them with water and made sure they had plenty to drink. As I drip milk into Nathaniel's drooping mouth, my hands shake, whether from alarm or the laudanum.

For hours we hover over him, cooling his skin and feeding

him milk, spoonful by tiny spoonful. Eventually, his breathing becomes more normal and he falls into a deep sleep.

"I think he will be alright, but I will stay up and look over him. You get some rest," I say meekly. Wracked with guilt, the least I can do is keep watch and relieve William.

"You sure you will manage to stay awake?" He shoots the question like an arrow, still angry and distrustful. Under his intense stare I drown in shame.

My voice is small: "I do not know how it occurred, William, but it shall not happen again."

At least the second part was true: God knows, I would be more vigilant in future. But it was a lie to plead ignorance. The cause of my oversight was likely to be the laudanum, the medicine I have kept hidden from view. A confession now would make the situation even worse, but I vow to destroy the bottle the next time I am alone.

William fetches some bread and cheese and passes some to me. We eat in silence.

I watch his face, dark and inscrutable in the early evening light, but he avoids my gaze, unwilling to forgive, not prepared to talk. I am not sure whether to be grateful or dismayed. Which is better, to be the brunt of harsh words or ignored in contempt?

As it was, we had barely talked since May Day. We existed, side by side, like a couple of pegs on the line outside, but never truly together. He avoided conversation; expressed his opinions through muttered comments and brooding expressions.

He pushes his chair back, removes his boots and makes for the bedroom. He nods when I bid him goodnight.

Alone with Nathaniel, I kneel by his crib. Sage and lavender hang at the end. Have they offered protection? Cleansed him, driven out any evil? They had not kept him safe from me - the mother who tended to her own comfort this afternoon at the expense of her child.

A wave of shock and remorse hits me, shaking my shoulders so hard it sends tears scattering on my arms and lap. I could have lost him! It would have been all my fault. *How could I have let this happen? How could I carry on living if he came to serious harm?*

Gulping for air, I'm overwhelmed by feelings of love and protection for him. And then it dawns on me. This is what has been missing since the day he was born. All this time I have worried about the love I have not felt, too ashamed to admit its absence to anyone. Yet now I feel it keenly, like a knife twisting inside my stomach. This afternoon has opened my eyes to what was there all along, unveiled my primal need to shield him from harm. I know now his loss would be a wound too deep to comprehend.

The candle flickers as the minutes turn to hours with me by his side. I wipe tears on my hands and the salt water sweeps across his forehead from my fingertips. His skin is still too warm, but his breathing is regular. Thank the Lord.

Despite the horrors of today, I am grateful.

Grateful Nathaniel is alive.

Grateful to be a mother.

Grateful for the bond linking us together that, before now, I had been too blind to see.

CHAPTER 13

Maud

Only two weeks have passed since I left poor Nathaniel in the sun and yet we have both changed considerably since that day.

It took three days for him to recover completely from the over-heating. I watched over him, cooling his skin with a sponge and fanning him, keeping him topped up with milk and boiled water. All the while I felt such shame, knowing my own actions were the cause of his suffering. But I am glad for it now. It has made me a better mother. I am more patient towards him and more aware of his needs. It is as though he realises it too: his cries are less frequent and he is more ready to smile.

At almost five months, he is showing many signs of wanting to crawl. More often than not, he will flip himself over to lie on his front, after I have put him on his back in the crib or on a rug. He tries to lift his head, manages it for a few brief moments, then his neck flops down and he becomes frustrated.

I got rid of the laudanum at the first opportunity, just as I vowed I would. The treacherous liquid was poured down the privy and I buried the glass vial in the vegetable patch. The next couple of days I felt groggy with a thick headache, but in a way the pain helped; reminded me how powerful it was, and the harm it could do. I shall never take it again.

In this frame of mind, I have had more energy and enthusiasm about the farm. Not a day has passed when I have forgotten to milk the cows. I am starting to make cheese again, to sell at the market. William slaughtered a male calf and I washed out its stomach and salted it to draw the rennet. When I added it to the hot milk and combed off the curds, the smell recalled me suddenly to the early days of feeding Nathaniel as a baby; those frequent occasions he would bring up his milk and the sourness would linger on our clothes and around his mouth. Those days were long and hard. They seem long ago now and I am glad for it. I am pleased to be moving forwards and coping better as he grows.

Just like Nathaniel, the piglets are taking steps to independence. We used a ring pig trough to wean them, each piglet having his or her own section to feed from, just like their own particular teat to suckle from the sow. They have taken to it readily. In a couple of weeks, we shall have to decide which to sell, which to keep.

The hens are laying well. I've been keeping track, splashing a dab of yellow paint on the eggs we are keeping so they stand out from those newly laid, to be collected for cooking. It will not be long before Nathaniel can help me with these tasks and it makes me smile to think of his chubby fingers scattering grain for the clucking, pecking birds, circling around tottering little legs.

I think William has noticed some change in me: I have felt his glance as I have been about my chores. There have been fewer occasions when he has questioned my judgment or my handling of Nathaniel, fewer black looks or shaking of his head. But there has been no acknowledgment in words. In fact, he talks very little. Harvest time is near, and, as usual, this weighs heavy on his mind. It is his responsibility to decide when to cut the crops: too soon, and they will be cut before their peak; too late, and bad weather could be their ruin. He is busy, maintaining equipment and securing labour to help when the time comes. But it is more than preoccupation with the farm. He does not trust me. In his eyes, I have made big mistakes and it will take months, if not years, to win back his faith.

CHAPTER 14

Bea

Last night was the longest I've ever known. Even without the baby kicking and pregnancy indigestion it would have been hard to rest, following the revelations of yesterday. How will I ever sleep easy here again?

I was awake for every change of hour, watched dark velvet midnight metamorphosize to pale grey early morning. All the while my mind was churning. *If there was some kind of presence in the house, what did it want? And why was it communicating only with me?* I tried to convince myself that there was no evidence to show it was dangerous. Perhaps Seb's head injury that night was unrelated? If so, the most physical harm connected with this 'presence', for want of a better word, were a few splashes of paint - an irritation to Seb, but less so for me. *Was there a reason why Seb's possessions seem to be targeted?*

Lying on the bed, every sense in my body was switched on, waiting for something to happen. *Was it with us now? Were we being watched?* And in the brief moments it wasn't occupying my brain, my thoughts strayed to my relationship with Seb – how he had looked for evidence of a relapse in me, as though waiting for the cracks to show. Previous episodes are part of our history, I get that, but it's stopping him from seeing what's going on now. His view is blinkered and prejudiced. He sees my mental state as the root of our problems, but he doesn't take responsibility for his own actions and behaviour. The best part of him is swallowed by work, leaving me with just moods and sulks. Doesn't he realise this has an impact on me too?

I'm not sure who I can turn to about any of this. My parents are in Essex and tied up in their own lives and Seb's mum is rarely around. I could call friends, but after the past few years I feel like I've lost touch, and it isn't something I can casually mention or drop into a conversation. Taken individually, the incidents seem minor, but pieced together they hover like the dark clouds before an imminent storm. It would be hard to land all of this on someone cold.

The ring of Seb's alarm clock comes as no surprise. I lay awake waiting for it, my back turned away. I pretend to sleep, not wanting to talk. He gets ready, quickly and quietly. Pausing before he leaves the bedroom, his eyes linger on me. I keep still, eyes shut. He turns and leaves.

After the car pulls away, I switch on my bedside light. My eyes ache and my head feels fuzzy from lack of sleep, but I'm still hyper alert. *What will happen today, while I'm alone? How will I deal with it?* I don't even have my own car yet, I've nowhere to go. But I must stay calm. *There's no evidence it's trying to hurt me.* I've no choice but to cope.

I think back to the help I've had in the past. *Focus on achievable goals.* Breakfast feels like something I can achieve. My stomach feels cavernous again, even though it's been squashed to a fraction of its normal size. I trudge downstairs in search of juice and cereal. Food in hand, I find my journal in the lounge where I last left it.

Between mouthfuls, I gather my thoughts, try to order what's happened over the past twenty-four hours and write it down. Reading it back to myself, it sounds far-fetched. *How can I get Seb to believe me?* He needs evidence. Perhaps I could record it? I can't obtain the smell, but I might be able to capture the noises. From now on, I must always keep my phone on me, fully charged.

I get dressed then tackle the painting materials from yesterday. Despite the colour reminding me of the unexplained spatters, I'm pleased with the annex: it's warm and cheerful without being too bright. I still find it hard to picture a cot in the middle, with our baby sleeping inside, but perhaps most first-time parents feel this way. It shall have to be built soon, ready for when he or she arrives.

There are no noises to distract me this morning, but I find myself moving quietly about the house, just in case. I look out the window as I fold away the laundry. It's slightly brighter today, the first signs of spring beginning to appear. The grass is long and scattered within it are tiny pearls of white, the heads of drooping snowdrops. Shoots and leaves of daffodils stand proud, their flowers tightly closed to shield from frosts that may yet strike.

A simultaneous knock on the door and a ping from my phone sends a bolt of energy through me. A quick glance at my phone and the app shows me it's Maureen – no reason for being so jumpy, but I can't believe I've forgotten her appointment yet again! I scurry downstairs to open the door. At least this time I'm dressed.

"Hi, please come in."

She insists on taking off her shoes, despite my protests. I thought she would usher me upstairs, like she did on her previous visit, but this time she loiters in the hallway. She's hard to predict, this one.

"Would you like a drink? Tea, coffee, something cold?"

"That would be lovely… whatever you're having."

Perhaps she's decided I need a little more support after reading through my notes last time. She follows me into the diner and exclaims as she looks upwards at the hooks on the ceiling.

"Goodness, this hasn't changed much over the years, has it? Imagine the carcasses that would have hung off those! I wonder what they used, to reach up that high?"

I smile and shrug, leaving her to scan the rest of the room's features while I make the drinks in the kitchen next door.

When I return, she's already sitting at the table. She smiles thanks as she takes the steaming mug and nods towards the range. "You can just imagine a family huddled round that, a kettle on the boil and some stew in the oven."

I'd rather not dwell on the previous occupants at the moment. I smile but steer the subject elsewhere.

"I'm sorry to burden you with home visits. We're going to buy another car soon – a family sized one, so that I can get about. Hopefully I'll be able to come to the surgery instead."

"Oh, it's no trouble. I do lots of home visits in the more rural areas. Your appointments will be weekly from now on as you've reached thirty-two weeks. We like to keep a closer eye on our ladies as they approach full-term." She takes a sip of her tea. "How have you been?"

"Oh, I've…" I look away. Why is it we can hold it together until someone expresses interest or concern? Her question triggers a wave of isolation and fear in me. Before I can stop it, my lip starts to tremble and my eyes well.

Maureen puts down her mug and stretches a hand across the table to clasp one of mine. Her voice is gentle, soothing. "It's perfectly normal to feel overwhelmed at this stage of your pregnancy. Particularly when it's your first and you've had a difficult time of it. Is there something bothering you?"

I twist a tissue in my hand. I don't know where to start.

"Have you managed to take it easy since I last saw you?"

How much should I share? It's tempting to offload my fears, but it's also nice to be treated like a sane human being, for once. I need to be cautious.

"I've tried to relax. It's not easy, here on my own. My partner's preoccupied with work, which doesn't help." I blow my nose. "I hear strange noises sometimes, which could be some kind of animal, but we haven't come across the cause any yet. Something about this house just makes me feel uncomfortable."

Warily, I look across to Maureen, gauging her reaction. To my relief, she shakes her head understandingly.

"I can understand that. It's a huge change for you and this is an old, atmospheric house. If you're feeling jittery, have you tried speaking to the previous owner?"

This suggestion is like a chink of sunlight. Of course, Mr Bryant! He did invite us to contact him if we had any problems.

"No, I haven't. Good idea. I'll give him a call later."

She looks at me cautiously, as if calculating how to phrase her next question. "And what about your partner? You mentioned he was preoccupied with work?"

"Yes. It's nothing new, but he promised things would be different once we moved here. I think he's finding it harder to put into practice than he imagined." I drain my mug and rest it on the table. "He can't really relate to how I'm feeling."

Maureen pauses before choosing her words. "Imminent birth can put a lot of stress on relationships. Do you feel in any danger from him?"

I shake my head.

"It's very important that you let me, or your GP, know if you ever feel threatened in any way. I know it's depressing and scary, but sadly incidents of domestic abuse often begin during pregnancy."

She reaches into a pocket of her bag and pulls out

a pamphlet entitled: "Preparing for baby: the effects on a relationship".

"If you're experiencing difficulties, you might want to explore counselling. It could help for both of you to talk things through with an independent third party, before baby arrives."

I thank her and leave the pamphlet on the table.

We make our way upstairs. Maureen tests my urine sample and examines me again. This time she lets me listen through the stethoscope. The regular 'whoosh, woo' noise is like a cross between fast moving traffic and a washing machine, and it makes me smile.

The baby is in a better position today, no longer in breech, but Maureen still has concerns about my blood pressure. It reads 150/100 mmHg, on the border between mild and moderately high. We talk about taking more exercise and monitoring it, and she schedules an appointment for the following week.

As I wave goodbye to her on the doorstep, I realise my first impression of her was wrong. She was a real comfort today and I'm glad to have her as my midwife. Her suggestion to call Mr Bryant was particularly helpful. Luckily his number is still saved in my phone from our house purchase conversations. I find it and dial from the landline. There's a long delay before he picks up.

"Hello?" his tone is wary.

"Hello, it's Bea Haddon – you sold the house to us?"

"Yes?"

"I hope you and your wife have settled into your new home. Sorry to bother you – I'm not ringing to complain or anything..."

I hear myself gush and stumble, but Mr Bryant seems more comfortable now he knows I'm not ringing to moan.

"We're doing fine thanks. You keepin' well?"

"Not too bad. I've unpacked most of the boxes, but there's

still a few lurking around. I hope you don't mind me calling. I've just been curious since we've moved in to learn a little more about the history of the house. Would you be able to fill me in?"

"Well, I'll try," he says, sounding hesitant. "As you know, we moved in early 2000. We bought it from an older chap who ran it as a pig farm. He wound up the business and then sold the house to us. He must've had the place gettin' on for thirty years – since 1970, there abouts? Before that, it was owned by someone who   inherited it from his uncle – lived in Dorset, I believe – and the place stood empty for a good few years then."

"I see." I have difficulty phrasing the next question, cautious of how it will be received. "And did you or your wife ever have any strange experiences in the house?"

There's a pause. Mr Bryant's voice is guarded when he finally speaks. "What d'you mean, exactly?"

There's no point holding back, so I tell him everything I've witnessed since moving in. I wait with bated breath for his response, which feels like an eternity.

"I'm not sure if I can help you, Mrs Haddon."

My hopes start to deflate, but then he continues.

"I always brushed it off, y'see, when Vics started hearing things."

There's a flutter in my chest. "What things, Mr Bryant?"

"Call me Andrew. Hard to remember exactly. When we moved in, place was a right mess. Had to start from scratch, y'know?"

I murmur in agreement, keen for him to get to the detail.

"Anyway, like I mentioned to you before, we wanted to start a family, but we had our problems – conceiving, like. Vics took it hard - hard on both of us, truth be told - but she felt it more. Lost her way a little. It was 'round that time she started noticing things. Noises. Can't remember the details. Always seemed a fuss about nothing to me, but she was having none of it."

I take a deep breath. It sounded all too familiar.

"I see. Do you think the noises were similar to the ones I've heard?"

"I really couldn't say, but she thought they were coming from the second bedroom – the one on the left of the stairs. Best person to ask is Vics herself – that is, if she's prepared to talk about it," he adds, awkwardly.

"I understand it might be difficult for her, but I'd be so grateful. I could meet her, if that's easier?"

"I dunno. She's out now but I'll have a word and see what she says. Let me take your number again."

I give him both numbers and thank him again before hanging up.

My mind races, like I've had too much caffeine, an odd mixture of gratification and fear. On the one hand, how I've felt in the house seems justified, more credible, now I know someone else felt similar. It's not just me, not just in my head. Knowing I haven't blown things out of all proportion makes me more self-assured.

On the other hand, my fears have been validated. Something is here. And it wants to be heard, but perhaps by a select audience. *Is it a coincidence it reached out to Vics Bryant and me, yet stayed silent for our husbands? What does it want? How will I maintain the courage to face it alone?*

I fix myself lunch and ponder what to do this afternoon. I promised Maureen that I'd keep active, go for walks. Now is as good a time as any, given it's not raining, and it gets me out the house. I feel I need time away to collect my thoughts.

I search for my wellies and thick socks. It takes some doing. Eventually I find them in a locked plastic crate outside, which once stored our garden equipment in Greenwich, hidden amongst plant pots, garden tools and camping seats. I look inside them, wary of spiders, and give them a good shake with my arms outstretched. Thankfully empty.

I head away from the road, across the fields towards the wooded area. Although the rain has been persistent recently, the ground is not squelchy; buffeted by wind, it's dried into hard firm ridges that I can feel through my boots, changing the swing of my stride and rocking my balance. The crisp blue of this morning has given way to a cold white sky, but at least it's bright. I zip my coat to the neck, trying to keep out the bite of the crystal air, and wish I'd put on my hat and scarf.

There's just enough space in the coat to stretch over my bump and I feel the baby writhe as I walk, a graceful swirl across the left side of my belly, like the twist of a sealion underwater. I wonder if he or she is enjoying the walk, taking advantage of increased wriggle room? Perhaps to him or her it feels like a dance, bouncing to the rhythm of my body?

Up ahead, the trees are gaunt. In the distance they look like feathers: the more delicate branches sway in the breeze, the sturdy resist the wind, solid and stationary. There's no-one within view – no tractors, no farm workers – and I have a pang of déjà-vu.

Where else have I seen this view? Then I remember my dream from last night. Similar, yet different. Then, the landscape was in the throes of a different season, the trees thick with green leaves. The ground was equally hard but from the intensity of the sun. It glared onto my skin and I had no hands free to shield by eyes from the piercing light; my arms were wrapped around a baby. A baby that didn't move.

Stop thinking about it. It's just a dream. I count back from hundred in intervals of sixteen to take my mind off it, I trick I remember from CBT.

I'm ashamed of how unfit I am. After only ten minutes walking, my breath is fast and loud. I used to make time for exercise at the weekends, but what with the move and trying to catch up with chores after long weeks at work, it's fallen by the wayside. Winter weather here has done little to encourage me out of doors. Now spring is arriving I need to make more effort, take a walk each day, build up stamina gradually, as Maureen advised. When I've had enough, I half-turn and retrace my steps back uphill.

Looming ahead, the house looks substantial and stubborn. So practical and functional, I imagine it would laugh at me should I share my terrors of what may lurk within. *Really, Beatrice? Do you truly believe in spooks? I have housed families for centuries, protected them from the elements. And yet you persist that some presence haunts my rooms. Are you letting your imagination run away with you; allowing uncertainty about moving here to cloud your judgment?*

Perhaps. But I know what I've experienced, and it sounds like Vics Bryant may have felt similar.

I refocus my thoughts back to my dilemma. *So, what am I going to do if the scratching returns?* I'd already planned to use my phone to record. I've never tried it before, so I experiment as I walk, using the video function to capture noise.

"One, two,

Buckle my shoe,

Three, four,

Knock on the door..."

It's a blessing I'm alone as I probably look insane. Playing back the recording, the camera image has captured the unattractive underside of my chin, but the nursery rhyme is barely audible. Hopefully the microphone will work better indoors.

I leave my boots by the backdoor until I can think of somewhere better to put them and switch on the lap-top in the lounge. Distraction is my best ploy: I'm going to use the time till

Seb returns to research a family car. Having access to a vehicle will help me feel less cut off here.

I'm so immersed in weighing up costs and features of various people carriers, I don't notice two hours pass. By the time I look up, the lounge has fallen into gloomy shadow. As I muster the energy to get up, the phone rings. It's Seb.

"Hullo. How're you doing?"

"I'm okay. Just been looking up some cars – have a few to show you when you've got some time."

"Great, well done. Why don't you save the pages on the laptop? I might have a flick through tonight."

"Well, we can look together if you like, when you get home?"

"No, I was ringing to say don't wait up – and I won't need dinner, thanks. The Claimant's being a complete arsehole in this case. Despite the Hearing starting next week, he's only just served a stack of new documents."

"Oh no."

"Yeah. If the Tribunal has any sense, they'll exclude them, but you know what they're like. Chances are, they'll be admissible, so we must get our head around them."

Great. Another evening on my own.

"Can't you bring them home and do it here?"

He sighs. "I would, but I know I'll get through it quicker here. Besides, whether I'm stuck here or stuck in the study, I'm still not going to be much company."

No, but at least I'd feel safer if you were here.

"Okay, but I hate not seeing you - particularly after how things were left last night."

He pauses. "I know. Are you feeling more… settled today?"

"I'm okay - I was alright last night, too. I saw the midwife earlier." I add quickly, "Everything's fine."

He sounds relieved, "Pleased to hear it. Won't be long now, Bea, and I can put this case behind me and concentrate on you, the baby and home. Hang in there."

We say goodbye. In my head, I have loads of questions for him. *What happens when the next case comes along? Will you be any different? When will you spend time with this baby? Or will he or she be consigned to your weekends, leaving me to cope Monday to Friday alone?*

I didn't mention to him my call with Mr Bryant. It's not worth it until I've spoken to his wife. I'll accumulate all the evidence and present it to Seb, just like a set of papers for one of his cases. But for now I use my journal to note down the gist of my conversations with Mr Bryant and Seb. It doesn't give me answers, but I feel better distilling the information, and transferring my irritation and anxiety into words on the page. They make more sense to me, in blue ink, rather than rattling around and tangling in my head.

I make myself an omelette with some leftovers and then feel overwhelmingly tired. Probably a combination of fresh air, exercise and lack of sleep. I scoop up my journal and trudge up to bed, yawning.

It's not long before I fall into blissful, undisturbed sleep.

CHAPTER 15

Maud

S omething is wrong. I sit bolt upright in bed, trying to work out what it is.

The room is brighter than usual. I heard William leave at the crack of dawn, hours ago. First day of harvest. He read the clouds yesterday and called upon extra help to cut the crops and I stayed up late last night making pasties to feed them all. When he left this morning, the light was thin and grey and I managed to return to sleep, making the most of a couple of hours before Nathaniel would stir.

And yet the baby did not wake me. This must be why I feel strange. I have been allowed to awaken under my own steam, a rare treat, his crib still silent.

I pad across the floorboards to the end of the bed, peer into the crib. What I see sends a cold bolt of terror through me. Nathaniel is lying face down, the white cotton sheets covering his body. I often find him in this position, but this time he is unearthly still, like a doll made from clay that has been discarded, arms by his sides. I spin his body over, my movements jerky and abrupt with fear. Yet he makes no response, like he cannot feel my touch or discern the sensation of being rolled over.

"No, no, no…"

I hear my voice, but it is as though it comes from someone else. I lift Nathaniel close to me. His skin is different, as white as the sheets I have pushed away, cool to the touch, his eyes closed. The soft mist of his breath is absent from my cheek; there is no rise and fall in his chest.

I gently shake him, try to wake him, but there is nothing: his arms and legs hang, head droops. Despite the warmth of the morning, his whole body is cold, so I wrap him in the covers and hold him tightly in my arms.

I must get help, I must get to William.

I fly downstairs, through the rear parlour, out the door, leaving it wide open behind me. My feet are still bare, but I am unconscious of pain from stones and sharp blades of grass. I look down at his face, searching for some sign of life that may have returned. Nothing.

Where is William? I scour the fields. Figures hover like black flies in the distance, the sun reflected in the swing of the scythes like glowing, gauzy wings. But I cannot make out which is him. I try to run, my legs stumbling over uneven ground; thick, scratching crops hinder my legs, like I'm wading through a bucket of grain. The sun seems unnaturally bright, its rays cruelly bearing down on us.

Almost within reach, faces turn towards me, alert that something is amiss. *How do I find the words?*

But in that moment, I realise it is futile. *Too late.* He has gone. Running to William will not bring him back. My legs stop, suddenly too weak to support my body. Figures now run towards me. Sinking to my knees, the scream that has been silently growing inside me unfurls from my lungs, cuts through the rush of my heartbeat, pierces the air.

CHAPTER 16

Bea

*B*ea,

You were fast asleep when I came in. 1am! Hope you're okay?

Bad news: got to take more statements for 3 witness in Ilford as a result of those docs. Pain in the arse. Good news: chance of coming home early. Will obvs need to work in evening though.

Preferred the Toyota to the Nissan. Could you find local dealer and book appointment at weekend pls?

BTW, where did you go in your wellies? Don't like idea of you falling over in the countryside alone. Text me when you're up.

S xx

I find the note on the table in the kitchen diner area. I didn't hear him arrive or leave this morning. Well, it's tough he doesn't like me walking on my own. Until I get a car, it's about the only form of exercise available to me and it clearly did me some good, if last night's deep sleep was anything to go by.

The lap-top is where I left it yesterday. When it flickers into life, I see that Seb didn't shut down from last night and tabs are still open from his searches. Most relate to the cars, but one captures my attention and I click on it.

Ted Barnes, psychiatrist based in Bungay.

Rage bubbles inside and my hand moves clumsily on the mouse.

How dare he! It's not for him to decide if and when I need help.

Too angry to cry, my instinct is to call him now, tell him what I think. But where will that get me? He'll just claim I'm over-emotional or irrational. No, I need to raise this when I'm calmer, face-to-face.

In the meantime, I find the number for the Ipswich Toyota garage and book an appointment for Saturday afternoon. As I'm toying whether to text Seb the appointment details, I almost drop my phone in surprise when it suddenly rings. The number is unidentified.

"Hello?"

There's a pause at the other end.

"- hello. Is that Bea Haddon?"

Instantly I guess who it is and pull back a chair. Whatever I'm about to hear would either reassure me or feed my fear.

"Yes, yes it is. Is that Mrs Bryant?"

"Yes. Call me Vic."

The cautious, quiet voice is at odds with her friendly request. She seems as nervous as I feel, probably not assisted by speaking over the phone.

"Thank you for taking the time to get back to me so quickly. Would you like to come over for a coffee perhaps? Andrew mentioned you're fairly close..."

Her reply is fast. "No thank you... that won't be necessary."

Unsettled by her abrupt response, I refocus my thoughts. "Right...I'm not sure how much your husband's told you..." I tell her about the strange experiences I've had at the house. The noises, the smells, the impression the house is listening, watching. Sensations perceived only by me, not Seb.

She doesn't interrupt. In fact, the line is so quiet, I wonder whether she's still there.

"I wondered whether you've experienced anything similar?" I prompt her.

Instead of words, there are uneven snatches of breath, sniffs.

"I'm sorry if I've upset you. Are you okay?"

She sighs and collects herself. "Sorry... didn't mean to get upset. I'm a whirl of hormones at the moment... It's just hearing it again..." The muffled sound of her blowing her nose is soon followed by a voice that sounds more controlled, decisive.

"Sorry. Like you, I was the only person to detect something in that house... and as you'll no doubt appreciate, it's hard going through it on your own. It's brought it all back, talking to you now... guess I'm partly relieved I didn't imagine it back then."

I press the phone hard against my ear, not wanting to miss a word she says.

"I don't know exactly when it started, but I know it was shortly after I discovered I was pregnant. I heard the scratching noise one afternoon, similar to how you describe. Never had a smell, though. When I heard it, I didn't think too much about it, but a couple of hours later, I started bleeding. That's when I lost my first."

"I'm so sorry."

Her voice starts to waver, but she pauses and recovers herself again.

"That was the pattern. The house'd be silent... no noises, no disturbances...You'll think I'm mad, but it was like the house was watching, waiting for me to fall pregnant and then...shortly afterwards I'd lose the baby. Three in total. Each lost before two months."

My heart beats close to the surface of my skin. I had never made a connection between pregnancy and the feelings I had in the house. Instinctively, my free arm wraps over my bump.

"That must have been awful for you. I'm sorry to drag it up again," my croaky words stumble.

"It was... and I couldn't understand what was making the noise or why I seemed to miscarry shortly after. Of course, the doctors thought my worrying brought it on - my fear of hearing the sounds caused me to miscarry, a self-fulfilling prophecy, if you like. But I disagree. It doesn't explain how..."

She stops short, as though rethinking her next words.

"It doesn't explain what?" I prompt.

She sighs again. "Look, I wouldn't normally say, given it's early days...but it's only right you should know. Andrew told me you're expecting. The thing is, after all that bad luck, I fell pregnant again. I took the test shortly before we left Oak Tree. That's why we were keen to move quickly...move to somewhere new. I'm nervous, of course, but this week we reached a milestone – I'm over two months now. I wouldn't say I was any less fretful this time: the only difference is, we moved house... moved before it was too late."

"Congratulations, that's great news,"

My voice is stiff. I am pleased for her. I know what it's like to miscarry, and she deserves her good fortune. But I'm also frustrated that the Bryants had sold their house to us, knowing the problems it could bring.

What did this mean for my baby? Am I to suffer the same fate?

Reading my tone, Vic is sheepish.

"I can only imagine what must be going through your mind right now. In all honesty, I wanted to get out of that house, after

I'd made a connection between it and losing my babies. Andrew didn't see it that way – he thought it was biological or triggered by the links I'd made in my mind. Even still, we would have said something to you...it's just that we had no idea you were pregnant. Andrew was shocked when he saw you get out the car that day."

Her voice changes, more forceful. "But please don't put too much weight on my experience. There's no reason to think the same would happen to you."

"Why not? We both heard things in the house. How do you know I'll be safe?" Fear makes me blunt.

"You're right, I don't know for sure. But your pregnancy is established – more than mine ever was. If something wanted you to lose it, God forbid, wouldn't it have happened by now?"

Possibly. She had a point, but there was no logic to this situation. We're clutching at straws, trying to find differences between our circumstances, to determine different outcomes. But there are no clear rules. No guarantee of my safety or the baby's.

"Please keep me informed, won't you? Let me know how things go? You've got my number now. You can call me any time."

"Thanks – I appreciate your honesty."

We hang up.

Rooted to the sofa, my brain whirs. I'm not going mad; my instincts are accurate. Vic Bryant felt the presence too. *But is this any comfort?* If anything, the situation seems bleaker. Until now, I'd told myself the presence had caused no real harm and was unlikely to do so, but Vic casts doubt on that theory. *Why would it not want her to be pregnant?*

I need air. Heaving myself from the sofa, I pull on my wellies, grab my phone and outdoor clothes and head out.

The wind has picked up since yesterday, roaring as it whips across fields, flattening grasses and battling with bushes. My scarf trails behind me, a streak in the wind, until I wrap it more tightly around my neck. I remember my hat today, but the weather is too boisterous: snatched from my head, I try to chase it across the field. It takes off each time I'm within two strides of it, as though taunting me in a game of tag. I finally catch it with the toe of my boot and stuff it firmly in my pocket.

I manage to reach the row of trees today: beautiful oaks, about thirty foot high. Craning my neck, I spot three nests cradled within the branches. How vulnerable they are, wedged so high within the boughs, at the whim of the careless wind. *Do the birds worry about their unhatched chicks, exposed to the elements? How can I protect mine, in this crazy situation?* I stroke my bump, praying I'm successful in keeping this little one safe from harm. I feel a swoop and nudge near my hand in response: he or she reacting to my touch for the first time.

The moment's interrupted by a beep from my phone. It's Seb.

All well? Did you see my note? S x

Damn, I hadn't texted him back. He must have arrived in Ilford. I turn my back to the wind and tap a response:

Hi. Yes thanks, all good. Toyota booked for Sat, 2pm. See you later, B x

I read it before I press send and shake my head. I could lose my baby. I fear something in the house is controlling my fate and a stranger has confirmed my fears. Yet your search history shows you believe I've derailed and need professional help to get back on track. All I can convey to you is information about some poxy car. *Was Andrew Bryant more supportive in this situation?*

On the way back to the house, I try to keep my spirits up by singing under my breath. After the interaction I'd had with the baby this morning, maybe he or she can hear? I read somewhere

126

that babies are able to pick out their mother's voice, even in the womb, and can respond to music. I'm not sure I'd classify my voice as music, but our shared experience this morning, the reciprocity of our touch, encourages me to try.

I enter the house through the backdoor, as usual. Instantly, I'm struck by a change in atmosphere. The house is almost too silent, like any sound has been sucked into its walls. Watchful. Listening.

I try to shrug off the feeling; after all, outside the air was alive with the rush of the wind and the sound of my song: the still air of the house is bound to feel quieter. I take off my coat and shove my mobile into my jumper pocket.

Then I hear something. Soft, but the unmistakeable sound of movement. It's coming through the doorway, beyond the hall. A chill rolls down my spine, like a finger trailing across the keys of a piano.

Can I do this on my own? Part of me wants to run back outside, to the openness of the fields. *No.* I need to find out. I can't let fear drive me from my home.

I brace myself, take slow quiet steps towards the door. My breath is loud.

There it is again.

It's coming from the lounge. Light, fluttering, like a deck of cards being shuffled by a pair of thumbs. In a split second, a small dark object soars across the door opening, left to right. I take a breath and step inside. My eyes dart around the room, trying to find the source of sound and movement. It confounds me at first, and I take in the debris spilling out from the fireplace: a clotted mess of straw and mud has tumbled from the chimney and a mushroom of black soot radiates from the grate, covering carpet, rug and coffee table.

As I move closer, I feel a swoop and waft of air over my head, a cloud of black dust billowing in its trail. I automatically duck, raising my hands above my head and yelp.

It's a crow. It stops to rest on the shade of a lamp, cocking its head to one side, eyeing me distrustfully. The fireplace wreckage must be the remains of a nest forced down by the wind. I move slowly towards the window fastenings. The loud sound of metal sliding against metal stirs the bird again, and as I open every hinged window, cool air gusts in. The bird senses the shift in pressure, and after a couple of minutes of me waving my arms and coaxing him in the right direction, he finds his freedom.

I fasten the windows, thankful to be rid of him, and reach for a discarded thick cardigan. Feeling cold and dizzy, I lower myself onto the sofa and take a breather. Birds don't scare me outside, but as it flapped in the lounge, I was acutely aware of the sharp claws and beak, the risk of being scratched or pecked. Pathetic really, given the size of him compared to me. But it was a strange coincidence that the nest should fall down the chimney today, when I had only just been looking at other nests perched in the trees.

Of course, I am relieved to find it was a bird and nothing mysterious, but the fact it was a crow unnerves me. Didn't they signify a bad omen? I'm sure they're associated with death. I'm not normally superstitious, but this house seems to unlock hidden fears.

Recovered from the shock, I fetch bin-liners, dustpan brush, duster and hoover. Where to start? Everything in the lounge is covered in dull grey soot. Thankfully, the nest has no eggs and I gently place it inside a bin bag on its own. I sweep the worst of the mess away with a dustpan and brush and run over the hoover to remove the last traces. The ferocious blare from the motor masks any other noise in the room. I find myself looking over my shoulder repeatedly, in case something is behind me.

Cleaning done, I put my wellies back on and seek somewhere to place the nest outside. It's unlikely a bird will use it, given it's tainted by my scent, but you never know. Just within reach, there's a hole in the wooden slats of the out-house. I tuck part of it in the hole, and it fits snugly. Far enough off the ground to limit the risk of predators, it also blocks one of the many gaps.

Returning to the kitchen, I can't believe it's already 2pm. I cut off a hunk of bread and heat up a tin of soup, which I'm so eager to eat I end up scalding the roof of my mouth. As I finish, I hit a slump, the adrenalin and exertion of this morning leaving me shattered. I soak the bowl in the sink, too tired to wash it up, and head upstairs for an afternoon nap.

I pick up my journal from next to the bed and roll onto my side to write.

4th March

Discover Seb has been looking into local shrink behind my back. So angry.

Black crow trapped inside lounge. Frightened the life out of me. Nest had fallen down the chimney. Trying not to think about what it could mean.

I can barely keep my eyes open, so I kick off my slippers and quickly fall asleep.

***

I wake with a start.

What was that?

A low familiar rumble, near my head, followed by a bang. Then silence.

The room is in semi-darkness. I heave myself up as fast as I can, curse as arms, half-asleep, clumsily navigate the bedside table searching for the lamp switch. Flicking it on, I see the bedroom door is closed. This was the source of the rumble and slam.

Who shut it?

My heart pounds in my ears. I'm too terrified to move

from the bed and try to recall what happened before I slept. I remember coming up for a nap but the time on the clock is now 6.30 pm.

What's that?

There's a different sound now, muffled through the door. But there's no mistaking the scratching again, coming from the spare room.

What do I do? Where's my mobile?

I take a couple of breaths and swing my legs out of bed, but before my feet touch the ground, I see my journal on the floor, pages splayed open. I never leave it like that. My throat constricts as I pick it up. Underneath my entry for 4th March, a word has been scrawled repeatedly, in writing that's not mine:

Leave Leave Leave Leave Leave Leave Leave Leave

The words are formed in loopy, old-fashioned handwriting, but by the end of the line the letters turn jerky and agitated.

"Shit!"

I slam the book shut, thrust it away from me on the bed, but still my petrified eyes are glued to its cover.

How can it be possible? Who did this? What does it mean?

My brain's blank. My only instinct is to get away - away from the book and the noise that claws my skull.

It's then that I notice the smell. The bitter, sweet smell of lavender and sage, smothering and sudden. The stifling scent swirls inside my windpipe, making me cough and gasp for air.

Shaking, I look around for my mobile. I grab it from the bedside cabinet, fingers fumbling over the keys as I try to set up the video. Crossing the landing, I put the phone near the wall of the spare room and press record. The scraping pauses briefly, then gets louder and louder.

"Stop, please stop!!" I hear my voice cry out. The sound pauses again, then continues, more frantic, more determined. I grip my head as it rips through me like a saw. I can't stay another minute. *Get away, get away!*

I almost trip down the stairs, legs and eyes moving at different speeds. My breath is shallow and fast. Terror turns movement into slow motion, bumbling and laborious.

The smell follows me downstairs, a sickly cloud. I shove my feet into wellies, grab my keys and coat and search frantically for my mobile, then curse as I remember leaving it upstairs.

Can't think straight, can't bear the thought of going back upstairs: must leave now.

I exit through the front door. Hands still shaking, I lock it behind me. Although it's a relief to be away from the noise and the smell, I don't know what to do. The steam of my breath catches in the electric light streaming through the glass panel of the door as I try to think. Kath's! That's my best bet. I lurch past the out-house towards the path.

Evening has set in. Crisp features in daylight have been replaced by vague blotches in sepia, brown and grey. With the landscape in shadow, lines between path, field and hedgerow are blurred and indistinct.

I think I've found the path, but my feet stumble over uneven ground, the ridges and furrows of the cold, hard earth impossible to distinguish in this light.

The texture of the surface under my feet changes, the road marking the end of our land. I turn left. There's no pavement or footpath, just a country road, but I am thankful for the tarmacked surface. I keep walking along what I think is the centre of the road and my ears trained for the sound of vehicles from front or behind. If anything comes, I'll move to the side, but I must be wary of the ditches between road and hedgerow:

in this light, they are invisible, but I know they lurk near and are deceptively deep.

How long was the distance between ours and Tanner's Farm? A couple of miles, if I remember correctly. Not far in daylight, but a different matter now. Seb would go ballistic if he knew, but what choice do I have? If only I had the torch on my mobile to guide me, or the chance to call for help!

On the murky road, I try to make sense of it all. *Who or what wrote in my journal?* Whatever is in our house has taken communication to a whole new level. Mysterious noises, flashes on video images, peculiar smells and the feeling of being watched could potentially be explained. Handwritten messages could not.

Leave: was it a threat or advice? Either way, I feel compelled to listen. Back at the house, I was inclined to interpret it as a danger and my reaction was to take flight.

What's to stop it following me here, out on the road? My skin prickles at the possibility. No, I can't think of that. It's too terrifying and beyond my control. Every strange experience I've had has been within the house. There's no reason to believe it will leave the four walls of the property to find me here.

Darkness diminishes visibility minute by minute. Before long I can barely see a couple of metres ahead of me.

The soft grumble of a car engine in the distance hums from behind me and I carefully find the righthand side of the road. The engine amplifies, the beam from the headlights casting a glow on the road between us. As it draws near, I tuck myself in as much as I can, but I've misjudged the space. To avoid being clipped by the wing mirror, I thrust myself out of the way. I lose my balance, toppling forwards into the ditch, arms flailing desperately as I try to grab something to steady myself. Wellies scrape the sides, seeking a grip. My left foot catches in the long grass, ankle twisting as the rest of me lands.

"Aaaggh!" my voice calls after the vehicle, but not loud enough for it to stop.

Coat, legs, and hands are clawed by the spiky hedgerow as I fight my way out. My right foot and hands have planted in the squelchy bottom of the ditch. *Yuck.* I feel the side of the bank with my hands and feet and manage to clamber out, back to the road. Tentatively I test my weight on the left ankle: it's sore but thankfully not too bad.

I continue my journey, shaken by how close I was to being hit or dragged along. *No more vehicles, please.*

I feel a different kind of fear to the one I experienced in the house; a tangible vulnerability. Nightfall in the countryside is so different to the city: in Greenwich, at whatever time of the night, the streetlight emitted a protective glow. You took it for granted; dark was never truly black. Here, darkness is complete, silently smothering the countryside. It's all consuming, a cloak that conceals the landscape and everything in it. I've never been afraid of the dark, but here on the roadside it's a present and physical danger.

Distance is hard to judge without markers. I'm cold, my coat providing limited warmth from the chill of the evening, the effects of adrenalin subsiding. Signs of spring in the daytime seem like a charade now. The wind has picked up again and rattles through the branches, buffeting my legs and pinching my skin with icy fingers.

With limited vision, my other senses compensate.

What was that?

I hear a distant clatter behind me, just like hooves on the ground, cantering at speed, but surely it can't be? Who would ride at this time?

It's getting louder, accompanied by a rattle, like the wheels of a carriage rolling across the ground. What farmer would use horses and carriage, when tractors have headlights?

Whatever it is, it feels like it's coming closer and I brace myself for the ditch once more.

Before it reaches me, all of a sudden there is a commotion, like something hitting the road then a cry of "whoa!" rings through the night. *Was that a neigh in response?* The clatter stops abruptly. Then silence.

As much as I strain my ears, I hear trace of neither horse nor carriage, as though they've been carried off with the wind.

Should I turn back on myself, to see if something's there? I hate the thought of leaving someone in trouble, but what I heard was vague and insubstantial. And I shouldn't spend longer on this road than necessary. No, I need to push on, find refuge with our neighbours, who would be better equipped to assist. I'm in no position to offer help to anyone.

Pushing this strange experience to the back of my mind, I continue to feel my way painfully slowly, as the road twists and turns. I wish I was more familiar with my location. I wear a watch on my wrist but have no hope of seeing it. It feels like I must have been walking for at least an hour, but it's so hard to tell.

As the road bends to the left, suddenly I can see lights ahead of me! Not the moving headlights of a car but static from a house. They drive me forwards, like a beacon, my feet moving faster.

Closer now I can see five peachy rectangles of light. Windows, hopefully from Tanner's Farm. Yes, I think I recognise it from our visit. I'm close enough now that I can see the moving picture of a TV screen through the window. The normality makes me want to weep with relief. I knock on the door and wait. Footsteps approach and the shadow of a man appears behind the glass.

John opens the door.

"Hello, who's that? Wait a minute... it's Beatrice, isn't it?

What the devil are you doing in the dark? Come in!"

As I cross the threshold, the tension that's kept me going, held me together, slips undone. My legs shake and start to fold so I cling to the doorframe to avoid crumpling to the floor. Overcome by sobs, my shoulders heave. John stares helpless; his hands try to support me but he's embarrassed and not sure where to put them.

He calls for his wife and Kath joins us. Without a word, she puts an arm around my shoulder and steers me towards the sofa in the lounge.

"Come in, take a seat. Take some deep breaths."

She kneels in front of me, her eyes locked on mine. She waits patiently while I breathe in, and slowly exhale.

After a few minutes I nod to signal I'm feeling stronger and sit back on the sofa. I look down. My coat and leggings have angry slashes, torn by the thorny bushes. To my embarrassment, hands and boots are covered in mud. I try to rise, intending to wash myself and remove the boots, but Kath puts out a hand to stop me.

"Don't you worry love. Can you tell us what happened?"

She takes a seat next to me and prompts John to put on the kettle.

"I will, but first, I think someone could be in trouble."

"Who? What do you mean?"

Just as I'm telling her about the sounds like horse and carriage on the road, John re-joins us with steaming cups of tea and takes an armchair opposite. I see them exchange strange looks. *Was it fear?* Or perhaps it was just concern for me.

"So, I don't know if something happened to the carriage driver, or one of the horses, or whether it was just the wind and my ears playing tricks."

Kath is the first to respond. "I don't think any help's needed.

Could have been the wind, and perhaps the distant neigh of a horse from our farm, or from Jess's place. No-one would travel in a horse and cart in the dark – not these days." She catches John's eye and he gives a small nod. "But what brought you out on the road in the first place?"

Where to begin? I tell them everything: the mysterious door that slides shut by itself; flickers on our video camera; the obscure scratching sound that only begins when I'm alone; the oppressive smell of lavender and sage that emanates from the same room; the sobbing message on the toy; the crow coming down the chimney; and most significantly, the entry in my diary, LEAVE written repeatedly by hand. I also relay the conversation I'd had with Vics.

Saying it out loud, I realise I must sound crazy or at the very least neurotic. *How will they react?* I expect a similar response to the one from Seb: I'll be told there must be a reasonable and logical explanation. They're kind people, and although they don't know the troubles I've had in the past, they'll likely suggest I take more rest or stay elsewhere for a little while. Their reaction couldn't be more different. They listen in silence, taking in my every word, their eyes dark. Before they speak, the shrill sound of the telephone makes us jump.

"I'll get it," John mumbles as he gets to his feet.

"Hello? Ah, Seb...yes, Bea's just walked over to us, no need to panic. Do you want to speak to her?" John twists his body and raises his eyebrows at me, phone pressed to ear.

Seb's words are indecipherable, but even from here I can tell he is talking loudly and fast.

John looks away: "Right you are... see you in a few minutes then." He replaces the receiver and shuffles back to his seat. "You've gathered he's on his way – he's back at the house. Sounds like he's worried."

John and Kath look at each other, seeming to communicate

telepathically in the way that couples do after many years together. John looks down and Kath speaks.

"You've been through a lot, my love, and there's so much to process. Did you tell Seb everything you've told us?"

"Most of it. He doesn't know about my call with Vics Bryant – and the writing in the journal and crow happened today - but I've told him everything else." I look at my filthy hands, rub the fingernails with my thumb. "He doesn't understand. He thinks it's all in my head."

"Have you got anywhere else you could stay? At least until the baby comes?" John asks awkwardly.

I sigh. "Seb won't leave...I haven't asked but I know what his answer would be. We don't have spare cash at the moment, what with the move and needing to buy a second car." I take a sip of my drink. "I've got family in Essex, but it seems a big ask for such a long stretch of time and I don't want to be away from him."

Before we can discuss it any further, there's a knock at the door.

"That'll be Seb," John rises. He opens the door and brings him straight through.

Seb's cheeks are pink and drips of sweat cling to his neck. His shoulders are hunched forwards. He fixes me with piercing eyes.

"What on earth were you doing, Bea? Why didn't you take your phone? I came home, calling your name: no answer. I rang your number, but heard it ring upstairs - found it on the floor in the spare room!"

"I know - I realised I left it there, but I couldn't go back for it. Can we discuss this..."

Seb doesn't let me continue.

"You're almost thirty-three weeks pregnant. You can't just

walk off into the night, without letting anyone know where you are and without your phone. Anything could have happened!" His eyes take in my dishevelled appearance. "Jesus! Are you hurt?"

"No, I'm fine, just a sore ankle and a few minor cuts..."

"So, what possessed you to walk out like that?"

My cheeks flush. "Seb, I want to discuss this at home...I was frightened, I didn't know what to do."

He looks at me as though I've taken leave of my senses.

"You're not on about the noises and smells again? Seriously, I can't believe you risked yourself - the baby - over that!"

"And I can't believe you won't take *me* seriously!" I hiss, shaking inside.

I mumble apologies to Kath and John. It's not fair to argue in front of them. They look like they want to say something yet feel too uncomfortable to do so.

Seb shoots a frown at me, before turning to them.

"I'm sorry if we've put you to any trouble. Must have given you a fright! We'll get home and let you enjoy the rest of your evening." Seb offers a hand to help me off the sofa, but I brush it away and get up unaided.

Kath rises too. She ignores Seb and looks at me, her face still full of concern. "It was no trouble, really. We're quite open about things here...there are lots of stories about this part of the county. People experience things... things from the past." She takes my hands in hers, "We don't pass judgment."

Seb cuts her short. "Thank you, but I think a good rest will do us both the world of good after tonight's excitements." He's keen to usher me out of the door and puts his hand firmly on my shoulder, "Apologies again, and goodnight to both of you."

I'm speechless with anger. Kath releases my hands,

reluctantly, and I nod a goodbye to her and John, who looks sympathetic but awkward.

We get into the car. My words fire like bullets as soon as we turn into the main road and out of view.

"I can't believe you apologised for me back there. How dare you! Particularly as they were actually going to help me!"

"Don't be ridiculous. What light can they possibly shed on a few noises and a smell? he snaps. "You need to calm down and listen to yourself, Bea."

"I had calmed down, before you turned up. But you don't even know what happened! Are you interested?"

"Yes, of course!"

"I fell asleep in the afternoon – I was exhausted after clearing the mess from the crow..."

"Crow, what crow?" Seb is shaking his head now, as though I'm speaking madness. "So, are you now telling me that a crow has been making these noises?"

"No! Let me finish – this is different. A crow and its nest dropped down through the chimney in the lounge this morning. Nothing to do with the noises upstairs. It was later in the afternoon – after I'd fallen asleep – when the scratching noise and the smell started up again, and this time I tried to record it. Worst of all, I found a message in my journal – the word LEAVE written repeatedly! The message is loud and clear, Seb: something wants us out."

He pulls up to the house as I finish telling my garbled account. I'm aware that it's not come out as clearly as it could. The internal car lights flick on as he turns off the ignition. Under the beam, his face is baffled and grim.

"Explain it again. Slowly."

He keeps his eyes forward, avoiding mine, as I explain everything that happened today clearly and in more detail. The light of the car dims. Still, he is silent.

"Say something, for Christ's sake! Weird shit is happening here, Seb! I'm terrified."

When he finally speaks, his voice sounds controlled, expressionless.

"I don't understand what's going on, Bea. It's good that you're using the journal, but now - now you're claiming it contains messages you didn't write?"

"*Claiming?!* What do you mean? I didn't write it!" my pitch rises.

He carries on, low and slow. "There's no other logical explanation." He is unclicking his seat-belt, no further point to be made, so far as he's concerned.

"No, you've got to believe me! I'll show you when we get inside. And we can play back the recording on my phone too." I'm trembling with frustration as I unfasten my belt .

We use the torch on his mobile to find our way safely to the front door. He takes my arm and I walk with difficulty, my ankle still throbbing. He lets go of me as he unlocks the door and waits while I take off my muddy boots. He helps me to clean my scratched, muddied hands then I lead him upstairs.

All traces of the pungent lavender and sage smell have disappeared. The journal is exactly where I'd left it, on the bed. I hastily flick through pages. *Please let it still be there.*

"Ah! Look!" I point triumphantly. Even on second sight it sends a chill down my spine. I watch Seb's face for a reaction, but it remains impassive.

"Well, yes, I can see it, but I'm still unconvinced about how it got there."

Fear flips to anger in an instant. "Why the hell would I write that, Seb? I'm not going crazy! Just because I've had problems in the past doesn't mean you can use it against me."

"No-one's using anything against you, Bea. I'm not ganging up on you! I'm trying to support you."

"Well, it doesn't bloody feel like it! If you were supporting me, you'd take this seriously, rather than trying to find a shrink behind my back!"

He winces. "It wasn't behind your back. You were asleep, I was browsing before bed."

"So, have you made an appointment for me, without my consent?"

He shakes his head, wearily. "No – no. You know how it is – sometimes it takes a while to find the right doctor and I wanted to be prepared. I'd never book an appointment without discussing it with you first."

"Right – I'll take comfort from that then," I retort, sarcastic. He tries to put a hand on my shoulder, but I shrug it off.

He sighs. "There's a difference between supporting you and believing you at the moment. I'm just trying to do the right thing. What you're saying doesn't add up."

"I know it sounds crazy, all of it, but it's real. And if you don't believe me, listen to the video recording."

We cross the landing. My mobile lies on the floor, near the wall. I stoop to pick it up, wincing as pain shoots up my back, my body bruised and jarred from earlier.

The video is ten minutes long, probably the default cut-out point. I turn the volume to max and hold the phone between us, playing it from the beginning. A fraction of my white, terrified face flashes into view, and then the frame focuses on the wooden beam of the ceiling. Only muffled background noise is audible. After a few seconds, we hear a sound. I press pause, scroll back. But it's only my voice, faint and desperate, shouting "Stop, please, stop!". No scratching, no scraping. My heart sinks.

Seb raises his eyebrow at me. "I can't hear anything, Bea,

apart from your voice."

"It's the crappy quality of the video!" I reply. But I'm winded, defeated. Even to my own ears, it sounds implausible. Then I remember Vics Bryant.

"I'm not the only one, Seb. Vics Bryant experienced problems here too."

He rests his temple on finger tips, his voice is tired. "What problems? When did you speak to *her*?"

"Earlier today. She rang me ... after I spoke to Andrew. You remember he said they had difficulty conceiving? Well, she's thinks it's something to do with the house. She miscarried three times after hearing the noises, and now she's carried for two months, living away from here."

Seb looks baffled. "I don't know what to say. I mean... she may have fertility problems, but I don't see how it has anything to do with the house."

"Well, I see it, and so does she. What happens now, Seb? All I know is, I can't stay *here*." My voice is firmer than I feel.

He shakes his head. "I don't know what's going on. I want to help you, really I do, but I can't handle this right now." His voice cracks. He takes a step down the stairs then lowers his bottom onto the landing. Sitting in this foetal position, he rests his head in his hands. After a while, he looks up at me, takes my hand and pulls me down next to him.

"I've got so much on my plate. Too much. My head was already whirring after speaking to the witnesses today. The case is a nightmare - more and more issues keep creeping out of the woodwork. I drove straight here from the hospital to write up the supplemental statements. I was looking forward to eating with you and finding some peace, getting the work done. But then this happens..." He shakes his head, looking overwhelmed.

"I can't believe... how can you talk about work now!" I shake my head, incredulous. "Seb, if you put all of the pieces together,

142

everything that's happened ...it's like some kind of horror story. Something strange is going on – something supernatural. It's terrifying!"

He frowns and looks at me with troubled eyes. "But that's just it, Bea. WE haven't had these experiences...all of these things have only happened to you. And when I think about it, you haven't been yourself since we moved in."

"No...no...that's not fair ...don't try and blame it on me. I'm not imagining things! Vics Bryant felt the same!"

"I don't know about Mrs Bryant... but I think speaking to her has made it worse... given weight to your fears." He sighs. "Ultimately, I don't want you to be here alone if it's going to make you scared and you end up doing something like this again - putting yourself and the baby in danger." Wearily, he rises to a standing   position, gripping the rail. "Maybe it would be better for you to stay with your parents for a while? Let's grab some tea and work it out."

He walks downstairs. I feel like shaking him, screaming at him, but I stop myself. Instead, I stay mute and tightly coiled like a spring.

I follow him downstairs and sit at the table while he makes noises in the kitchen. I've no appetite, but I know the morning sickness will return if I don't eat.

He puts a plate in front of me and tucks into his hungrily. We're both silent, lost in our own thoughts, but his eyes dart towards me. I concentrate on swallowing forkfuls of food which catch in my throat.

How can I make him see sense, open his eyes to what is going on around us? John was right – we should stay somewhere else. If Seb supported me, we could seek help together. We could move to my parents temporarily until we figure out what to do. But his reaction makes it abundantly clear that I'm in this on my own.

LEAVE. A single word, but it makes my throat constrict. Is

something trying to protect us, send us away before we meet harm? Or is it an order, a threat? Either way, it shouldn't be ignored.

At the end of the meal, he stacks the plates and breaks the silence.

"I can only think of one solution, Bea. Just hear me out. I don't want to go over what's happened again, there's no point. But I feel like this has been building – like you're struggling to adjust here. I get it: it's a huge change for you, leaving work, London, your friends and all the unknown challenges that lay ahead."

"No, Seb, that's not what's happening, I'm not -"

He closes his eyes, like he has to make a conscious effort to be patient, and holds up a hand to ward off my protest.

"Clearly, you're not okay. It would be a lot for anyone, but you've taken dangerous decisions. I can't focus properly on my work if I'm worried about what's happening here. And while you're feeling like this, I don't think it's a good idea for you to be left alone."

He pauses, looks into my eyes. It takes all my effort to hold in tears of anger.

"I think you should spend some time at your parents. You could come with me to the station tomorrow. The Liverpool Street train stops at Colchester, and you could change there for Chelmsford. Have a week with them, or however long you need, enjoy a change of scenery. And I'll pick you up at the weekend, so we can take a look at that car."

To him, it makes perfect sense. I have to admit, it gives me a chance to escape and feel safe, time to plan what to do. But I hate his logic behind it. Like I'm losing the plot and can't be trusted on my own. A threat to myself and the baby.

"Okay... I'll ring my parents. But not because *I'm* a danger – something here is a danger to me. I just wish you could see it."

He nods and leaves the table. Although we've reached agreement about what to do, there's much that's unresolved between us.

I'm left to do the dishes and make the call to my parents.

CHAPTER 17

Bea

"**H**ello?"

Mum's clipped, familiar voice answers. The normality of it jars with the strangeness of the day. I call home weekly and usually it's an opportunity to catch up and exchange news, particularly in recent years since I've been married. Today, however, the sound of her voice is a comfort, taking me back to my younger self, looking for support and advice. A strong urge to break down and sob wells within me, but I manage to keep my voice calm. I don't want to worry her.

"Hi Mum... it's me."

There is a pause. "Ahh, darling... it's unlike you to ring at this time! It's a Tuesday. I play bridge on a Tuesday."

Since she's retired from nursing, her life has been crammed with social engagements, sometimes with, often without, Dad. I usually call at the weekend, after breakfast on a Sunday, when I'm unlikely to intrude on her plans.

"Sorry, I won't keep you. I just wondered if I could come and stay for a while?"

An even longer pause.

"Is something wrong, Beatrice? I thought you had your work cut out for you after the move?"

"No... well, yes I do, but I could just do with a rest," I bite my lip, conscious of my half-truth. "I just keep finding more and more jobs to do here, and it's difficult to take time to put them to one side and concentrate on preparing for the baby."

"I see. Is everything okay between you and Seb?"

I'm thankful she can't see my face. "Fine. Actually, it was his idea. He has seen how tired I am and wants me to take it easy for a bit."

I can't face telling her what's been happening here at the house. I don't have the energy or the strength to face the risk of her doubting me too.

"Plus, it would be nice to spend some time with you and Dad. I'd not seen you since we've moved."

I strike a chord here. I know she felt guilty for not having helped us to move in, but her and Dad couldn't fit it in around Dad's work commitments.

"Ah.. well, fine. What date were you thinking? It might be nice around Easter..."

"No Mum, my due date's in April! I was thinking of tomorrow."

"Tomorrow?" She is incredulous. "But that's rather short notice, darling...we're going out to dinner with the Athertons."

"Well, I could come with you... or fix something for myself at home. I really don't mind."

Silence again. I know she doesn't like surprises, particularly if they involve changing plans. But it's not often I lean on her for anything.

"I won't be any trouble, honestly. I'll take a cab from the

station when I arrive... I can cook for myself, and I'll sleep wherever there's a bed that's made up. You just carry on as normal."

"Yes... that will be fine. Although it wouldn't hurt to give a little more notice in future. Must go, I should have left five minutes ago. See you tomorrow."

"Bye." The line is dead.

I didn't expect Mum to be overjoyed at my spontaneous visit. I knew she loved to see me and my sister, but she liked to plan things in advance.

My parents have encouraged my sister and I to be independent from an early age, sending us to boarding school aged eleven. They made sure we had a great education, and that we could stand on our own feet, but it's had an impact on how we interact. We've never really spent much time together as a family from our teenage years onwards, and although we get on well enough, there's a distance between us, particularly since I've been married. Still, perhaps the slight detachment in the relationship with my parents built a stronger one elsewhere. Harriet and I are extremely close, united by the same upbringing and sharing similar passions - art, books and theatre - looking out for each other, sharing secrets.

I take a suitcase from the wardrobe and begin filling it with a week's worth of clothes. It doesn't amount to much, given I'm wearing maternity jumpers, jeans and leggings on rotation. I'm just zipping up when Seb's footsteps can be heard on the stairs.

"How did it go with your mum and dad?"

"Oh, the usual. Mum answered. She was taken aback but the suddenness... but she's okay with it."

"Right." Seb nods, knowingly. "Hopefully your visit won't be too disruptive. Did she say if your dad was going to be around?"

"No, sadly not."

Dad was a doctor, a general practitioner, who had attempted to retire many times, but kept getting drawn back to work. Well, that was his line. We had our own theory. Perhaps each time he tried, he realised that he didn't fit in with Mum's lifestyle, so he gravitated back to work, where he felt appreciated. He was currently working part-time, but filled the rest of his week with golf.

"Well, hopefully you'll get to spend some time with them both. I've got at least another couple of hours work before I call it a night. I'll try not to disturb you when I come up." He kisses me and is about to leave when I grasp his arm.

"Everything that's happened today.... I know you don't believe it, but I'm not sure you should be here alone. I'm frightened what could happen."

He eyes me warily. "Bea, don't worry about me."

"What about that accident in the kitchen? When we first moved in."

"That was stupidity and tiredness on my part. I'll be fine. I think we'll both be fine in a week or so's time."

I remove my hand and he drifts out the room.

It's enough for me to recognise his view hasn't shifted. As far as he's concerned, it's all in my head.

CHAPTER 18

Bea

W e leave the house before sunrise. Not long ago, this used to be normal for me: wake at 6.15, quick shower, bit of make-up, grab breakfast and be on the platform for the 7.21 to Charring Cross. My routine has changed a lot since then so the alarm at 5.30 is a rude awakening.

My ankle aches, less so than yesterday, but with each movement I sense a bruise on a different part of my body. Seb carries my case to the car: the wheels are no match for the uneven ground. The rain and wind still rage since yesterday, roaring through the trees and rattling branches against the metal roof of the outhouse, like a prisoner banging a plate against his cell.

In the dozen or so steps it takes to get to the car I'm drenched, the wind kicking the rain against the fabric of my trousers, spraying my face and whipping my hair into my mouth. Seb mutters something about installing external timer lights on the outhouse as he puts my case into the boot.

We buckle up and he pulls away, the headlights catching the streaks of rain, gunning in diagonal lines. Something dark lies on the ground near the outhouse, captured in the beam, and as we drive past, I realise it's the nest I tried to rescue yesterday. Knocked off and discarded by the wind, it was unlikely to offer protection to eggs and baby birds now.

Neither of us is talkative. Aside from the rain and wind, the only sound emits from the wipers, moving rhythmically across the windscreen, one slightly squeaking each time it reaches a point on its arc.

Seb is first to speak.

"You'll send me a text, won't you? When you reach your parents?"

I smile. Typical Seb. He was so aware of earthly, corporeal risks, like tripping down steps or taking a dodgy cab. Those he understood and sought to protect me from. Yet danger that was ethereal or unexplained, he dismissed. Perhaps this is the difference between him and me: he only gives credence to things that have a practical solution, whereas I'm more emotional and receptive of things I don't understand.

Harriet was right: *He's not comfortable with anything outside his experience.*

Now I think of it, it explains a lot about our relationship. There's no denying Seb and I are opposites in many respects. Sometimes we balance each other out. He brings order, organisation. Without him, we wouldn't have the busy diary, the fantastic holidays, the memorable day trips. I, on the other hand, bring emotional connections: special Christmases, birthday celebrations; thoughtful notes; the details that make our house a home. When we work well, we are immense, each providing skills the other lacks. When we don't, it feels like we're different species, each with their own needs, moving in opposite directions. In the past, when we've been at loggerheads, we've managed to work things out. After a rocky day or so, we've overcome the problem by talking it through and seeing things from each other's perspective.

This time it's different. The problem seems unfathomable and our explanations incongruous. I think we're dealing with some kind of supernatural force in the house. I don't know what it is or whether it's trying to help us or scare us. He thinks I'm showing obsessive, anxious behaviours I've exhibited in the past, leading me to misinterpret normal occurrences and act irrationally. At the moment, I see no way of bridging the distance between us.

We approach the station, which is a bustle of light, cars and people in stark contrast to the rest of our journey. Clearly, we're not the only ones mad enough to commute from the sticks.

Seb drops me outside and drives off to park the car and I wheel my case inside the station. There are queues of people in line for tickets and to pass through the   entrance barriers. Electric information boards display details of the next trains on the four platforms.

"It's Platform 1, as usual. I'll carry your case for you over the bridge," Seb says, having caught me up.

He shifts his lap-top bag to his back and takes my case from my hand.

We join the stream of commuters heading for the London bound train, moving like a shoal of fish, some clutching coffees or newspapers, others listening to music headphones or scrolling their phones. Synchronised, yet anonymous: this could be the commute from Greenwich, or anywhere else for that matter.

Seb is watching me. "Do you miss it?"

"Partly. Obviously not the cancelled trains and overcrowded carriages. But reading time and London, yes. I miss work more. Don't get me wrong: I appreciate having time to get things straight, but I miss the stimulation."

He nods. "Well, like you say, there's plenty of time to decide what you want later on. We don't need the second income –

financially - but maybe you need work in your life?"

"Hmmm." I can't imagine living without my career long term, but I hope he's not suggesting its current absence is behind my experiences at the farm. Perhaps I'm being paranoid. I look into his face. "You'll take care of yourself, won't you? Ring me each night to let me know you're okay?"

He gives a wry smile. "And you nag me for being over-protective. Look, I'll try, but you know what it's like in the lead-up to a hearing... Okay?"

I nod. There's time for a brief hug, and Seb's lips briefly skim my cheek as the train slowly pulls onto the platform. The trickle of people already on board is a fraction compared to the crowd trying to align themselves with the automatic doors, determined to secure the best seats. My bump guarantees me one, but Seb stands.

The 6.29 is a fast train, stopping only at Manningtree before my destination. When we pull into Colchester, Seb helps clear the way for me as the opening doors bleep. I briefly squeeze his hand as I pass him and exit. He remains on board, in the throng for London Liverpool Street. The doors beep again as they close, shrill and discordant. We wave as the train pulls away, then he looks away, fumbling in his pockets for his phone.

I stay watching until I lose sight of him, a tear streaking down my cheek. It feels wrong, parting while things are unresolved. Going separate directions when we should be side by side.

The train for Chelmsford arrives within minutes. It's full, but not crammed like the London bound carriages. A kind older man offers to help me with my case, and I find a spot where there's space for me and my luggage under the table.

Normally the rocking of a train sends me to sleep; I find the movement and sound so hypnotic. Today is different: despite being frazzled, I'm too wired to drift off. I try reading my novel but can't focus. Every few   paragraphs I'm distracted, my brain flitting back to the house like a nagging pain that can't be ignored.

Why would something want us to leave? What was it, and what connection does it have with the farm?

Questions but no answers. My brain is too foggy to process any of it. I try to shut them from my mind and look out of the window.

Leaving Colchester, views of fields and farms flash by, blocked occasionally by high, overgrown banks. Towns, housing estates, factories and commercial buildings dip in and out of focus. My ears pop as we roar through long tunnels, window images vanishing as though black blinds have been wrenched down and then suddenly released to reveal the scene on the other side of the hill.

We rarely stop: the stations of Marks Tey, Kelveden, Witham and Hatfield Peveral are far apart. The names ring vague bells from my childhood, but the fleeting glimpses of them are unfamiliar. My memories of Essex are more urban. Saturday afternoon trips to Romford market to buy material from the stalls, my toes frozen numb and the air vibrant with stall holders shouting the prices of their fruit and veg. Cycling to my grandparents' house in Margaretting, where I'd be spoilt rotten with sweets and magazines. Bitter-sweet fragments of senior school, the joy of the friendships, the pain of unrequited teenage crushes. Returning home stirs up many memories.

Arriving at Chelmsford, the station is busy, mainly with people arriving for work. There's already a long line at the taxi rank. It feels warmer here. No wind to whip across fields and fens, no foggy dampness, only office blocks and concrete slabs, people and traffic. How different it seems! From the queue, I see a snap-shot of the city. The cathedral spire stretches above the rooftops; flashes of shop signs and advertisements shout for attention, a very different appeal to the rugged natural landscape in Suffolk. Which do I prefer? It feels too soon to stake a claim, but I'm surprised to notice Suffolk has started to seep under my skin. Although I welcome the bustle of people here, Chelmsford seems louder, brasher than I remembered. How would Greenwich seem now? An assault on the senses, perhaps. This shift in my perceptions unsettles me - at the moment, nowhere truly feels like home.

As the cab pulls away, I think back to when I last visited. It's been a while – a few months, at least. Now I remember. It was the weekend we told mum and dad about the baby. That was memorable, for all the wrong reasons. Many couples share their news at the end of the first trimester but we'd had to wait a little longer before sharing ours, keeping quiet until Enid, Seb's mum, returned from India, so we could tell both sets of parents at around the same time. Their reactions couldn't have been more different: Enid was thrilled to bits, sobbing with joy; Mum froze in surprise. Eventually she congratulated us, along with Dad, and explained her initial shock because she had no idea we planned to start a family.

Overall, my parents' response was under-whelming, but, in fairness, they knew nothing of the difficulties we'd had. Of course, Enid knew, having helped us financially. But I didn't want to involve my parents in the all the times when we were hopeful or desperate during IVF. It was bad enough dealing with it ourselves, without having to relive it through them.

After our announcement, there had been lots of follow-up questions: where did we intend to put the baby in our small house? How could we consider keeping the mini when we needed a family car? What are the schools like in Greenwich? Why hadn't we relocated somewhere before starting a family? By the end of the weekend, we were glad to be back on our own in Greenwich.

It was easier telling Harriet. She was thrilled and couldn't wait to be an auntie, even planning her trip so that she could be back in time for the birth.

"It's just here," I point to the driver.

The cab draws up outside number 58, Bay Tree Close. The familiar sight of the 1930's mock-Tudor beamed house makes me smile. I take in the window frames, in need of a lick of paint, no doubt a source of disagreement between Mum and Dad. She somehow thought my dad was responsible for keeping the place spick and span. Dad, however, was largely indifferent to the upkeep of the house yet begrudged paying others to do it. In our family, many household projects met a similar fate, an impasse of wills.

It was clear Mum had been busy planting bulbs for the spring though, some beginning to bloom. She was less keen on maintenance; weeds poked through gaps between paving slabs on the driveway, some clinging to the wheels of Harriet's lilac Micra, as if claiming possession.

I stand in the porch, ring the doorbell. Mum answers. Her eyes briefly take in my bump, the suitcase, before she smiles, then she notices the empty milk bottles in the rack on the doorstep.

"Now why has he left those? Honestly, how can they be any more visible? Come in, darling. No, no, leave that," she wafts her hand in the direction of my case as I make to lift it. Her head twists back and tilts up as she shouts. "Duncan! Beatrice is here, come and get the case."

She kisses both my cheeks as I cross the threshold, awkwardly embracing, conscious not to squash my bump.

"How was the journey? I hope people volunteered their seats for you? Although, I have to say, sometimes it's hard to discern whether someone is pregnant or overweight. So many plump young women these days."

"It was fine thanks, and yes, I had a seat on both trains."

As I'm speaking, Dad breezes through. He smiles at me

fondly, puts an arm over my shoulder and squeezes it. He's been doing it ever since I hit puberty when he seemed to conclude it was more appropriate than a hug.

"Hello love. You okay? Looking tired."

"Thanks, Dad, you look well too," I reply, although in his case it's true. He's lost a few pounds, and there was a lightness in his step.

"Ah well, I've gone back to the tennis club. Just once a week."

I notice mum purse her lips.

"I'll take this up to your old room," he says as he disappears upstairs.

Mum ushers me into the lounge. Easing myself into the sofa, the room is like a time capsule to me: very little has changed. The highly patterned carpet had a myriad of purposes, when Harry and I were kids. The green swirly shapes were "home" when we played musical statues with our friends. When it was just the two of us, we pretended the shapes were steppingstones, in a raging sea or stream of lava we had to avoid on our treacherous journey to the sofa "ships". Mum preferred us not to play in this room - too many ornaments and lamps perched on numerous pieces of furniture - but sometimes we snuck in for an illicit game, before our noise gave us away and we were ordered upstairs, to the playroom. Rooms designated for playing were never as much fun.

"So, how are you feeling? Not long to go now. I remember this stage well: can't wait to get it over with, I bet."

I shrug. "Hard to say - I'm not feeling prepared for the next bit either! I'm definitely more tired now, even though I have trouble sleeping. Blood pressure's slightly higher than the midwife... oh shit!"

Mum frowns at my expletive just as Dad walks through the door.

"What's that about blood pressure?"

"I'd forgotten about my midwife appointment next Tuesday. I'll have to cancel it. Dad, would you mind taking my readings that day, and I can text them to her?"

"No, of course not," his face looks concerned. "Everything else okay?"

"Yes, fine, I'm only slightly higher than she'd like. We're just keeping an eye on it."

"Well, you look a little grey. Time to have a rest. Drink?"

I ask for coffee, and Dad predictably lectures me about the caffeine. I opt for water instead. When he returns from the kitchen, their eyes fix on me, expectantly. Mum can hold it in no longer.

"Lovely as it is to see you, darling, why exactly have you come to stay? We don't often see you on your own, and ... it is close to your due date. Is something up?"

I knew this was coming. She was unlikely to be content with the explanation I'd given on the phone. Luckily, I've given some thought about how to respond. My parents see life in black and white: both with science backgrounds, they were unlikely to be open to the possibility of supernatural presence in my house. The less said, the better.

"No, no. It's nothing for you to worry about. Obviously, there's been a lot to get used to, over the past six weeks or so. Leaving work, moving house... living in the countryside. I know you haven't seen it yet," I glance up and see them with awkward expressions, "but it's so different to living in Greenwich. And something about the house makes me feel uncomfortable when I'm alone."

Mum frowns. "Well, it's understandable, darling. It will feel quiet at first, and perhaps a little lonely. But you've bought it now. I don't mean to sound unsympathetic, but haven't you just got to get on with it? Unless something else is wrong?"

She looks at me pointedly and I find myself avoiding her gaze.

"Well, yes, Seb and I are on slightly different pages at the moment...but it's nothing serious." I rub the skin around my thumb. "I've not mentioned it before, but I've had some issues with anxiety in the past, when we were trying to conceive. We both feel I could benefit with some company and a change of scenery – just in case it flares up again. Particularly as Seb's caught up in a case and can't really spare the time."

Inside, I wince. I feel like I'm giving Seb's version of events credibility, blaming my own mental state on the need to leave. But I don't feel I have much choice. My parents need more from me but I don't want to talk about everything that's happened. The chances of them understanding and believing it were slim, and I couldn't face being judged by them too.

Dad looks concerned. "Now you mention it, you did seem distant around that time. I thought something might be going on, but I didn't want to pry. Wish I had now - perhaps we could have given you more support?"

I shake my head. "There's nothing you could have done or said. At the time, I didn't want to talk about it."

"Did you have any medication – when you had anxiety before?" Dad asks.

"Not for a long while, in case it affected our chances of having a baby. I've used CBT though, which has helped to an extent."

Mum looks agitated.

"Well, I can't believe we're hearing about this for the first time now. We're your family, Beatrice. We want to help you – and to know what's going on. You and Seb, it's like you're sealed off from the rest of us. It's always been the same since you met him."

I tense and she looks like she instantly regrets her comment.

She always seems reserved around Seb. I don't want to open this can of worms so I change the subject.

"That reminds me, he's going to pick me up at the weekend so we can check out some family cars."

She presses her lips together. "That's if he can spare the time. He's seems a little too preoccupied with work, if you ask me," she checks herself again and adds, "but it will be nice to see him."

I nod. "I think I'll go and unpack my stuff."

"Of course. I'm going to finish off some bits in the garden then, before lunch. Let us know if you need anything, won't you?"

I smile and head upstairs.

Like the rest of the house, this room has remained largely unchanged since my teens. The patterned navy curtains match the lampshade and bed-side light. The terracotta carpet is patchy, bleached and worn from sunlight striking the same spot each day. The key difference between now and then is the bed, an upgrade from single to double, once Seb and I had married (and certainly not before).

The window overlooks the garden. Mum's kneeling on her cushion, gloves on, attacking her borders with a ruthless energy. She's wiry and determined in all she does, her elbows jutting out at angles, the rest of her tall, thin body folded neatly. I knew it wouldn't be long before she'd find a distraction to keep her busy, and I was thankful to escape upstairs away from further questions.

I move from the window and sit at the dressing table. The drawer still contains the hair pins I used to keep my unruly curls in place. Now they are too short to restrain, reaching just below my chin when pulled taut. The mirror catches only a section of me: you'd never know I was pregnant, only head and shoulders captured within the wooden frame. The woman staring back at me has changed considerably from the reflection I used to see: a girl who fretted about her looks, the absence of a boyfriend, being alone. That girl didn't realise relationships are not always the antidote for loneliness.

This reminds me: I haven't texted him.

Hi, I've arrived safely. All okay this end. Hope work is going well. When are you planning to pick me up at the weekend? I told them you'd visit, B x

He replies, a couple of minutes later.

Pleased you're okay. Will let you know as soon as I can – I'll call. Try to enjoy yourself, S xx

I unzip my case with the intention of unpacking, but each drawer is crammed full of linen and clothing   belonging to my parents, the wardrobe similar. Clearly not my room anymore, I'll get by living from my suitcase.

My old journal I left at the farm; I couldn't bring myself to bring it after the sinister message. I pick up a new notebook I'd packed in case I found it helpful for research or recording my thoughts and place it on the dressing table.

I pull out my lap-top and open Harriet's last email. She'll be surprised when I tell her I'm at Mum and Dad's and it's about time I told her everything that's happened. I get comfortable and begin my reply. At least I know she'll take me seriously.

I click send and hope for a swift response.

CHAPTER 19

Maud

I cannot face them. Not today.

I sit in the corner of the rear parlour, dry eyed and empty. Around me people chat and make polite conversation, a soft murmur in the background. I avoid their eyes. They are probably relieved. No-one can find the right words to say to me.

My mother has prepared some refreshments for the mourners. The smell of beer and meat makes me nauseous. Food has been too much for me to stomach since that day.

My mind cannot escape the picture of that tiny coffin: too small, too soon, tied to our cart as we made our slow procession to the church. He did not need a team of pall bearers to carry him to his grave. Instead, he was propped on the shoulders of my father and William, William's face fixed to hold back the tears that had wracked his body last night and many nights before.

We have not found comfort in each other. If anything, Nathaniel's death seems to have driven a deeper wedge between us. William barely utters a word, but then I give him little opportunity. He leaves before I awaken, stays out for luncheon and, more often than not, I have gone to bed before he returns, having left his dinner on the table or on the range to keep warm. Morning drifts to night, without sound or marker. Some days I have struggled to get out of bed at all, not having reason or inclination to tend to my duties on the farm, my role as mother no longer required.

The few occasions when I have caught his eye, I can see it: the harsh glint of blame, a dark ferocity in his eyes that has not found its way to his lips. Not yet, at any rate. But I can tell it is brewing.

Was I at fault? Not in the way that William might imagine, a carelessness for the life of our son. But perhaps I failed him in other ways, before the day he passed. *Was his death a punishment for my love being too slow to arrive? Did God take him from me because I was too selfish and scared to love him from the start?*

In the darkest times, I dwell on Nathaniel's screams that haunted me in the dead of the night, his fury at odds with his tender age. *Was it a spirit that possessed him? Did it take his soul once and for all that night?* I can ask no-one these questions, but they spin in my head, night and day, preventing me from mourning my son, making me buzz with nervous energy.

"Maud, everyone is starting to leave. It's time to say farewell."

William stands in front of me. I had not noticed the shadows creeping in. It is the time that fills me most with dread, knowing night lies in wait, when my thoughts echo louder in the darkness.

I meet his gaze. He is hardly recognisable as the man I married eight years ago: dark crescents hang beneath his eyes and with less flesh the skin clings to his bones, making his features more pronounced – eyes large, nose and chin protruding. The light that flickered across his features has been snuffed out. I dread to think what he sees in mine.

I struggle to my feet and follow him to the front parlour. I

163

am half-conscious of the neighbours and family members who kiss my cheek or clasp my hands, and nod vaguely in response to their well-intentioned platitudes. I cannot focus on anything they say; it is as if I am under water, with sounds indistinct and faces blurred. My mother captures my attention and brings me up to the surface. Her embrace is fierce, her words comforting.

"You might not feel it now, but you will get through this Maud. Burying a child is the 'ardest thing you will ever do." Her voice falters and her eyes gloss as she loosens her grip and looks me in the face. "You won't remember, but you had a brother, thirteen months younger than you. He was only with us for five weeks. It broke me - but I had to pull through, for your father and the rest of the family. You will find your strength too."

The moment of candour passes and her body turns, fingers on the latch as she leaves.

I have never known of this brother. It explains my mother's brittle manner, her tough exterior. But we are different women in different situations. I wonder whether I can follow her footsteps, with a husband increasingly remote and without a family dependent on me.

After they have all gone, William and I sit at the table in the back parlour in silence. He looks towards the darkness beyond the window, pained. I rest my head on my forearms. Today feels long and unreal, like a fever dream. Closing my eyes, the questions come flooding back. *What if Nathaniel was here now? Would I be a better mother? Could I have protected him from evil, kept him safe from harm?*

I do not know, is the honest answer. I would like to think I would treasure every day, anticipate his every need. But perhaps we would still find ourselves in this position. Maybe I was never meant to be a mother.

"Perhaps we'd best wash the plates then head for bed?"

William's voice is low and thick and breaks the silence. I

lift my forehead in acknowledgment but have little energy to respond. After a while he sighs then moves to his feet, collects plates and tankards, pumps water to heat on the range.

I know I should help but my body won't budge. Nothing seems important anymore.

CHAPTER 20

Maud

It came to me last night in a dream.

So often I've struggled to sleep, after Nathaniel left us, but last night was an exception. I can't recall any of the details, but I awoke knowing exactly what to do. How good it feels to waken with a sense of purpose!

Nathaniel's things must be cleansed to free them from the spirit that took him. We have mourned our son but have given no thought to the evil at the root of our loss. It still lingers in our house. What if it strays elsewhere? These past four weeks I have been drifting aimlessly. Why on earth did I not think of this sooner?

I've put a large kettle of water on the range and, while it warms, I gather all his possessions: bedding, clothes, toys... there is much to do! Altogether the pile collected at my feet is three armfuls. Thank goodness the weather is brighter today, bestowing on us the last dregs of the autumn sun. The washing can dry outside when I've finished.

The water is now in the tub, but I think I need more than the usual soap and washboard. Lavender will purify and sage will ward off the bad spirits... just as the pharmacist said. I take the dried sage from Nathaniel's crib and leave the steaming tub to fetch fresh lavender from the garden – we have plenty left over.

As I bend to snip a few sprigs, I hear a voice behind me.

"Hello, Maud."

Straightening and turning around, I see Emily. She is walking up the path awkwardly, her tummy vast now. Beyond her, I notice her cart and the farmhand patting down the horse. He nods in my direction, and I feel my cheeks flush, this time with shame. The woman who swooned at his attention back in May is very different to the one who stands here now.

"I was uncertain whether you would be glad of my company - you seemed to wish to be left alone last time," her words stumble. Then her mouth drops as she notices my clothing and she lowers her voice: "Maud, what are you doing in your night wear? You'll catch cold."

"I'm fine, just busy." *What business is it of hers?*

She pauses. "Are you quite well? You don't seem yourself?" Emily's forehead is creased, and she moves closer towards me. "Perhaps we could have a cup of tea inside?"

I balk at this. *Inside? Has she taken leave of her senses?* It is not safe for her or her unborn baby in this house. *What if the spirit takes possession again?* Who knows what could happen. And I have only just started to cleanse Nathaniel's things. I quickly block the door with my body to prevent her from entering.

"Maud?" Her face looks more worried now, and she seems uncertain whether to stay or leave, her head swivelling back towards Joseph.

"Emily, I don't think it's safe for you now. This house is not the place for children – born or unborn. And I am very busy. Perhaps we could meet another day?"

"It is perfectly safe for me, Maud. I am well – but I have concern for you."

I smile tightly. "Do not worry about me, Emily. I am well, truly. Thank you, good day."

Her face is aghast as I step across the threshold and close the door firmly behind me. She does not move for several minutes but then I hear her footsteps retreating, and in time the wheels of the carriage roll down the hill.

Now I have seen her off, I can concentrate on the task in hand. I add sage and lavender to the water, then scoop the first clothes. As the small smocks and undergarments billow in the water, I remember the last time I washed them. Little did I know, as I scrubbed his soiled cloths, that he would not wear them again. I feel the familiar pang of grief but bury it. It is important to do this task well. I scrub each piece with soap on the washboard, inside and out. Then again and again, just to be sure.

I do not notice him until he's right behind me.

"Maud, what are you doing?"

I jump in fright. "I could ask you the same, William Catchpole, creeping up on me like that! Particularly when there's work to do outside."

"It is lunch time, Maud."

"Oh, I had not noticed the time." I feel my face flush.

"Emily stopped to speak to me on her way by: she is worried about you."

"Well, Emily should mind her own business, particularly when others are only looking out for her and her baby."

William does not look convinced, and I see his eyes taking in the night dress I am still wearing, and the wet garments in the tub.

"You've not answered my question. What's going on?" He

picks up one of the wet rags, opens out a tiny, dripping smock, bafflement on his face. "Your hands are red raw from scrubbin', but you're not even washing our clothes. They're Nathaniel's."

I look down at my hands. Usually hardened from washing on the farm, today they are livid and covered in blisters, yet I had noticed no pain.

"Well? Why did you tell Emily it was unsafe inside?" William's voice is impatient, his eyes agitated.

"Because it is, William – until I have banished the spirits away." My voice is small and I look down.

"Spirits? What are you talking 'bout?"

I ignore his question, seeing no point in trying to reason with him in this mood, but then his hands grip my upper arms.

"Get off me!"

"Then answer my question, Maud. What's this talk of spirits?"

How does he not understand? I sigh.

"The spirits William - the demons that plagued our son in the night and took him away from us!"

He looks at me, slack-jawed, eyes troubled. Then, after a few moments, he abruptly walks out the door without saying a word or having eaten a morsel.

I am glad to be left in peace.

CHAPTER 21

Maud

One morning, William snaps.

Perhaps he was weary of making his own meals and eating alone. Perhaps it was coming home to find curtains still drawn and the house left in the same state as it was the night before. Perhaps he did not know what to do with a wife who was unable to rise from her bed.

"I am telling you, I cannot look at it any more!"

The desperation in William's voice matches how I feel inside. He is holding the crib, Nathaniel's crib, and I cling to the other end, unable to let go.

"You cannot just forget about him, William! He was our son... I need his things near me. I will not be rid of them!"

"Of course I know he was our son! I do not need to be reminded of that! Pity you needed to be reminded of your maternal duties while he was living!"

I stagger back, winded, losing grip on the crib. A look of shame flits across his features momentarily, recognising he has said too much. But it is too late. He has confirmed my suspicions. He thinks I was an unfit mother. It was always implied, but this is the first time he has said it straight. The first open conversation we have had since Nathaniel's funeral, and his words slice like a knife. The loneliness and pain that's been brewing for months explodes.

"You monster! He has been in the ground for little more than two months, and this is how you comfort me! Shame on you, William Catchpole." My head burns, my body rigid as a pole, fists clenched. I glare at him.

He flinches. "I am the monster? Maud, you should look at yourself. I came home yesterday to find you rocking in the chair in the front parlour, with Nathaniel's doll in your lap, in some dream with your eyes open. Last week I find you all agitated scrubbin' his clothes, saying you were washin' away bad spirits. You are either hysterical or mute, Maud - I never know which version I'm going to get."

"Liar!" Rage takes over and I storm towards him. Two fists land on his chest in the time it takes him to lower the crib to the flqor and clasp the top of my arms. I wriggle in his grasp, then give up, close my eyes and take a few deep breaths. Steady myself.

What does he mean? My memory is blank of all William's accusations. I have no memory of scrubbing Nathaniel's clothes since he passed, although my hands have recently been very sore and blistered. Last weekend I made a salve of lard, honey and oatmeal to soften and soothe them, to no avail.

Did I rock in the chair with Nathaniel's toy? I admit taking some comfort occasionally holding Nathaniel's playthings, or breathing in the smell of his cot and clothes. But I cannot recall William ever finding me in this way. I am normally careful to express my grief when I am sure to be alone.

Am I forgetting these times or is he trying to trick me? I do not know. Panic rises inside of me, and I lash out in any way I can to free myself from his grip.

William's eyes are scared as he draws me closer, no doubt to prevent me from striking him with my legs.

"Maud, take control of yourself! I'm not lying. Those things happened as plain as me standing in front of you now!" He shakes his head, baffled and confused. When he speaks his voice is quiet, barely audible, the words too painful to be said or heard.

"If I'm honest with myself, you've not been yourself since the day he was born - like you're only partially here with me. Now I'm afraid his death may have tipped you over the edge."

"And where were you, William, when I was strugglin'? Where was the love that I needed from you?" I fire at him, the questions long spent bottled inside.

He loosens his hold, voice expressionless. "We each have responsibilities. I was runnin' the farm, you were tendin' to our child. I did my job." His stare is heavy with the words he holds back. He turns away from me, stares out the window, distancing himself from the spoken and wordless accusations.

Something inside me yields. The sobs come fast and I gasp for breath between them. I hate the sound they make, exposing my vulnerability and the hurt he has caused, but I cannot control it. All the while my mind races back over his accusations.

Did I fail in my responsibilities?

The past six months are shrouded in mist. I am plagued by the thought, night and day, that I could have done better, but when I try to remember examples, they seem hazy and incomplete, as though the memories belong to someone else. Sometimes I spend hours at home trying to remember the details. Even the picture of Nathaniel in my mind is a blur: I see him as a baby, but it could be any child. I struggle to remember the features of his face, his little body. I must have looked at him countless times, every day, and yet the image is fading. It makes me shake with regret; not only have I lost him, but I am losing my memory of him too. *Will I soon forget the sensation of his skin, the weight of his body in my arms?*

To William, I am silent. He knows nothing of my pain and fears - no doubt he would use them against me. The man has no compassion. He knows the wife standing before him now is in anguish, yet he fails to offer the comfort of his shoulder to capture her tears, or an arm to steady her waist. Instead, he sinks to a seat, buries his head in his hands. After a few minutes he looks up and keeps his eyes trained on the view outside the window again, avoiding me. His voice is more controlled.

"I don't know how to make it better, but I know this: keepin' all his things around us is no help. We need to carry on, as much as we can. I have turned to the farm, but what about you? Half the time you're asleep. The rest, you don't register when people speak to you. Even turned Emily away." His mouth droops and his eyes disappear behind a heavy brow. He turns towards me, shakes his head slowly, then looks away. "Something has got to change, Maud."

I am silent, trying to make sense of what he says. *Emily was here?* I can't recall seeing her since the funeral, and even then, she was one of the faceless mourners in the room. I have no memory of any conversation with her.

Am I distant? Perhaps. But then so is he, and it is much easier for him to use work as a distraction. I am bound to this house, alone. I may be struggling, but I am trying my best. *Why can he not see that?*

His focus shifts towards me, and his voice becomes softer. "I know it is hard. I am not suggesting we forget him. Per'aps we could keep the crib and his christening gown, but hide them from sight? Maybe conceal them in the eaves upstairs. That way it will always be with us, but we don't have to look at it all the time. And the rest of his things could go to the church, pass them on to those in need."

I breathe out slowly. It feels like the aftermath of a storm;

anger and tears have washed away but I am left exhausted and uncertain. With a handkerchief I wipe my face and consider William's idea. This house is full of Nathaniel: the bucket and cloths; the rug he used on the floor; the clothes I made for him. I cannot deny a glimpse of each smarts the open wound, but I need some physical possessions to bind me to him; without them, it is like he made no imprint, a mere footprint in the sand washed away by the sea.

Perhaps this suggestion of keeping his gown and crib, but concealed from sight, is a good one - still present but not a constant source of pain. I give a small nod.

"We are agreed then. Thomas will help me put up a wall in the eaves tomorrow. You could gather Nathaniel's other things for the curate."

And with that, he leaves, farm to attend.

Feeling weak, I make myself a cup of tea. Brace myself for the task ahead.

It does not take long to find all his clothes, blankets and toys. Most of them are in a pile in our bedroom. I close my eyes and hold one of his smocks to my cheek, painfully soft, knowing it had once wrapped over his body yet I cannot picture him in it. I inhale the cotton, hoping it will trigger my memory. Nothing. It smells freshly laundered, with a hint of lavender and herbs, like the sprigs attached to his crib.

Could I have cleansed his clothes, as William said?

Why can't I remember?

Panic stirs again. I feel as though I am losing grip on things around me: the ground shifts under my feet and memories slip by like wind through the leaves. I cannot recall things I have done, people I have seen.

It is too much today. Weakened by the argument, I cannot battle with my memory too. I find a sack for Nathaniel's things and start filling it.

CHAPTER 22

Maud

A week has passed since the argument with William, and I have become better at pretending.

I visited the curate with the bag of Nathaniel's possessions for the poor. He was pleased to receive it – said many would be grateful for his clothes and toys, particularly during the winter months ahead when times were likely to be harder. I did not struggle to hand them over; I am detached from them now, they are but cloth, wool, and wood, insignificant compared to the child they once wrapped or entertained.

For the last few days, so far as William and the farmhand are concerned, I am much improved. The woman who spent time moping indoors has become useful, more apparent. I gathered blackberries and made a jam. Windfall apples I have pulped by hand for cider and others I have picked from the trees to prepare a chutney to see us through the winter. The cows have been milked, the animals fed. I killed a chicken and turned it into a stew with the last of the runner beans. The cottage is clean and tidy. I've even taken more personal care, tending to my appearance, arranging my hair.

Inside, it is a different story. I can fill my time with chores and activities to keep me grounded, to stop the panic rising, but I cannot silence the questions churning in my mind. Each day I've gone through the motions of living, without sense of purpose or enjoyment. So long as I keep up appearances, William will not ask any questions. There is no point trying to talk to him. He does not understand and will make no attempt to do so.

There is the sound of voices outside. William and Thomas. I put down the knife and carrot I was scraping, wipe my hands on my apron. I know why they are here. In their hands they carry the strips of wood and hammers.

"Are you ready, Maud?" William is hesitant, wary of my reaction. I nod and he looks relieved. No hysterics today. We trail though the rear parlour and make our way up the stairs.

The crib sits ready in our bedroom, Nathaniel's christening gown folded neatly inside. All three of us take a last look at it. I kneel to the floor and stoop to kiss the initials William had carefully carved at the head of the crib shortly after he was born. My throat thickens with this memory, us as new parents, closer then, unaware of the struggles that lay ahead. Strange that this picture stays with me, yet so many others have drifted away.

I struggle to my feet and wrap my arms across my body, holding back the emotion. William nods then picks up the crib and pushes it into the eaves. I turn to leave the room, my feet carrying me back downstairs.

Overhead they hammer the strips of wood.

I continue preparing the vegetables, tears silently rolling down my cheeks.

CHAPTER 23

Bea

<u>5th March</u>

Pissed off. Seb no longer collecting me for appointment at garage. Says it will be quicker for him to go alone as he does not have the time to come via Chelmsford - too much preparation for the case on Monday! Would have been nice to have had opportunity to test drive the car too, given I'll be using it. Dad offered to drop me off, but I don't want to put him out. Mum didn't openly criticise, but her silence over dinner indicated what she thought.

Seb didn't mention whether he'd experienced anything unusual in the house, but I'm not sure whether he'd let me know if he had. He noticed the leaflet Maureen left (about managing relationships during pregnancy) – seems more concerned about the impression I may have given to her of him!

<u>6th March</u>

Apparently meeting with Toyota went well – Seb negotiated a good deal on a people carrier. Should arrive in 4 wks. He apologised for yesterday and for me not having a chance to test drive it, but he seemed to think I'd like it. He sounded preoccupied, but said it was work. Client kicked off about the costs. Steve now scrutinising Seb's handling of the case – Seb very stressed.

7th March

Very tired today. Baby moving about more at night-time, making me restless.

Mum cooked roast. Feel hypocritical enjoying the smell of cooked meat!! Must be a pregnancy thing. Dad tried to tempt me with a slice of turkey, but I resisted. The herb in the stuffing reminded me of smell in spare room - sage. Must look it up.

8th March

Mum meeting a friend for lunch, Dad playing golf. Relieved to have house to myself. Used time to do a bit of sleuthing, find out if there is any meaning to the things experienced at the farm.

Googled uses of lavender: " most often used for **protection**... thought to drive off the evil eye and chase away demons and evil spirits. Fashioned into a cross, it was hung over doorways and at entrances to homes to protect inhabitants against evil spirits."

Was protection deemed necessary in our house at some time? If so, why? Who might have used it? Dread to think.

Found similar entries relating to sage: it was used in exorcisms (!) and was also connected with the Virgin Mary and cleansing, sometimes placed at altars. Sprigs were used outside homes to ward off bad spirits and bad people. Seems similar to the use of lavender.

I looked up meaning of a crow in the house. A sign of bad, important news, potentially impending death (!!). I'd normally laugh at such ideas, but combined with everything else, I'm apprehensive about returning to the farm.

Haven't spoken to Seb since Saturday. So much for him keeping in touch.

9th March

Rang Maureen with blood pressure stats. Dad seemed to think it was okay – 125/80. An improvement. He insisted on testing my urine too, but all fine. Maureen was a little curt. Don't think she appreciates me gadding about at short notice, missing my *appointments. Got the impression she thinks I'm not taking my pregnancy seriously. She doesn't realise everything else that's going on. Booked again for next Tues.*

I put the notebook to one side. Dad is taking me to play golf later on. It's never particularly appealed to me, but it's a way of keeping mobile and spending a bit of time with him.

Over lunch, the phone rings. Mum picks up the receiver in the hallway, within sight of the kitchen table.

"Harriet, lovely to hear you darling! We're just having a spot of lunch with Beatrice...oh, you knew she was here? Ahh, I see. It never occurred to me to reply to your email, given it's an update to everyone. I wouldn't want all those other recipients of your message to read my message... oh, you can, can you? Ahh, well, I shall have to ask Beatrice to show me how to do it... Where are you? Quito? How are you getting on there?"

There is a long pause while Mum nods her head at the phone, listening and murmuring in acknowledgment of Harriet's flow of information.

"Coming home next weekend?" Her eyebrows shoot up, and she turns to Dad and me, still sitting at the table. "Was that planned? I thought you had another week. Everything's okay?"

She appears convinced by Harriet's response as she turns to face me.

"Yes, Beatrice is here. Would you like to speak to her? Okay, 'bye darling, safe travel back."

Mum beckons me to the phone, and for some reason whispers. "It's Harriet. She wants to say hello but she hasn't got long on her phonecard."

I press the receiver to my ear. There's a faint buzz and Harriet's voice sounds faint and slightly tinny, but it's lovely to hear her after so long. It must be the longest time for which we've had no spoken contact.

"Hello you. Heard Mum's stage whisper just now! Listen, I've decided to come back early, spend a bit of time with you in Suffolk..."

I interrupt: "No Harry, don't cut your trip short for me..."

She interrupts back. "I insist. I've seen as much as I can safely see in Ecuador. I'd like to go further North, but near the borders with Colombia it can get a bit dicey: I'd need a chaperone and I'm not sure it's worth the risk. Besides, I want to see your new place and, more importantly, you - particularly after reading your email." She drops her voice, "I doubt you've told Mum and Dad - it sounds terrifying! I don't want you to spend time there on your own, especially without a car."

"Well, if you're sure, that would be amazing."

"I'm sure. See you on Saturday. I'll be jet-lagged – flight gets in around 6pm at Heathrow, and I'll get the train across to Mum and Dad's. 'Bye for now! Get some rest!"

I replace the receiver, feeling lighter. Up till now, I've avoided thinking much about returning to Suffolk, the days alone in the house, wondering what would happen next. I'm much happier returning with Harry.

Mum and Dad are finishing lunch back at the table.

"So, Harriet will be going back to Suffolk with you?" Mum's bright eyes fix on me. "I hope she's not relying on her car getting you there. That thing hasn't been driven in over three months!" She takes a sip of her tea. "Mind you, I'll be pleased to see the back of it, cluttering up the driveway."

I grin at her. "Might mean you'll have to do some weeding."

She rolls her eyes. "It's a pity she couldn't leave it in London." She opens the dishwasher. "It will be lovely to have both of our girls under one roof though – rare these days." She gives me a small smile, but there was concern in her eyes as though still unconvinced about my reasons for being here.

Dad chips in, "Ready in ten minutes?"

Golf turns out to be more difficult than I thought. Even if I had the aptitude (which I don't – hand-eye co-ordination has never been a strong point), my bump hinders the swing of the club, much to our amusement. Eventually the repetitive stooping of my back becomes too uncomfortable, so I give in and traipse after Dad around the course, followed by a drink at the bar.

By the time we get home, the last of my energy has drained and I head upstairs.

I awake three hours later to find my room in darkness and my body cold, but thankfully clearheaded. A swirl of movement in my tummy stirred me. Finding myself in a semi-foetal position, mimicking the baby inside me, I uncurl my stiff body.

Checking my phone, there are three missed calls from Seb. I press dial.

"Hi. Where were you?"

"Asleep – phone must have been on silent."

He detects the coolness in my voice. "Sorry, I've not called for a couple of days – I've just kept my head down."

His voice sounds brighter than it has been. Hearing him gives me comfort and I can't stay grumpy with him.

"Missed you – even if you have been distant and distracted. How's the hearing going?"

Seb gives me a run-down of the hearing so far. "I reckon the client is likely to succeed, although they've been such a pain in the arse about the fees, I'm not sure they deserve it! How about you? What's going on in Chelmsford?"

"Some good news. Harriet's coming home early, and she's going to stay with us for a while in Suffolk!"

Silence. "Okay - good."

"What's wrong? I thought you'd be pleased."

"I'm just surprised that's all."

"I thought you preferred me to be with someone?"

"Yes, you're right. It makes sense."

I can tell by his voice he's a little put out that I've invited Harry to stay without talking to him first.

"So, will I be bringing you both back on Sunday?"

"No, Mum's looking forward to seeing the back of Harriet's car. We'll drive it over on Monday. At least we'll have something to get us about while we wait for the new one."

"Well, I'll give Sunday a miss then – use the time to build the cot."

"Okay." I'm disappointed but his suggestion made sense.

"Everything okay at home?" I can't resist asking.

"Fine, very quiet without you. It'll be good to have you back."

I smile. "Yeah – I'm missing you too."

We say our goodbyes and I start to feel more hopeful. It'll be good to see him next week. I just wish I felt differently about the house. My last weeks there are a blur now, the intangible experiences there far removed from my familiar, safe family home. It managed to stay silent for Seb: no mysterious occurrences or communications.

Will it remain so for me?

CHAPTER 24

Bea

"**G**od, look at that amazing bump!" Harriet laughs.

She seems wary of it at first, but perhaps it's my imagination as her stringy arms soon wrap me in a hug. The chill, dark air seeps around her in the open doorway and we usher her in. She looks tired after her long, delayed flight, her frame trim and athletic after her adventures.

"You look radiant, Bea. Must be exhausting carrying that around with you though. Can we sit down? I'm shattered."

Harriet dumps her massive rucksack in the hallway. Mum, Dad and I stayed up, not able to settle until she was safely home. Now we're all in the lounge, staring at her under the bright electric lighting. I expected her to look younger and more care-free on her return, judging by the exciting experiences she's had. Instead, shadows pool under her eyes and although she's clearly happy to see us, her face shows strain. She talks about the chaos at the airport for a little bit, and the temperature drop being a shock to the system, but she's desperate for sleep so we all head for bed.

The past few days have been uneventful. Mum insisted on

going shopping to buy a few clothes for the baby. It should have been a fun experience, but she disapproved of many of the gender-neutral items I favoured, and in the end, we returned with a few babygro's, vests and hats and a grumpy atmosphere between us. I'm grateful Harry is here now to break the tension.

I creep around the next morning, wary of disturbing her in the room next door. She emerges just after eleven, still yawning.

"Can't believe I've slept for over twelve hours, and still feel like shit!"

"It will take a while to adjust."

Downstairs, we find Mum's out – no doubt at church - and Dad is reading the paper. He lowers it to talk to us.

"Sleep well?"

"Not bad, thanks. Just need more of it!"

Dad nods as she sticks four slices in the toaster. "What was your favourite country?"

"Hard to say. I liked bits from all of them. The salt plains were spectacular in Bolivia - I saw flamingos!."

"Strange enough, when I was doing the crossword the other day, I discovered that flamboyance is the collective noun for flamingos!" Dad smiles.

"Nerd," Harry grins.

"What about the rest of it?" he asks.

"Well, I enjoyed a pampas trip– we saw piranha and capibara. But I got fed up in La Paz - my day pack was stolen while I was there. Clouded my judgment of it a bit."

"Oh no - you never told us that!" Dad frowns, "What happened?"

"Didn't want to worry you. I wasn't in any danger – they grabbed it from the overhead rail on a bus then got off at the next stop. I didn't realise until it was too late. Should never have left it there - felt stupid and angry, more than anything else. At least I had my money and passport safe in my security belt."

He shakes his head. "What else did you enjoy?" Mum and him tend to go to the same place in France on holiday and I can see Harriet's trip has really captured his interest.

"Overall, Argentina was my favourite. I could happily move there," she clocks the look on our faces, "if it wasn't for friends and family here, of course. Buenos Aires is beautiful, in a shabby-chic kind of way." She turns on the tap to fill the kettle. "It felt like going back in time - how I imagine Paris might have looked, before the war. The tango scene was amazing. Even had a few lessons myself!"

"Dance with anyone interesting?" I raise my eyebrow.

Harriet pulls a face. "Oh, you dance with lots of people, that's how you improve. I'll have to show you my photos later."

The toast pops and she slathers it with butter, marmite and jam, groaning with pleasure. "Haven't had decent jam for three months and marmite was like gold-dust. Found it in a shop in Quito, but it was extortionate."

We hear the click of the front door. Dad retreats behind the newspaper. Mum breezes into the kitchen, unfastening her mac.

"Good to see you're both up, but please don't eat too much now - you'll lose your appetites! Lunch will be around 1.30."

"Thanks Mum. Think I might take the car out for a spin, check it's okay, but I'll be back for lunch." Harriet pops the last piece of toast in her mouth and stands up.

"I'll keep you company," I smile at her. I'm surprised when she looks a bit uncomfortable.

"I won't trouble you, Bea, I just need a few bits and pieces before we leave for Suffolk tomorrow. Why don't you stay here and rest?" She flashes a smile and quickly leaves the room before I have a chance to argue.

"Car keys in the cupboard under the stairs!" Mum shouts after her.

She returns an hour or so later with a bag of shopping and disappears upstairs with it as soon as she gets in.

When she comes down for Sunday lunch, a little later, she is quiet and that drawn look on her face is more prevalent. I thought perhaps she'd had difficulties with the car.

"How was it, getting back into driving?"

"Oh – it was fine. She took a few goes to get started, but eventually decided to move. My breakdown cover's still valid anyway, should anything happen. Do you want to set off after breakfast tomorrow?"

"Fine by me."

It's the first time in ages that we've sat around the table to have lunch together, just the four of us. Harriet tells us more stories of her travels: the characters she met, the places she'd seen. She tells the stories with animation, but I can tell something is wrong: something she's holding back.

"What's wrong?" I ask, as Mum and Dad disappear into the kitchen, Dad carrying plates and Mum fetching dessert.

"We'll talk about it tomorrow," she quickly replies, taking a sip of water as Mum returns with a crystal bowl in her arms. I can already tell from the layers of over-bright colours gleaming through the glass that it's trifle, one of Harriet's favourites. The spoon squelches as it dives through the layers, scoop wobbling as it comes up for air. I decline, reminding Mum again of my dislike of custard. We look at Harriet expectantly, but she regards the spoon warily.

"Not for me, thanks mum." She looks pale, sips more water.

"But it's your favourite! Surely, I can't have got it wrong for both daughters?"

"I'm just so full after lunch. Maybe later?"

186

Mum makes a disapproving noise and taps the spoon on the side of a dessert bowl, unburdens its contents with a splodge and hands it to Dad. She serves a smaller portion for herself and sits down, irritated that her efforts had not been fully appreciated.

I wash up while Harriet shows her photos to Mum and Dad on her phone. They hold it at a distance, trying to focus their eyes on the tiny screen. It's probably the most united I've seen my family for many years. As I listen to their voices from afar, the occasional laugh, I try to fix it to my memory. Something positive to remember, whatever happens next.

CHAPTER 25

Bea

Mum and Dad wave us off on doorstep. I feel a lump in my throat as we say goodbye. Harriet would be returning to them, after her stay with me, but there was no firm plan of when I would see them next, although they promised to visit once the baby arrived. I still can't picture that scenario, even though it is just around the corner.

In the car we're quiet at first, each locked in our own thoughts; the main sound over the drone of the car was the Sat Nav, directing us on our journey. I twiddle with the radio.

"We didn't really get a chance to talk about it at home. Are you okay with returning to the house? I can't believe you had to face all that on your own," Harriet glances at me again before fixing on the road.

"Not looking forward to spending time alone there, that's for sure. It's a huge comfort to have you with me, but at some point, it'll be just me. And the baby."

Harriet nods grimly. I can tell she thinks the environment I've described was not one she'd want to raise a baby in.

I tell her about the research I did while at Mum and Dad's: the uses of lavender and sage and the superstitions concerning crows.

Harriet whistles as she sucks in a breath, gently shaking her head. "I wouldn't put too much weight on the crow – sounds like old wives' tales to me – but the herbs! Made the hairs on the back of my neck prickle! Is there anyone you could ask, about the history of the house?"

"The Bryants didn't know much – they lived there for six years before us. They bought it off a farmer who ran it alone for thirty years. Before that, it was owned by someone who inherited it and never lived there. I've no idea of the history before then. Maybe the neighbours might know something? Perhaps we could call on Kath while you're here."

"Good idea." She changes her tone, softer, more cautious, "And how are things with Seb?"

"I don't know: confused, mainly. I missed him while I was at Mum and Dad's, and I think he feels the same, but it really hurt how he refused to see things from my perspective back at the house. I felt like he was using my old problems against me – you know, the anxiety and stuff."

Harriet nodded, thoughtful. "I understand. He's your husband, he should stick by you. But you have to remember, it hit him hard, Bea, when you were ill." She presses her lips together. "He was so worried about you, as was I. You'd been through so much and we felt helpless. Part of him just wants to protect you, I'm sure. I bet he can't wait to see you."

I nod, turn my head towards the side window. I know she's probably right, but I find it hard to think straight. When I look back on those few weeks at Oak Tree Farm it feels like nightmarish but also ridiculous. Viewed individually, many of the incidents that terrified me are innocuous. But no matter how I try to rationalise or make light of them, I still return to the last one, that chilling message scrawled in my journal: *Leave, Leave, Leave*. There's no explaining that. Thinking about it now, my shoulders tense and I recall the pit of despair in my stomach.

Thank God I'm not returning alone.

For the rest of the journey, we speak occasionally, listening to a 90's station, our conversation turning to the songs and the memories they trigger. As we draw closer, I grow quiet again, my tummy fluttering, this time from anxiety, not movements from the baby.

"*Your destination is on the left.*"

"So, just up here?"

"Yes."

She catches the apprehension in my eyes.

"You'll be okay," she briefly squeezes my hand that rests on my bump before replacing her fingers on the gearstick. Turning left off the road, she takes a deep breath as she sees Oak Tree Farm for the first time. "You weren't joking when you said it was isolated, Bea."

The house looks cool and tranquil in the bright midday sun. A very different image to the sombre, grey landscape I left behind, in wind and rain. In the space of ten days, promising buds have started to burst into colour. I've always loved daffodils and narcissi, like sunny stars. As we pull closer, I notice the land in the shade of the house is still muddy and grim. I try to push aside the negative thought that the house seemed to drain joy from anything close to it: I need to be more positive on my return.

Harriet stands back to survey the rear of the house.

"Well, it's certainly bigger than your place in Greenwich. Are you going to give me a tour?"

I walk her around the grounds first. We peer through holes in the outhouse. Shards of light pierce through the gloomy interiors of the barn.

"Wow, this is huge. If this was patched up, you could convert it into a holiday let," Harriet suggests.

We reach the front of the house and it's lit up by the sun. The view reminds me of why we bought it in the first place: neat, proud, full of opportunities. From here, the fear I'd felt inside the walls seems implausible.

Harriet reads my thoughts. "It looks lovely, as if butter wouldn't melt…"

Having collected the bags from the car, I lead her inside and put the kettle on. On the table, Seb had left a note for me, which I read with a smile:

Welcome home!
I've made a veggie shepherd's pie in the fridge for later and there's some broccoli to go with it. Should be home about 7pm.
S xxx

I saw Harriet take in the diner, apprehensively. "It feels different inside. Like time's stood still! It would put me on edge, staying here alone."

"Hmmm. Here, let me show you the rest of it while the tea brews."

I guide her through the house, pointing out the places where strange occurrences had taken place. I share with her the plans we have for each room too, although they feel inconsequential after everything that's happened. Seb has kept the place very tidy, but he's moved my journal downstairs. I tense just looking at it. Harry notices.

"Is that where you found the message?"

I nod.

She gestures towards it: "Mind if I take a look?"

"No. I think you need to see it."

She flicks through the pages until she lands on the last one inked. Her eyes widen and she shakes her head.

"No wonder you were terrified." She quickly closes the book and returns it to the table, clearly frightened.

"I think that cuppa might be good now."

We sip our drinks in the lounge, discussing how the message could have been written. She suggests I may have written it in my sleep – after all, people have been known to do all sorts of things while comatose. But to my knowledge I'd never done anything like that in the past, plus I didn't know how to write in that script.

Draining our tea, we venture upstairs. In the annex, sunlight streams through the curtainless windows, making the golden walls sing. The cot stands proudly in the centre of the room. Seb must have built it yesterday, the packaging neatly stacked to one side with his toolbox. The baby twists inside me, almost as if he or she already feels territorial about this room and its furniture. I feel a flutter of nerves: the imminent birth feels real now the baby's bed has been built. Guiltily, I vow to spend more time thinking about it rather than allowing occurrences in the house to usurp my energy and attention.

Harriet notes the bags and boxes of other baby equipment, and I show her Seb's paint splattered shoes.

"I see what you mean… not much I can do about those, but I'll help you get things straight, tomorrow Bea. You'll need to put curtains up in here too."

"The spare room's through here…"

We cross the stairwell. Seb has cleared away his stuff on the desk ready for her arrival. She dumps her bag on the bed and looks around. Although she says nothing, her eyes linger warily on the back wall.

"It was there I heard the sounds. I don't think you have anything to worry about though: whatever's causing it seems to enjoy putting on a show just for me," I grimace.

The rest of the day passes pleasantly, both of us unpacking

our things, putting on a wash. Taking advantage of the weather, Harriet joins me for a walk across the fields. Early spring sunshine glows on my face and I feel calmer than I've done for several weeks. The company certainly helps, and not for the first time I'm thankful to have Harriet as my sister. We've always been close, able to communicate so much without lengthy explanation. Perhaps it was being sent away to school together. Whatever the cause, I'm glad of it. It's also the reason why I know, without a doubt, that something's troubling her. She's quieter than usual and from time to time I catch that look on her face. But I know better than to keep asking her before she's ready to share.

It isn't long until Seb comes home. Harry's in the shower and I'm heating up dinner when I hear the back door open. Nervous anticipation tingles as I turn to him, worried about how things will be but also excited to see him again. When I see his face, I know it's okay. His eyes glint with the same hopeful apprehension. He grabs me in his arms and squeezes so hard, I gasp, and he loosens his grip with a laugh.

"Sorry, didn't mean to smother you." His voice turns softer. "Missed you, Bea."

I glow inside. "Me too."

My throat swells with emotion, the relief of being close to him, after my period away. But it's more than that. In past weeks we've moved out of sync with each other, emotionally apart. Holding him now is a powerful reminder of how important he is to me.

He notices me gulp. "What's wrong?"

"It's nothing... it's just that recently we've kind of lost sight of us, what with the baby, the move, the Hearing, the troubles here... and I was just reminded." I give him an extra squeeze. "I don't want to lose us again."

Seb smiles and strokes a stray curl behind my ear. "We're

always together, Bea. Even if we don't always see eye to eye."

Just then, Harriet walks through the door, hair wrapped in a towel. She smiles at me, over Seb's shoulder, as though she knew it would all be fine. Seb turns round and gives her a hug.

"Don't suppose you have a hair dryer?"

"No, sorry, we don't have much call for one here."

"Never mind, I'll drip dry. I'm used to it by now – went without one for most of my travels." She unfurls her towel and drapes it over the back of her chair, teasing out tangles with her fingers.

Dinner is a pleasure, the three of us catching up, reminiscing, so much so I almost forget the reasons behind Harriet's stay. For some reason, the baby is sitting directly over my bladder. I nip to the bathroom, yet again, while Seb tells Harriet about his recent Hearing.

The hallway and bathroom feel cold, silent and dark after the warm chatter of the diner. My fingers reach for the light cord, but they knock against something, sending it to the floor with a clatter. After the light has fizzed into action, I see it was Harriet's toiletry bag, its contents spewed over the floor. I bend over to gather everything together and there's a knock on the door.

"Everything okay in there?" It's Seb. The noise must have travelled.

"I'm fine, just knocked over something in the dark. I'll be out in a minute."

The last object I pick up is a white plastic stick with a blue tip. I thought it was a toothbrush at first, then with an intake of breath I realise it isn't. It looks like a pregnancy test. The window shows two clear blue lines. Positive.

I bury it at the bottom of the bag, then sit on the toilet, mulling it over. So that explains Harriet's drawn face, my suspicion that something else was bothering her. I remembered her reaction to my joke about the tango dancing. Perhaps she met someone in Argentina? How long ago was that leg of her trip?

No, I shouldn't speculate. I feel like I've been snooping in her things, like a nosey sister prying through a diary. I didn't mean to discover her secret, but now that I have, I will confront her, when we're next alone. It isn't for me to second guess her story.

CHAPTER 26

Bea

My opportunity to talk to Harriet about her pregnancy arises naturally the following day.

I wake up before her, ravenous as ever, frying eggs in the kitchen. She comes in, looking like death warmed up. Her skin has a greyish tinge, those shadows ever present under her eyes.

"Morning! Would you like egg on toast?"

She turns even paler, and before she can answer, her eyes blink open in alarm and her hand shoots across her mouth as she darts from the room. I quickly turn off the gas and follow. I find her bent double over the toilet. When it passes, she shudders, passing tissue over her mouth and flushing the chain.

"Are you okay?"

She rinses out her mouth then straightens. We look at each other through our reflections in the mirror.

"You know, don't you?"

I put my hand on her shoulder. "Yes. It was an accident yesterday. I knocked over your toiletry bag and the test slipped out."

Harriet nods, dismally, and slumps down to perch on the corner of the bath. "It's such a mess, Bea. What on earth am I going to do?"

My sister, normally in control, sobs silently on my shoulder. Gently, I persuade her to come and sit in the lounge so I can fetch her juice and something to eat that won't turn her stomach. By the time I return, she's stopped crying, but her eyes are red and forlorn, staring into the distance beyond the window.

"Here, tuck into this. How far gone are you?"

"About seven weeks. It happened in Buenos Aires. I met him at Spanish school."

"Where's he from?"

"Wales– he's called Rhys. I really liked him; bright, funny... kind. Down to earth. We saw each other for a couple of weeks. We both agreed we didn't want anything serious. I needed some space after Marcus, and Rhys' travel plans were different to mine. He wanted to travel to Patagonia, to go the Welsh settlement there, in Chubut. We left things open – talked about meeting up once we were both back in Britain. But I don't have any expectations."

"Does he know about the baby?"

Harriet closes her eyes and sighs. "No. I've got his email and mobile number. We've exchanged a few light-hearted messages, but I've not mentioned this."

"And what do you want?"

"To keep it. I've always wanted children one day; I just didn't expect it to be like this. Without a partner." Her lip trembles, on the verge of tears again. "It's not just that. I've taken three months sabbatical from work. I can't imagine how they'll react when I tell them I'll be off again in six months to have a baby. And I'll need to work full-time to keep my flat – how does that fit with looking after a baby?"

Her voice spirals into a wail. I cuddle her clumsily, bump getting in the way.

"Other mums do it, Harry, and if anyone can, you can. The partners in your team know how committed you are - I'm sure they'll be fully supportive. Let's face it: they don't have much choice."

Her breathing calms down as she takes a few breaths and leans across the coffee table to grab a tissue.

"If he's a decent person, I think you should tell him. Who knows where it could lead?"

She nods slowly. "I'll think about it." She squeezes my hand. "I feel better for telling you. I had such a strange night's sleep. I think I must have been worrying about the pregnancy."

My interest is piqued. "Oh?"

"Can't remember much...but I do know I was holding this baby, bundled up in my arms. I was terrified, something was wrong...I was trying to find someone, anyone, but I was in this empty field..."

I freeze. My heartbeat races in my ears.

"What, Bea, what have I said? Are you okay?"

"I had a dream that was very similar – not last night, but in the last week I was here. In mine, the baby wasn't breathing, that's why I was desperately looking for someone. I had no shoes on my feet."

We stare at each other, Harriet's eyes dark and round.

"It feels like too much of a coincidence. Why would we have had the same dream?"

"I don't know but we'll have to talk about it later. Maureen is due to arrive shortly. Would you mind clearing up while I get ready?"

Maureen arrives at 9.30, punctual as ever. Harriet

apologises for still being in her pyjamas and offers to make her a cup of tea then I take her upstairs.

"Any changes?" she asks, as I move onto the bed.

"Not really. The readings I sent to you were better though, weren't they?"

"Yes, they were. Obviously, you benefited from a change of scenery. I've updated your file. Let's take the reading for today."

She wraps the band around my arm and turns on the machine. The squeezing effect makes me think of a boa constrictor, and I'm glad it's only around my arm. Maureen's face frowns.

"It's slightly higher again. Whatever you did in Chelmsford, you need to do it here. Put your feet up. Take advantage of your sister being here. Time to relax now and stop worrying about sorting out the house – other than the baby essentials, of course."

I say nothing but it's hardly any wonder my blood pressure reads higher here.

She listens to the baby, and lets me listen too. The repetitive whoosh of a heartbeat is comforting, like the sound a shell makes when I press it to my ear. At least he or she is doing well.

"Now would be a good time to start planning for the birth. Are you sure I can't tempt you with a home delivery?"

I laugh. If only this delivery would be as easy as internet shopping. "No thank you. I think I'd rather make a mess in the hospital."

"Fair enough. In that case, I'd book a tour, if I were you. I think they're running one next Saturday. You'd have the chance to see the labour unit and the birthing pool."

I thank her and show her out, dialling the number for the hospital as soon as she's gone to secure a slot for the tour. Harriet joins me in the hallway just as I end the call.

"How did it go?"

"Fine – my blood pressure is a little high again, but it's hardly surprising, is it?"

She nods thoughtfully. "I know. I've been thinking about that similar dream we had. You don't think we've seen a film or tv series some time ago where there were similar images, and something about this landscape or house here has triggered the memory of it? That's the only logical explanation I can give. And obviously we've both got babies on our minds."

I pull a face. "It's plausible, but I can't remember watching anything like that, can you? And it felt so real – like it was my child– the surrounding fields so similar to here." My foot reaches for the first step of the stairs. "There's not much point dwelling on it - the more I think about it, the more anxious it makes me."

A different thought concerns me more, although I'm wary of raising is.

"Harry, there's something you should know. It may be irrelevant but it's a judgment call only you can make."

She leans against the doorframe. "Sounds serious – go on."

"Vics Bryant said she thought something in the house was responsible for her miscarrying. She never seemed to reach two months. If she was right, maybe your baby could be at risk if you stay here."

Harry nods slowly, her lips set in a grim line. "Thanks - I hear what you're saying, but there's no way I'm leaving you. That's my main concern at the moment."

I almost knock her off balance as I grab her in a hug. "It means a lot Harry, but don't think you can't change your mind. I'm going to head upstairs and make a start on sorting the baby stuff if you want to join me."

"Sure."

We tackle the car-seat first, fiddling with the straps and

working out how it attaches to the car. I knew Harriet would be interested in helping me whatever her situation, but I sense the vested interest in her understanding how everything works. It certainly feels less daunting than wading through it alone.

Packaging is removed from blankets and clothing, piled up ready to be washed. The steriliser instructions are easy enough to follow. It's when we unpack the breast pump that Harriet's eyes widen in mock-horror. I attach the last piece together, a conical shape reminiscent of a miniature gramophone trumpet, and plug it on. The pump noise drones like a lawnmower. We look at each other and she's the first to laugh.

"Rather you than me."

"Don't worry – I'll keep it for you!" My voice turns sober. "When are you going to tell Mum and Dad?"

Harriet frowns as she puts the instructions in a pile on the side. "After the first scan, I think. Dad will be okay, I reckon, but I'm dreading telling Mum." She looks at me. "Would you come? To the scan, I mean. Of course, you'll have your own baby by then, but I'd feel less nervous if you were with me."

"Sure. We'll figure something out. How long are you intending to stay here?"

"A couple of weeks, if that's okay with you. Then I'll be back at work – which seems an alien concept at the moment! I'll commute from Mum and Dad's initially until the tenants leave my flat at the end of next month."

She's telling me about her tenants when my phone buzzes. It's a notification about the front door sensor again.

"Look at this, Harry." I show her the message and replay the video footage from my phone, but we lose connection in the middle.

She raises herself off the floor, "Let me go and check."

She returns soon, puzzled. "There was no one there –

couldn't see what triggered it."

"Hmmm – it's not the first time. I thought I saw a flash of black once, but lost the recording."

We spend time figuring out how to set up the pram in different configurations and are just putting the pieces back in the box when I hear a sound. I put one hand out to still Harriet and with the other place a finger across my lips. We both listen intently. There, I hear it again. It's the scratching. Harriet locks eyes with me and nods her head slowly, acknowledging she can hear it too. Part of me wants to weep with relief, knowing I'm not alone. The other part fills with dread, wondering what will follow.

Noiselessly, we tiptoe across the landing, into what has become Harriet's room. As before, it's coming from behind the wall. Slow, deliberate strokes, seeking attention. Harriet looks frightened but I take her hand and crouch down on the floor. The pair of us place our ears to the wall, listening, waiting. I hadn't thought of it before, but I now have a clear sense that only one animal, being, whatever it is, is making the noise: each scrape is distinct, not overlapped.

"What do you want? What are you trying to show us?"

My voice makes Harriet jump. We both hold our breaths waiting for a response. The scratching picks up pace and there's something else: a different sound, a different movement from inside the space, like something rocking or tapping, close to the ground. Harriet looks terrified, makes to get up, but I put out a hand to steady her. Although my body buzzes, I feel braver this time. Maybe it's having Harriet with me, or maybe I'm just more determined to unravel the mystery.

"It's no good Harriet. I've got to know what's behind that wall. I'm going to need your help. Can you fetch the toolbox from the annex?"

She nods, stumbling to her feet. When she returns, we open

it and take a look; there are all manner of tools inside but none which look perfect for the job. I want to make a hole but not a massive one. I grab a dibble and mallet, first scoring a mark in the wall with the dibble to keep the tip in place, then whacking the handle with the mallet to drive it into the wall. The first two attempts do nothing and on the third the mallet rebounds off the curved edge of the dibble and I lurch forwards, losing my balance.

"Stop!" Harriet looks alarmed. "There must be a better way. Is there a drill?"

She's right. My mind races, trying to think of when I last saw it. Got it. It was when I was searching for my wellies. It's in the plastic crate in the garden. I describe where it is and Harry's off.

Without Harry's reassuring presence, fear starts to creep in. I'm not sure if it's the perspiration cooling my skin or whether the temperature in the room has dropped. Alone, the scraping sound gets under my skin, clawing at my skull. The baby inside me is aware something's wrong: he or she is kicking me on my side. I take some deep breaths to calm myself, but as I inhale the air seems to change - thicker and charged. Then the pungent smell of lavender and sage hits, heady and stifling as it was before. I cough, try to clear it from my airways, but it's everywhere, like a gas spreading to every crevice.

Tightness pulls across my chest, like it's being compressed. I panic, struggling to breathe. Not enough air to scream or shout. Just as I feel I can stand it no longer, I hear Harriet's footsteps on the stairs then she bursts through the room, drill in hand.

"Oh my God, that smell!" She puts her hand over her mouth, trying to block it, opens the windows, then helps me off the floor. Fresh air wafts in. I stand near the window, gripping the sill while I clear my lungs and head. As my heart starts to slow, the scratching sound stops.

"Are you alright?" Harry puts her hand on my shoulder. "I can see why you've struggled, Bea. Something's definitely here, and it wants to be noticed by you... and, I guess, me too. I don't know how you've dealt with it on your own till now."

I nod, still catching my breath.

"Do you still want to do this?" She points to the drill on the floor.

"Yes... I need to know what's behind that wall."

Free from the insufferable scratching, Harry and I tackle the drilling of the wall, methodically, practically. I fetch an old towel to place on the floor and plan to drill two holes: one to peer through, obviously, the other through which to shine a torch, to give us some light. We agree to make them just under a foot apart, a few feet off the floor.

Harriet insists on holding the drill. I think I scared her earlier with my clumsy slipping. I cringe as the angry roar of the machine rages through the house, the drill penetrating the surface, sinking a centimetre deep, then jolting in Harry's arms, resistance giving away suddenly to air as she hits the cavity. One thing's for sure: if there was something living in the space, it would have scarpered quickly, faced with that racket.

"One done. Do you think it's big enough?"

We decide to enlarge it, inserting a screwdriver and wiggling it. The plasterwork flakes easily after the initial hole has been made, and suddenly a larger chunk comes away, showing the horizontal strips of wood beneath. The pest control people were right: it's lathe and plaster.

Once we've made the hole large enough for my eye, we make the second.

"Moment of truth. Will you hold the torch while I look?"

I feel giddy and shaky, but I'm determined to see this through. I kneel and bend slightly, placing my right eye to the hole. The torch clicks on and then a weak beam of light pierces the black. It sweeps across in an arch, then drops lower to swoop back.

"No, it's no good, I can't see anything. Can you move it more slowly, horizontally? A bit like painting, from left to right. That's it. Now do it again, slightly lower this time."

Harriet tries, but the chink of light reveals nothing and leaves part of the space in darkness, the trajectory limited by the size of the hole.

"Let's try and make the holes a little bigger. We've come this far, we can't give up."

Once we've chipped away more plaster and wood, we repeat the process. This time, I gain more of a sense of the size of the space, the light catching the edges and corners through the murk. It's about 3 feet deep, running the width of the wall, but the ceiling slopes down irregularly, split by the beams of the roof. The air stream that meanders out of the hole smells old and dusty, no doubt partly caused by the plaster dust, disturbed after many years of rest.

I put my eye closer to the opening. Despite the larger holes, I can distinguish nothing in that space: nothing to explain the noises, nothing to suggest the presence of animals. With disappointment and frustration, I'm just about to tell her to give up when something catches my eye.

"Stop! Keep the torch at that height but swing it slightly more towards the right...a little more...there! Hold it."

The shape that had caught my attention is scarcely perceptible in the gloom, dark and brown, more or less in the middle of the floor, like a box with no lid. It measures no more than three feet long and a foot wide, about a foot and a half high. It looks like it was made from wood, guessing from the dark colour.

"Can you move the beam down a fraction?"

"What is it? What can you see?" Harriet's voice is impatient, eager, but I keep her waiting until I can be sure. The refocused beam catches the bottom of the object, which is not square and flat, but curved upwards, like an upturned coat hanger.

The breeze from the window, or the draft from holes, seems to wind its way behind my neck, tickling down my spine.

"A fraction to the right," my voice falters.

The same shape is at the other end of the object, except they aren't coat hangers. They're rockers. Fear catches in my throat.

Eventually I find the words.

"Harriet, it's a crib."

CHAPTER 27

Bea

W e sit on the floor, side by side, facing the drilled holes, the air heavy with questions. Harry wanted to see the crib for herself. Now that she has, she too is numb and silent, but is the first to speak.

"Why would someone entomb a baby's crib? And why nothing else? I mean...could something else have been sealed off with it, that's since rotted away? Perhaps it was once a cupboard?"

I shrug. "I don't see how it could have been a forgotten cupboard. People don't usually remove the doors and seal off the contents. As for what else was, or is, in there, we can't say with certainty, can we? There may well be something else hidden, perhaps inside the crib."

We look at each other.

"Does it seem like too much of a coincidence to you that we dream about a baby, and then we find a crib?" Harry stares at the holes then turns to me. "Bea, I don't think I can sleep in this room tonight."

"No, I don't blame you. We can fix up the sofa bed in the music room."

I wonder how Seb will react.   He won't be happy about the holes! More importantly, when we tell him Harry witnessed the smell, the scratching, he'll have no choice but to accept something is going on, that it's not in my head. This crib gives weight to our sensations, tangible proof that there's something strange in this house.   But part of me dreads upsetting the atmosphere between Seb and me, particularly as things feel more positive since I've returned from Chelmsford. I just hope he'll understand.

Harry breaks my train of thought.   "How are we going to find out who lived here – the person or people who hid the crib?"

"There's a chance one of the neighbours might know.   I'd start with Kath."

"Good idea. Let's call on her tomorrow. In the meantime, I'll move my stuff downstairs."

As we get up, Harriet wraps her arm around me.   "Don't worry. We'll get to the bottom of this."

Seb returns early. Harry and I are in the kitchen, preparing tea, as he arrives. A wave of trepidation ripples through me, anticipating his reaction to our discovery upstairs. Harry keeps her head down, chopping vegetables.

"Good day?"

"Yeah, not bad. Enjoying the calm before the next storm! Might be roped into a corporate deal next week, but shouldn't be too bad. You two?"

Harry and I exchange quick glances and I take a breath.

"You're not going to be thrilled, but hear me out, Seb."

The post is in his hands. He pauses flicking through the letters, meets my eyes, and puts it down.

"We made an important discovery.   Harry and I were working our way through the baby stuff when we heard the scraping noise again..." my voice is thin and tight, "...and then that overpowering smell seemed to seep from the wall."

Seb exhales heavily and closes his eyes.

Harry is quick to chip in, knife suspended mid-chopping. "Seb, I experienced it too, all of it. It was weird, how it came and left so abruptly. I'm amazed Bea has managed to spend time on her own here after that; I don't think I could."

She nods to me in encouragement, and I continue to explain. "I decided I had to get to the bottom of it, once and for all. We drilled two holes in the wall in the spare room. When we shone a torch through one, we saw a crib inside the cavity."

His eyes grow wide, then look pained, words firing from taut lips: "Haven't you just made things worse? I thought we'd agreed not to disrupt the room, knowing the baby, our baby, is going to arrive shortly?" His knuckles are white as he grips the work surface behind him. "Has it made you any happier, knowing there's a crib in there?"

His reaction is no surprise, but I'm still desperate to persuade him, make him see there was no real choice. I rush towards him, feel like shaking him, but instead grip his upper arms, look him straight in the eyes.

"Seb, we had no choice. I can't carry on being scared stiff here. Of course, the crib has raised all sorts of questions in my mind - many of them terrifying - but I'd rather find out than pretend it isn't happening!"

"But how does it end? Are you going to know when to stop?"

My hands drop from his arms. Still, he questions my judgment, my sense of proportion. I struggle to keep the anger from my voice.

"I don't know exactly – how could I? But Harry's heard it… smelt it too. At least you have proof now that it's not all in my head." I sigh, releasing some of the tension in my shoulders. "If this is going to be our family home, I need to investigate it - you must realise that! And Harriet will be here for a couple of weeks.

She'll make sure I don't become overwhelmed."

Harriet agrees, sharing with Seb the plan we'd already made to contact Kath.

He is quiet, leaning back to rest against the kitchen units, staring at the kitchen floor. It's clear he's struggling with everything he's heard. Eventually looks up.

"Alright - I can't deny you've had some strange experiences here. I don't know what the answer is. I still believe there's a logical explanation, somewhere. Perhaps a draught in the roof caused the crib to rock, and that made a noise like scraping? Perhaps there's a sprig of lavender up there, and the breeze carries a waft through the roof into the room, from time to time? I don't know... but for me, the answer's not ghosts or spirits..."

I start to protest, but he raises his hands, fingers widespread, signalling for me to stop and hear him out.

"Having said that, while we've been apart, I've had time to think. We don't always have to see eye to eye, but it's important we respect each other's views. If this is something you need to explore, to feel safe here, then so be it. I'll support you."

I wrap my arms around him, tears of relief flowing down my cheeks. Those three words mean so much. Knowing he's behind me makes the situation less daunting - it will all be okay. I kiss his lips. He holds my cheeks but moves apart with a smile, conscious of Harry in the room, who was doing her best to disappear into the background under the haze of flour from her pastry making.

"There's one condition though," the smile in his eyes sobers. "You've got to pace yourself, take regular rests. Try not to get worked up. I'm thinking of the baby."

It was an easy point to concede. "Agreed."

"Good. I want to see this crib now. Give me a call when dinner's ready."

After he disappears from the kitchen, Harry turns to me, a triumphant look on her face. "That was definitely a step in the right direction," she whispers, passing me the peeler.

While the potatoes bubble away and the pie cooks in the oven, there is banging overhead. I leave Harry in the kitchen while I see what Seb is up to. I find him stooped, through clouds of dust. I cough and cover my mouth. He is swinging the mallet to strike the wall in the spare room, the circular holes Harriet and I made earlier replaced by a large ragged tear and the dark hole beyond. An old sheet lies over the bed and bedside table, a dustsheet on the floor. With every bash of the mallet, particles billow, shards of wood and chunks of plaster fly. I stand and watch from a distance, wincing with every smash and crack. Seb, sensing my presence, turns around.

"I thought you didn't want to make a mess."

"No, but I thought I'd finish what you started."

With four more strikes, the hole extends to the floor and is large enough for him to lean into, his lower half remaining in the room. He strains, pulling backwards towards me, dragging and clattering what I imagine to be the crib across the floorboards inside the cavity. He lifts it through the hole, trailing dark, furry cobwebs which cake his arms too. He places it on the floor and brushes himself down. He looks up at me then we both stare down at it. The crib is solid and simply made from dark wood. The surface was probably once polished but it's hard to discern now, covered as it is in thick layers of dust, smeared away in places by Seb's clammy fingers. It stands low on the floor, resting on the rockers I had glimpsed earlier. At the head, it looks like the wood has been damaged, but as I wipe it with my fingertips, I realise it's a carving: the initials N. C. Seb notices too, his face grave and covered in beads of sweat and dirt.

Inside the crib it's thick with filth in the place that must have once held a baby. As I touch it, the surface moves and I flinch. Not just dirt, but some kind of cloth. Carefully, I ease my fingers underneath, lift. It's grey with dust and age, and falls apart in my hands, but it's gauzy and fine, like a christening gown, presumably once white and flowing.

"What do you think happened to the child who slept here - he or she who wore the gown?" Seb's voice is soft. "Whoever it was, it seems likely they had the initials N.C. Nora? Norman?"

"I don't know, but my gut instinct is that it wasn't a happy ending."

"We don't know that. For all we know, he or she could have become an adult, even a parent." Seb rationalises. "People keep mementos of children from when they were small, don't they? Doesn't have to be sad or sinister."

"But why hide it behind a wall? No-one does that for a child who thrived and simply outgrew it."

I replace the remains back in the crib, straighten up to face Seb. His face bears the same sadness I feel. He reaches for the torch and peers back into the cavity, the light catching the exposed beams and the contours of his profile. He flicks off the switch and the hole returns to inky darkness once more.

"No, nothing else there." He motions to the crib. "I'll tidy up here and give it a clean. Perhaps I'll put it downstairs in the kitchen when I'm done - make it look respectable for the poor mite."

It seems he's reached the same conclusions as me. N.C. probably died as a baby. Possibly in that very crib. Somewhere in this house.

CHAPTER 28

Maud

F rom every room in the house, I smell the damp musty odour of plaster curing, the lingering sign that my husband has decided it is time for us to move on. The last remnant of Nathaniel has been boarded away, behind the wall in our bedroom that he rendered and plastered with Thomas. In the meantime, we rattle around in this cottage, pretending life is normal.

It doesn't matter what we remove from view – crib, gown, blankets – this place will always be overshadowed by Nathaniel's loss. The cracks in our marriage run too deep for us to start again. It took long enough for me to fall pregnant back then and now I am twenty-six. Neither of us has any interest in lying together. The rush of attraction that drew us together has long since passed.

I cannot keep track of the days. Was it last week we argued? Or was it the week before? It involved the crib, but I could not tell you what else. Whenever I try to recall anything, my head feels foggy: like the steam trailing from a locomotive, memories blur, wisp then blend away. If I had not buried that vial of laudanum, I would swear I was still under its influence. Perhaps it is nature's way of protecting me from the pain of the past. Or perhaps it is just my own steady deterioration.

There's an ache behind my eyes, whether from the damp smell or the tension in the air. A storm is brewing, no doubt about it. We have had more than our fair share of rain over the past couple of weeks. Time to feed the animals before the downpour.

The hens know what is in store and circle round my feet before I have even begun to scatter their food. I used to take pleasure in observing their ways, talking to them. The large one, with the lighter streak on her chest, has always been the bossiest: the others wait until she has had her say and her share of the seed. Now I barely notice them. My hands dip into the bucket and fingers disperse the grains and seeds mechanically, my mind elsewhere. Reaching the bottom, I return to the house to fetch the pail for the pigs.

They have grown fat. Before long the majority will be sold, or slaughtered. I wonder if their mother can tell them their fates, or is she too in blissful ignorance? Are we better off knowing our babes are not long for this world: to have the chance to say goodbye and breathe them in until the hour beckons? Or is it kinder to remain unaware, even when the time is nigh? I know which I would prefer, but I cannot speak for the pigs.

The swine demolish their swill within seconds - peelings, dinner remnants, oats and corn. Most days they scoff more of my dinner than I manage: I pick at my plate, unable to muster an appetite.

Just in time. Clouds hover thick and ominous. The wind has picked up and is stirring the leaves on the ground so they spiral, like giddy dancers, and the first drops of rain fall heavy on my head and shoulders.

I take shelter in the house, but as soon as I cross the threshold, I sense I am not alone. *Who would creep into the house unannounced?* The hairs on my arms stand as my eyes scan the back parlour. There! My head spins as I catch a movement to my left, going out the door to the front parlour.

"Who is there?" My own voice sounds too loud. I follow the movement, heart thumping as I tip-toe.

The front-parlour captures most of the morning light, what little of it there is today. At first all appears as it should: everything in place, no unwanted visitor. Then there is a flash of black in front of my face, a swoosh from left to right, and I hear myself wail before I can make sense of what I see. In seconds I realise it is a crow who must have ventured in the house when I left the back door open to feed the animals. I feel foolish, then fear. What was it that my mother used to say about seeing a crow indoors? Destruction and bad luck? Heaven knows, we have already had our share.

I close the door of the parlour and open the window. A gust of wind blows inside, cooler than it felt before. I wave my arms to encourage the bird outside and eventually he flies over my head to freedom. I close the window behind him, shutting out the wind and the rain.

Alone at luncheon, I pick at some leftover crumbs of bread. The rest of the afternoon I try to carry on my usual chores but the feathered visitor has left me unsettled. *What danger lies in store? To whom does the omen speak – William or me?*

Distracted, I make foolish mistakes. The meat catches in the pan on the range and I forget to season the dumplings. While our evening meal cooks, I fetch my mending and take a seat at the table near the window, making the most of what is left of the afternoon light.

The rain is heavy now. Drops bounce off the ground and beat a muffled drum on the thatched roof. In the distance I hear a grumble of thunder, followed by a bright flash in the sky. I draw my shawl around me: I dread thunderstorms. To me, they feel unearthly. It is unusual for us to have one this time of year, more likely to strike in the summer, not mid-October.

William is out selling some of the hay today. I hope he has already made delivery and is riding back – the bales would perish in this weather. God willing, he finds shelter somewhere safe.

I turn back to my sewing. How my mind wanders today!

Before I finish darning the second hole in a sock, I hear something over the rhythm of the rain, like a high-pitched mew. I stop sewing and strain my ears. It stops. Probably an animal, a cat or something. We have plenty of wild ones here, and they do not care for the rain.

A few minutes later, I hear it again. Louder this time, not as sharp as a cat. It seems to be coming from somewhere in the house. Not another trapped animal, surely? One is more than enough for a day. This time it shows no sign of stopping. I cast off my last stitch and pierce the needle through the cushion.

As I step out of the rear parlour, the sound is louder and recognisable. I stand motionless, a chill running down my back. It is the sound of a baby's cry, and it is coming from upstairs.

There is no time to think, my feet just carry me. My memory of his face may have faded, but I would recognise that wail anywhere. It is Nathaniel. He needs me.

The cry is louder in our bedroom. It echoes in my skull, turning my headache into a searing pain. All I can think of is Nathaniel. I must reach him. But where is he? The room is empty. Then I remember. His crib is behind the wall. He must be there. I must get to him, before the spirit does. I mustn't fail him this time.

I fall to my knees. The plaster has not dried completely, there are patches where it is light and dark. I scan the room, looking for anything that will help me break through the wall. Nothing. His cry changes – more desperate, like he is struggling for breath. I must get to him, using my bare hands if I have to. I scratch at the surface of the plaster, clawing with my nails, frantic. Sharp, fiery pain shoots through the tips of my fingers, but it does not stop me. I keep clawing, grating away at the surface, now streaked with blood. There is a sound downstairs but I ignore it. Reaching Nathaniel is the only thing that matters.

"Aaaaggh!"

A firm grip clenches my shoulders, drags me to my feet, takes me away from the wall. I lash out at whatever it is that keeps me from my child.

"Maud, Maud! Stop! You must stop!"

I am wrenched around and see William, a horrified look on his face. But I have no time for him now: I turn back, desperate to save my son.

This time he scoops me in his arms, one wraps under my shoulders, the other behind my legs. I try to wriggle free, scream, but he has me firm.

"William, William! I am trying to save him! He is trapped behind the wall! He is crying for me, William! I must protect him from the spirit!"

He throws me on our bed, and uses his weight across my legs, his hands on my arms to stop me from breaking free. I try to fight back but he is too strong.

"Who Maud, who are you trying to save?"

"Nathaniel of course!"

"Maud, listen to me! Nathaniel is dead! You cannot save 'im, he has gone! It is only his crib behind that wall!" William is sweating and panting, terror in his eyes.

"No, you are wrong! He was wailing, I heard him over the storm. I need to get to him before it is too late!"

"Maud, calm yourself! You must have heard something else. I promise you he is not here. He is in heaven now, Maud. He has no need of our help now!"

The wind is sucked from my chest and the room turns black, just like that awful day in the fields, with Nathaniel in my arms.

When I come round, a wave of remorse hits me and my body trembles. There is no pressure on my body now, but I lie on our bed, my eyes floating on the river of tears trickling over my cheeks and dropping from my chin. William looks down at me, eyes wide. He sees my fingers, then looks across the room to the blood-streaked plaster. Fear and repulsion distort his features.

"What have you done, Maud?" His voice is a whisper.

He picks up my hand and raises my palm so that we both can see. Where fingertips should be there are bloodied, ripped ends. Jagged nails hang tethered from some, others have lost the nail completely.

I should feel pain, but I feel nothing. Just exhaustion, unable to move from the bed.

Without another word, he gently covers my body with a blanket and draws the curtains.

CHAPTER 29

Maud

I t is an effort to open my eyelids, swollen as they are and crusted with tears. I have no idea how long I've lain here but the sharp pain in my fingers is unbearable. I raise a hand slowly in the half-light of the room; dark stains of blood crust the tips and where nails should be the flesh is exposed and raw. The sight sickens me. I rest my hand back on the bed and focus on lying as still as possible.

The curtains have been kept drawn. William has slept elsewhere, but he has checked on me a few times: given me a little bread and beer, emptied the chamber pot. I heard my mother's voice at one point – I believe she may have peered at me through the door. I felt the weight of her stare and then she disappeared. I did not have the energy to talk to her or anyone else.

I can hear a carriage approaching from afar. It is not the kind of cart normally used about the farm; I can tell by the clatter of the hooves that it is drawn by at least two horses. The rattle and clacking gets louder until it stops outside our house. There are male voices - I hear two, I don't recognise either. One stays outside: the footsteps of the other approach our cottage and there is a rap on the door. He enters, talking to William and my mother; I detect their voices but not their words.

The tread on the stairs is heavy, purposeful, filling me with apprehension. The door to my room opens.

"Ah. So this is Maud? Let us open the curtains to take a better look."

William reaches over me and pulls them open. The light feels harsh on my eyes, and I raise a hand to my brow, forgetting to keep still. The pain makes me wince. The stranger and my mother gasp.

"Oh Lord, what have you done to yourself, Maud?"

It is my mother. Her voice quivers but she comes no closer to the bed. The man does. Without asking my permission, and despite the pain that flashes across my face, he takes my wrists and examines the fingertips. I take an instant dislike to him. He is portly with large, white whiskers and half-moon spectacles perched on the end of his nose. His eyes are dark and as hard as flint.

"Why did you harm yourself, Mrs Catchpole?"

"What do you mean? I did no harm to myself. Who are you?"

"I am Doctor Aspall. Your husband arranged for me to attend to you. I am referring to your hands, Mrs Catchpole. You have severely damaged your fingertips and nails, some have been removed completely."

I look at my hands.

"I know they are damaged but not how it occurred. I assume it was some kind of accident …"

But I sense this is not the correct answer. My memory has been hazy of late. I vow to keep quiet.

"You do not remember?" The question is aimed at me but Doctor Aspall looks meaningfully in the direction of my mother and William. "Well, I'll tell you the explanation you gave at the time. Your husband said he found you trying to rip down the wall over there with your bare hands. He said you believed your son, Nathaniel, was buried and crying behind it. The son who died three months ago. Do you remember that?"

"Nathaniel?"

Despite the pain, I twist my body frantically searching for Nathaniel's crib in the room. *Where is it?* Although I vowed to keep quiet, I cannot help myself.

"William, I thought you were looking after Nathanial - where is he?"

Doctor Aspall, my mother and William all look at each other, as if conveying some secret message, but no-one is answering my question.

Where is my child? Why will no-one tell me?

I feel myself starting to panic. I try to get out of bed but the searing pain in my hand catches my breath, and the room spins after having spent so long in bed.

Dr Aspall places a hand on my shoulder and pushes me back down. I flinch.

"Don't worry yourself, Mrs Catchpole. Nathaniel is at peace. It is you we want to help."

I try to wriggle away from him. "I don't need your help. I just want to know what's going on." I turn to William and my mother, my eyes pleading. "Why is he here? What has he done with Nathaniel?"

But instead of helping me, they look away, embarrassed, as though I have said something foolish.

"It is best if you do not struggle, Mrs Catchpole. I can give you a sedative if necessary. I will just have a word with your mother and husband outside."

They disappear behind the door to the room opposite, close enough for me to catch some of what they say, but not all.

"....most likely cause is puerperal insanity...seen examples before associated with infant mortality... sufficiently satisfied to provide one of the signatures for the certificate ... St Felix's could provide the second, if you, Sir, are willing to authorise the journey."

St Felix's is the local asylum in Melton. I have heard tales about it, and none of them happy. *William cannot mean to send me there?* It must be a mistake.

Footsteps retreat downstairs, but thankfully William and my mother return to my bedside.

"Oh, thank goodness that horrible man has gone! Why does he talk of St Felix's? Surely it is for lunatics, not for the treatment of injured hands?"

William and mother are stony faced. William draws up a chair next to my bed and eventually finds his words.

"Maud, it is for the best. The past nine months have taken their toll on you. I thought we had turned a corner recently – you've been more involved in the farm, looked after the animals, kept the house well – but then I found you up here." He looks down at his hands, which shake a little until he clasps them in front of him. "We worry you might harm yourself again...while you're still confused in your mind. There is no other option."

Surely he cannot mean this? Have I misunderstood his intentions? But his eyes are grave and sad.

"No William, not there...please! What about Nathaniel? Who will look after him? I know I make mistakes, William, but I will try my best, I promise! He will be safe with me!"

It is my mother who answers this time, in a pained voice. "For heaven's sake, Maud, he has gone. He died, we buried him, there was a funeral. If you cannot remember that, you have to accept that St Felix's is the best place for you right now."

Her voice gives way at the end and she reaches for her handkerchief.

The room spins as her words sink in. I remember a coffin, now. I remember holding his still body in my arms, and the world caving in around me. Yet I also remember the sound of a baby crying behind the wall.

If he's dead, what was the wailing I heard?

Was it the spirit trying to trick me?

It is too much. Too much for my head to comprehend. Fear and confusion render me mute and immobile.

Laboured footsteps again on the stairs. Dr Aspall returns with another man, holding a heavy linen garment over his arms. William beckons my mother and they disappear out of the room, heads bowed. The doctor dresses the wounds on my hands with a tenderness that was absent in his dealings with me earlier. He helps me to my feet. He asks me to hold my arms above my head, then he and the other man ease the garment over my body. It's weighted down and the arms are exceptionally long, falling beyond the end of my bandaged fingers. The other man takes the drooping ends and crosses them over the front of my body, tying the ends behind my back, swaddling me like a new-born babe only upright, my legs remaining free.

I do not resist. What would be the point? This doctor and William believe they can determine my fate. I have no power in this room to argue otherwise.

I am carried downstairs in case I fall. They walk me through the back parlour, past William and my mother, who has turned away from me and is sobbing on his shoulder, and out the door to the carriage.

I sense William watching from the doorway as I am assisted into the carriage, and then as the horses are instructed to walk on and the wheels begin to roll.

But I do not look back.

It is the last time he will see me alive.

CHAPTER 30

Bea

My foot knocks something under the bed. It's my new journal; I must have left it there before I fell asleep. I search for my watch and find it under my maternity notes. Slipping it on, I adjust my limp curls in the mirror. 'Pregnancy Bloom', poppy cock: my face seems to have aged five years since we've lived here, eyes permanently tired, skin blotchy and flaky.

10.38. Drats. We were supposed to be at Kath's eight minutes ago. Harry's waiting for me at the bottom of the stairs.

"Ready?"

I lock up the house and climb in the car next to her. The baby's lying low again, right on my bladder, making me feel like I need the toilet when I've already been three times this morning.

"Which way, left or right?"

"Right."

I'm stirred by a flash of deja-vu, remembering my visit with Seb a few weeks ago. Although, of course, I'd since made the journey by foot in the dark. My face flushes as I think about the impression we must have made then: me sobbing, bleeding and frightened, Seb furious and controlling. I hope Kath doesn't hold it against us.

I needn't have worried. She opens the front door smiling as we get out the car.

"Hello! You're looking well, Bea. And this must be Harriet – pleased to meet you. Come in, come in."

She walks us through to the kitchen. There's a delicious smell.

"Just waiting on a tray of scones in the oven. Come take a seat."

Jam, cream and butter are on the table ready and just as she pours our tea, the oven bleeps. Tempting, golden fruit scones are put on a plate before us.

"I'd wait a few minutes or they'll take off a layer of your mouth! Now, how are you Bea? You mentioned on the phone that you'd spent a week or so at your parents?"

I fill her in on the past couple of weeks, pausing when I trace my way back to the last time I saw her. My cheeks burn. She seems to have a sixth sense for my thoughts.

"Please don't be embarrassed. You clearly had a real fright that evening, and who can blame you, after what happened?" She beckons for us to take a scone. Still warm, it splits easily against my knife, releasing a puff of steam. I plan my next words carefully, watching the butter on top darken and liquefy.

"Actually, I wanted to ask you about the house."

"I gathered," Kath's face is expectant, attentive.

"Yesterday we found an old crib buried into a cavity in the wall upstairs. The initials "N.C." have been engraved on the side."

Kath's gaze becomes serious and fixed, as though focusing on something not in the room. With no prompt, I continue.

"It might sound far-fetched, but I think the crib is somehow connected to the noises I've heard in the house. I feel like something is warning me... telling me not to stay there." I don't tell her about the message in my old journal, not wanting to lose her attention and fearing it might be too much to handle at this point. "Do you know anything of the history of our house?"

I wonder whether Kath has heard me, her gaze still fixed, but then she seems to make up her mind and addresses us.

"I don't want to give you further cause for concern but it's only fair that I share what I've been told. The way I see it, you're scared already. A bit of folklore... history, however you choose to look at it, might help you."

Harry and I exchange glances, and I nod to Kath, encouraging her to continue.

"This farmhouse has been in my family since about 1880. My parents bought the freehold from the local estate owner, back in the 1940's just after the war, but mother had lived here with her parents, and her grandparents were here before that as tenants. My mother's grandfather, my great-grandfather, was actually the nephew of a chap who lived in your house. I can't tell you his name - passed away before my great-grandfather moved here - but I can tell you the story I heard about him."

A chill runs down my back. Even my baby is intently still, curled up inside me, listening to Kath's every word.

"Apparently, the man who lived in your house was married... had a baby. But the child died. I don't know how or why, but obviously we're talking about Victorian times - deaths of infants were not uncommon then, sadly. It was said that his wife, again I don't know her name, was never right after the baby passed. In the end, he called the doctor and had her declared insane. A carriage from the local asylum, St. Felix's, in Melton, near Woodbridge, came to take her away. But she never made it to the asylum - threw herself out the carriage while it was travelling at speed. Died instantly. It was treated as suicide, which was considered shameful back then. Her husband died a couple of years later."

Harry and I exchange frightened glances across the table.

"I'd not like to say whether that sorry story has anything to do with your experiences, and I can't vouch for its accuracy, but I do know this: there hasn't been much happiness at Oak Tree Farm. Poor Vics and Terry wanted children but never seemed to have any luck. And my family have never known there to be children at that farm." She reaches across the table and takes my hand, attempts a reassuring smile. "But, of course, you'll be the first to break that tradition, my dear, you are so very nearly there."

I'm speechless. Such a tragic story would resonate with any expectant mother, but given it's my house, it knocks me sideways.

Silently, I try to process what I've just heard.

Did the crib belong to the poor baby who died? Was it once rocked by the hands of his mother, later driven insane by grief? Or am I trying to make connections to local folklore, which may or may not be true? Something about the story strikes a chord, consistent with my experiences. Surely, it's too much of a coincidence that a baby had died and we had found a buried crib. I can't imagine what the mother must have gone through.

Harriet saves me from the need to speak, but I can tell by her tone that it's affected her too. "So... thank you for sharing that... do you know when it was supposed to have happened?"

"I don't know specifics, but like I say, my great-grandfather came here in the 1880's, and his uncle must have died shortly before that. Probably lived in your house in the 1870's or 1860's? Around then."

"And are you aware of any history of strange experiences in the farm – perhaps connected with the story?"

Kath shakes her head. "I wouldn't know. Nothing that's ever been confided in me."

Harry nods, her face serious when she glances at me. We're silent, contemplating the story and how it could relate to our experiences.

Eventually I find my voice. "You mentioned the mother fell from a carriage. Where did this happen?" I had a feeling I knew Kath's answer before she spoke.

"People say it was the main road out there – I'm not sure where exactly."

"Perhaps I heard it replay – that night I came here."

It makes no sense, of course, having taken place many years before, but it offers an explanation for what I heard; the clatter of hooves, the commotion and the urgent instruction to stop.

Kath's expression is bleak. "I have to say, it went through my mind."

Thank God I hadn't tried to investigate that night! I don't want to think about what I might have seen.

Harriet intervenes again. "I'm just thinking...it would be helpful if we could trace the people who lived in the farm – perhaps the people from your story. Terry told Bea the owner before him ran it as a pig farm for thirty years, and before that it was inherited by someone who lived in the West Country who never lived here. But you mentioned something about farming tenants in Victorian times. How did that work?"

Kath nods, happy that she can provide some concrete answers. "Before the war, much of the land was owned by the local lords, and plots were leased to farmers. Here, the land owner would be one of the Lords Huntingfield of Heveningham Hall. The Hall is still privately owned today, although, of course, they sold off most of their land after the War, including the plots for this farm and yours."

"Right. So, it would have been owned by Lord Huntingfield, but our farm would have been leased to someone else. How could we find out the names of the tenants?"

"Well, there would have been records, of course, held by the estate. The family up at the Hall sometimes offers tours… open it up to the public - one way to keep the place ticking over. You could try there?"

"Great. Could you write it down for us please? Also, the name of the asylum you mentioned."

"No problem. Of course, it's not an asylum these days – it was converted into flats about twenty years ago."

As Kath drifts off to find some paper, Harry reaches across the table to squeeze my hand.

"All seems close to the bone, doesn't it?"

I nod.

When Kath returns, our chat returns to more normal matters while we eat scones and drink tea, although my mind wanders back to our earlier conversation. I can't wait to talk about everything with Harriet in the car.

"So that was a revelation, wasn't it?" Harriet checks the road before pulling out of Kath's drive.

"I know…that story…so dark and morbid…but it could fit, couldn't it?" I air the fear that's been brewing ever since my call with Vics Bryant. "To me, it seems like whatever's in our house doesn't want babies to live there."

Harry pulls a face.

"Think about it, Harry: who are the people who've sensed something there? Me, you, Vic – what's the common factor?"

"We're female?"

"Yes, but more than that – we all are, or were, pregnant. Perhaps it's the ghost of the mother – maybe she can't bear the thought of other children living in that house – not when hers died."

"Is that what we experienced in our dream, do you think?

Reliving the death of her child? Her face is pale and grave.

"Maybe. The nightmare left me with a strong sense of despair and terror."

As soon as she parks the car, Harriet can't get the seatbelt off fast enough, tries to clamber out at speed, muttering something about feeling sick. She makes it out the car, bends double and retches. I sweep her hair out of the way, rest my other hand around her shoulders as she contorts in spasms. When she's finished, exhausted and sobbing, I hug her close.

"I know. It's horrible. Hopefully it'll pass when you hit three months. It did for me."

She accepts a tissue to wipe her eyes and mouth.

"Thanks...I think it's the shock...I don't normally feel this bad after I've eaten." She looks at me. "Look, I said I'd stay here with you, and I will, if that's what you want. But do you think it's safe for you and the baby?"

"I don't know, but I don't have much choice. I mean, nothing's clear, is it? If there's a danger, what is it exactly? Even if I went back to Mum and Dad's, when would be safe tor return? I can't just leave Seb here, indefinitely." I fumble in my bag for the house keys. "Don't get me wrong: I'm not easy with this. But unless I have solid evidence of potential harm, this is our home and we have to stay."

Still trying to locate the keys, I hear something on the other side of the door. Tap, tap, tap. A rhythmical beat. Peering through the rippled glass, I detect movement.

I freeze.

"What is it? What's wrong?" Harry whispers.

"I saw something."

My quivering fingers brush the keys at the bottom of an inside pocket. I grab them and struggle to turn the key in the lock with shaking hands. Every sense is alert, body tense. The door creaks open.

Sunlight from the kitchen-diner window streams directly onto the crib by the hearth. It's like a spotlight on a stage. In the glow, the crib rocks to and fro, fast. Swaying rhythmically, of its own volition, tapping the stone floor with each rock. Within a split second, it ceases abruptly, as though conscious of being watched.

I'm speechless for a few seconds, eyes fixated.

"What did you see?" Harry says impatiently.

"The crib - I saw it rock – just as I opened the door."

"Shit!"

We enter apprehensively. The crib remains stationary. Still, obedient, deceptively innocent. With a fearful hand, I try rocking it. It requires some force to move it.

"No breeze or draught could rock this."

Harriet puts her arm on mine, white faced. "I thought I heard something, but I didn't see it move – you were blocking my view." She turns on the tap. "Do you want a glass of water? I definitely need one."

The running water, mundane and normal, is a welcome sound. I close my eyes and take some deep breaths. *It's all starting to feel too much.*

"Are you going to tell Seb about Kath's story – and the rocking crib?" Harriet hands me the glass.

"Maybe." I take a few sips. "Although I'd rather present him with something substantial, after we've had a chance to investigate the previous occupants."

As we drink silently, leaning against the kitchen units, we keep one eye on the crib in case it rocks again, although my gut instinct tells me it would not do so under our direct scrutiny. With each gulp I try to pick a way through the fears crowding my mind.

I close my eyes again, exhale, long and steady.

I speak my thoughts aloud, for my own benefit as much as for Harriet's: "I need to assess what we know and focus on what I control – it's the only way I can cope here. I can't change what's going on: I have to accept strange things are happening... unanticipated disturbances beyond my control. But I must focus on the fact I've never been in actual danger, have I? I've been scared, yes, and I've felt like I had to get out, get away - but not because I was directly threatened."

"No... but..."

I turn to her. "It's not like I've been pushed down the stairs, or hurt in some way, is it?"

Harry puts her hand on my arm, speaks gently. "True, but dismissing it – seeing it as just a noise, smell, sensation - easier said than done, isn't it? How would you cope on your own – or with a child?"

I shrug. "What choice do I have? Seb would never agree to moving out – we couldn't afford the additional expense anyway. No – I need to focus on controlling my fear - think of ways to calm me down or how I can get out of the house at speed." I change the subject, unwilling to think about it anymore for now. "And what about you? Have you given more thought to contacting Rhys?"

"Funny enough, he contacted me last night. He's flying into Heathrow in a few weeks, just after I start back at work. He'll be in London with friends for a few days and wants to meet up while he's there. I'll be staying with Mum and Dad...but I could meet him after work."

"That's a start."

She nods. "I'll play it by ear, but I'll try to tell him about the baby. Obviously, it's going to be a shock for him. And things between us may feel very different now we're both back on home soil." She places her glass on the counter, folds her arms across her. "The distance doesn't exactly help, him in Cardiff, me in London. I don't know...it's all such a mess."

"One step at a time, I guess. One of you could relocate, change jobs – you never know," I give a wry smile, "buy somewhere - a place in the country!"

She manages a half-smile. We've run low on levity recently and it gets me thinking.

"We should all go out tomorrow... after the tour of the hospital. Makes sense while we're in Ipswich anyway. And it gets us out the house."

"Are you sure you want me to come? Isn't it a special time for you and Seb?"

"Well, the alternative is you staying here alone – would you be comfortable with that?"

Her eyebrows knit. "No, if I'm honest. But I don't want to cramp your style. Maybe I could stay in the car or go to the town while you're in the hospital?"

Later, when I tell Seb our plan, he nods but looks disappointed. I can tell he was expecting us to make the trip together, just the two of us, but he says nothing and remains quiet all evening.

The following day he's still quiet and sullen. We drop off Harry in the town centre and continue to the hospital car park. Once he's parked, I broach the subject.

"Don't you like having Harry over? You've seemed moody ever since I mentioned she was coming with us today."

He pauses a little too long. "I do...you know I think she's great. But I'd like to get back to being on our own again – prepare ourselves."

"There's time for that, she'll be leaving next weekend. She's a great comfort to me, Seb. In fact, I don't even want to think about how I'll cope after she's gone."

"I know…well, at least you'll have your own car by then. I forgot to mention - the dealership rang yesterday and said we could pick it up any time after Friday."

I nod, but I think to myself that a car can only go so far in making me feel safe. It was no replacement for a sympathetic sister.

CHAPTER 31

Bea

"**A**nd this is the birthing pool. You should indicate in your plan if you'd like to use one, although, of course there's no guarantee it will be available on the day. We deep clean it between each birth."

"Good to know," I whisper, and Seb grins in response.

We wait patiently in the queue behind the other fifteen couples, all keen to inspect what turns out to be a glorified bathtub. I eye it, doubtfully, unable to imagine climbing in and out, bulbous and naked, in the throes of labour. I take a sneaky glance at the other women, wondering who will pop first. I'd say I'm in the top five, based on hugeness, but looks can be deceptive. The next time our paths cross could be on the labour ward or pushing prams around Ipswich town centre. Both options seem so unlikely, so remote from what I know.

The automatic doors swing open and a man with a harried expression pushes a wheelchair at speed. A heavily pregnant woman sits on it, face creased with pain, teeth bared, knuckles white clenching the armrests. He bends his head, talking to her, trying to reassure, as they make a beeline for the reception desk. I can't take my eyes off them, imagining myself in that position in a few weeks' time.

Seb nudges me, bringing me back to the present.

"Are you okay – did you have any questions.?" The midwife showing us round is staring at me, and other pairs of eyes follow suit. I flush.

"Sorry – think I'm already developing baby brain. No questions from me. Thank you, it was very helpful."

There are a few chuckles and sympathetic glances. The midwife smiles and carries on.

"If you haven't already done so, please pick up your birthing pack from reception. It should answer any questions you may have, plus it provides details of services you may find useful after the birth, like new baby groups, baby weigh-in clinics and breast-feeding support contacts."

The tour is over and we're left in the maternity reception area, encouraged to engage with other soon-to-be-parents. Seb is keen to chat with a cluster of couples who already seem to know each other. We introduce ourselves but I don't catch their names. I can't stop thinking about the pair who arrived like a whirlwind earlier. Other aspects of our tour also linger with me: mechanical beds, birthing stools, tips for what to bring and what to leave behind. I can't process any more. I let the voices wash over me, internally willing us to leave and find Harry. Eventually Seb says our goodbyes, I smile vaguely and follow him out of the door.

Out of ear shot, he turns to me, irritated. "You zoned out back there. It was a great opportunity to meet some others in the same boat."

"I couldn't absorb any more info, Seb. There's a lot to get my head round...not to mention other parts of my body. Besides," I'm tetchy now, "who's to say we'll have anything in common with them, other than the fact we're about to pop a baby?"

"And who's to say we won't? I know it seems daunting – the

birth and everything else. But that's why it could be helpful to get to know others who are going through it." He presses his lips together and takes my hand. "The biggest burden falls on you, but I want to help as much as I can. I don't know if you heard, but that lot met through the local NCT group. Perhaps we should think about joining?"

I give him a tired half smile, squeeze his hand. "Maybe. I'll think about it."

We meet Harry in town for pizza and cinema. It's odd how a social evening, once normal and part of our everyday life, now feels flippant and surreal after everything that's happened. I try to enter into the spirit of things, but in the darkness of the auditorium, I find it hard to focus on *Murder on the Orient Express:* my mind wanders back to the crib and our plans to discover more about the history of the house and its inhabitants.

The following day, I search the internet for more information about Heveningham Hall. There's very little. I can't find a website or any contact information online. Then I remember the local papers we receive on Thursdays, festering in the pile of unread post in the lounge. They may have a use now.

After leafing through the first couple, my heart sinks. No relevant articles or information. With the third, I hit gold; there's a half-page piece on Heveningham Hall. The owners, Lord Marcus and Lady Fiona Huntingfield, were re-opening the house at the start of spring, and it listed dates of events and a contact number for arranging guided group tours. Mrs Turbiton is the marketing manager and I make a note of her number.

Now that I've made a connection between pregnancy and the spiritual occurrences in the house, Seb's presence in the house is an enormous comfort. At weekends and in the evenings, it's like a cloud disperses, making way for shared jokes and lighter conversation. Harry and I feel safer then. When the time comes for him to return to work on Monday, my stomach knots and I brace myself to expect the unexpected.

Keen to find a reason to leave the house, I phone Heveningham Hall. After several rings, it's answered by Mrs Turbiton, whose London voice bears no trace of the local accent.

"Can I help you?"

"Yes please. My husband I have recently moved into the area - Oak Tree Farm in Ubbeston. I believe it was once part of the Heveningham estate and was leased to tenant farmers. I'm interested in tracing the history of those who lived here and wondered if the Hall has kept any records?"

"Interesting. Well, I know there are some records, but they haven't all been retained. You may be aware the estate has sadly suffered two fires. But you are welcome to view those that are accessible. When were you hoping to visit?"

I try to keep my excitement in check. Although Mrs Turbiton agrees to see Harry and me in the afternoon, the chances of finding the records intact are slim.

We set off at 1pm. The day had started misty and uncertain, but the clouds had given way to tentative sun rays. As we pull into the long, majestic drive, the pristine lawn is a sharp contrast to the surrounding countryside of wild hedgerows and fields. The house stands vast and regal, the symmetry of the Palladian columns and austere stone façade broken by the scaffolding erected on the East side of the building, where windows are shuttered and all three stories are in much need of repair. Harry follows the drive to the empty and small visitors' car park.

"What do you think? Back entrance or front door?"

I point to the front, but as we approach the massive arched door, squarely in the centre of the building, we feel uncertain and out of place. I pull on a rod with a handle, hoping it won't fall off in my hand. It's stiff with rust and age, but I hear the faint tinkling of a bell from somewhere within. We wait outside for what seems like an age, shifting weight uncertainly from one leg to the other, when a well-dressed woman in her forties opens the door. She looks from me to Harry but settles on me.

"Mrs Haddon? I'm Vanessa Turbiton, marketing manager for the estate."

"Yes, please call me Beatrice. And this is my sister, Harriet. Thank you so much for agreeing to see us."

She beckons us in. In contrast to the exterior, the entrance hall is grand but inviting. Our scruffy trainers sink into sumptuous red carpet with a patterned border, which also lines the stairs directly ahead of us. From here, the curves of the stairway are visible, gliding through all floors of the building, drawing my eye upwards to the domed glass roof which bestows glints of light on the decorative features and surfaces below. Gilded paintings hang in clusters on the walls, along with elaborately arranged armoury and the decapitated heads of bear, moose and deer.

"Impressive, isn't it?" Mrs Turbiton smiles, watching our eyes soaking up the rich interior. She leads us to a door on the right and into a drawing room, carpeted and curtained deep blue and lined in bookcases, dominated by a large walnut desk in the centre. We continue, out through a different door. As we wind our way through corridors and connecting rooms, the décor becomes less splendid, more functional, until Mrs Turbiton stops in a room unlike the others. Far from grand, this room looks more like a museum or library. It's crammed with ugly metal shelving that blocks much of the thin light filtered through the small obscure glass windows or that that emits from the solitary ceiling pendant. Files, books and labelled boxes are stacked high, their arrangement suggesting they were kept for posterity rather than requirement.

"It's not the best of rooms, I'm afraid. It's supposed to contain just the archives for the house; all the old records and plans relating to the estate that have survived. However, since the restoration works, it's become the dumping ground for any paperwork that's been displaced or without a home."

Surveying the stacks of shelves, the prospect of finding the information we need is daunting, to say the least. The astute Mrs Turbiton reads our minds and gives a reassuring smile.

"Don't worry: I've worked here for ten years and have a good idea where everything lives. In fact, I had the chance to scan through some of the archives after our call and I've found the accounts for the estate farm tenancies dating back to the nineteenth century. I've put them on the table in the corner."

She leads us past the rows to a table underneath the windows and signals for us to take the two plastic seats.

"Please could you wear the cotton gloves when you examine the books? It helps to protect them. And of course, please refrain from drinking or eating in this room. I'll leave you to browse. If you need anything, I'll be in the room next door, on the left."

Alone, Harry and I ease our fingers into the gloves and reach for the first in the pile of books, each volume bound in burgundy leather and numbered on the spine. Carefully, I open the yellowed pages. As expected, the handwritten script is scrolled and slanted, difficult for the modern eye to read. But I notice on the first page there are numbers in the left column and names of farms and cottages next to them: Number 1 – Stonehill; Number 2 – Brow Farm, and so on.

"Perhaps this is the index to the other volumes? Each book may relate to a different plot on the estate."

We scan the list of farming plots. Number 4 was Oak Tree Farm. Harry and I lock eyes. Volume 4 was in the pile of ledgers. We carefully extract it. The leather crackles as Harry eases the cover open. Oak Tree Farm is written on the first page. On the next, the date written is 8th April 1794, the tenant recorded as Mr Edmund Sawyer, and next to that a column with the rent received.

"That's too far back. Can we skip forwards?"

"Where to?" Harry turns to me, fingers poised.

"Maybe it might be easier to work our way from the back. Trace the ownership of the farm from the most recent accounts back to the 1860's – that's the date Kath suggested."

We carefully thumbed through the ledger to the last written page. The last recording for rent received is 1945, the tenant is Terence Fairly. His name appears in 1928, and before that the tenant was recorded as Archibald Cross.

"Archibald took the tenancy in January 1910, before the First World War. I wonder what happened to him then?"

"Who knows, but farming was an exempt profession, wasn't it? Who took the tenancy before him?"

"Benjamin Truss – he seems to have struggled to pay rent on several occasions, look."

We scan back to find Benjamin's first recording in 1892. Before him, we find Albert Wooltorton, from 1869 to 1892.

"It can't be Albert. Kath said her great-grandfather moved into her house in the 1880's, but his uncle, who lived at Oak Tree Farm, had died before he moved in. Albert was still alive and present in Oak Tree Farm in 1892."

"Perhaps it was the tenant before him, then..."

Totally absorbed in our task, we turn back the next page in eager anticipation. The previous tenant is recorded as William Catchpole. He left the farm in 1869. We scroll through the entries relating to his payments, which appear to be regular. His first is recorded in 1859, a short tenancy compared to many of the others, only ten years. But a shiver runs down my spine when I consider his name.

"Catchpole."

Harry nods slowly realising the significance. "That could be the surname associated with the initials on the cot – N. C."

I make a note of the lineage of former tenants who lived in our house, but my hunch is that only one will prove to be significant: William Catchpole. *Who was he? Who were the members of his family? What were the circumstances that caused him to leave in 1869?*

Driving back from Heveningham Hall, Harry and I buzz with triumph. It felt like we had made real progress in unlocking the story of the house and its former inhabitants, but it raises more questions than it answers.

"So, do you think William was the husband who tried to have his wife committed to an asylum?"

"It's the best clue we've found so far. If the C stands for Catchpole, what might the infant's first name be?"

Mrs Turbiton, helpful as ever, had made some suggestions about lines of enquiry. Now we have William's name, we could use an ancestry website to find out the name of his wife. Apparently, the website records the census information, which includes the name of every adult in residence at each house for every year ending with a one. If we checked it for 1861, the only year ending in one during the Catchpole tenancy, we could find out her name and age at that time. Mrs Turbiton also recommended that we contact the local vicar and explore the graveyard, to see if we could find where the Catchpoles were buried.

By the time we reach home, light is starting to dim. It's late afternoon. The colours of the landscape are muted and the air is chilly as we step out of the car. I approach the house excited and preoccupied with our plans, so much so that I fail to recall what happened the last time Harry and I returned to the house together - the rocking crib. It's brought to mind like a slap round the face the moment I open the door. The air inside the house is heavy and charged, like the prelude to a storm. My eyes are drawn to the crib, this time not rocking but lying overturned by the hearth. Harry reaches for my hand as we stand looking at it, her skin cool with sweat.

"Leave the door open, in case we need a quick exit," I

murmur.

Wordlessly, cautiously, we drop hands and split to search each room on the ground floor, heads turning and eyes skimming every surface, checking for other signs of disturbance. Harry shrugs and gives the thumbs up in the music room, where she has been sleeping. I find nothing untoward in the lounge and downstairs bathroom. I point towards the stairs and we climb quietly, cautiously, me in front, Harry at the rear. The only sounds I hear are the pad of our feet and our shallow, quickened breaths. No scraping. No movement other than the two of us, creeping towards the spare room.

A quick inspection shows nothing appears to have changed. The hole remains from Seb's demolition, the cloths lie folded on the floor where he hoovered and. It's when we cross the landing and step into my bedroom that I sense it. That smell again, faint this time, but unmistakeably sage and lavender. Harry notices too and she makes towards the annex, our last room to inspect.

She gasps sharply, arms wide blocking my entrance.

"Christ, look at this!"

"Harry, I can't see, let me past."

She moves slightly to one side, as though reluctant or unable to move any closer to whatever has frightened her. As I squeeze past, I understand why. The baby clothes we had neatly sorted and stacked have been flung all around the room. Everywhere is covered in specks of beige, which I assume are grains of sand, until in the next second my eyes reach the cot. What looked so pristine several days ago has been reduced to a wreck. The mattress is gouged, disembowelled, the sponge interior having exploded fibres everywhere. The wooden headboard and rails had been tortured and defaced - gashed and clawed by something powerful and sharp.

My legs start to give way and I allow the wall to support my body as I slide to the floor, on top of the mess. My breathing is erratic. I'm too shaken to cry. My forehead drops to my palms, shutting out the sight of the ruined room around me. I feel Harry kneel to my level, her hand squeezing my arms and shoulders, trying to soothe away the fear and desperation.

"How? How am I going to bring a baby into this? I won't be able to let him or her out of my sight!"

For once, Harry has no answers. Now I've let panic take over, I find it hard to stop, the pent-up fear and frustration I've tried to contain now spiral and expand out of control, mixed with anger. I struggle back to my feet.

"What do you want from me? Do you want my baby, after losing your own – is that what this is? Or are you trying to drive me out of here? I don't know, but I'm fucking sick of it!" The cry is startling, interrupting the silence and the heavy atmosphere hanging in the air.

I hear no response but I'm stunned and overcome by shooting pain through my abdomen. I gasp and clutch my bump.

"What is it, what's happening?" Harry panics.

The pain subsides as quickly as it arrived, but then returns, equally intense, grasping my lower body. I can't speak until it passes.

"It could just be Braxton Hicks contractions, but they're bloody intense!"

The next wave silences me again, teeth clenched, mouth grimacing.

"They seem to be very close together! I'm ringing for an ambulance."

Harry rummages in her shoulder bag for her mobile and makes the call. In the calm between contractions, I try to remember the last-minute items for my hospital bag, thankfully still sitting in the corner of the room unharmed.

"...yes, the contractions are about a minute apart..."

Her eyes widen as they give her instructions. When she comes off the call, she takes control of the situation, fetching pillows to support my back and clean towels.

"Could you get my water bottle, toothbrush and paste and deodorant for the bag?"

While she's fetching the items, she calls Seb, who, I gather, is utterly terrified judging by her responses.

"...Yes, don't worry, the ambulance is on its way... Yes, I've got it... I'll meet you at the hospital...Yes, of course, I'll let you know."

I have no concept of time, only conscious of the contractions, easing back then surging forwards in powerful waves. Harry supports me as we attempt the painstakingly slow journey to the bedroom, each small step interrupted by a contraction. I lean on the bed, bracing myself for the next juddering crescendo. The room slips out of focus. My concentration centres on the peaks and troughs, each contraction a steep incline to overcome before the next one arrives. At the next peak, wet trickles between my legs, pools at my feet. For a split second I'm confused and embarrassed, believing the pain has made me urinate, but Harry grabs a towel.

"Your waters must have broken! Don't worry, the ambulance will be here soon!"

I'm vaguely aware of the doorbell and commotion around me, people in green jump suits, monitoring me and asking Harry questions. I'm told we'll move downstairs after the next contraction. It comes with an intensity like none before it, and then I'm being carried down the stairs. We don't make it to the door before the next one arrives and I cling to the doorframe waiting for it to pass. The next minute, I'm helped into the ambulance.

What happens next, I can't say in any detail. One minute,

I'm lying in the ambulance, monitors strapped near my heart and between my legs to the baby's head, an oxygen mask clamped over my face, taking the edge off the pain contorting my body. The next, I'm wheeled through hospital corridors, doors swinging, reassuring voices of masked robed medics, fluorescent lights flashing above. It is a nurse who holds my hand, not Seb. This is not what we planned. My legs are splayed; people are watching me, checking monitors.

The crowning is unbearable. It's like a dental procedure, when your mouth is stretched open, taut and wide, only this hole must expand far wider to accommodate the great descending mass. I'm told to push, to pant, to hold back. It's happening to me, but I've no control over it. Each push feels futile, with no power or impact, yet I focus on it with all my might, fighting to stay on top, not let myself sink.

Just when I feel I have nothing left to give, there's an instant alleviation of pressure.

"That's it! Baby's head is out!"

I'm barely conscious of the nurses and Harry who congratulate and encourage me. With less pain, I deliver the rest of the baby and the placenta.

"It's a girl!" Harriet is crying, but with joy and relief.

For a few precious moments, I have my daughter in my arms and we say hello for the first time. She is angry, red and beautiful. If only Seb were here to see her! Intense joy floods over me but it's short lived. Within seconds, the room blurs and spins. She's scooped away.

Her cry is drowned out by the beep of a machine, the shout of instructions.

The last sounds I hear.

CHAPTER 32

Bea

"Hey... How're you feeling?"

I wake to find Seb is not beside me in bed. He is sitting, stooped over me, hand reaching for mine. Although he smiles, his dishevelled hair and pinched brow show concern. The lighting is too bright and unnatural, and I remember I'm in hospital.

"Wuh..."

I try to sit up, but feel a sharp pain in my arm, which is uncomfortably restricted. Seb rises out of his seat to stop me as I notice my forearm is attached to a drip, a bag of blood dangling above my head. My whole body aches and groans.

"Don't try to move too much. You had to have a transfusion - you lost so much blood after the birth. Feeling okay - ish?"

"Achey and a little cold." I look around, feeling a sudden surge of panic. "Where is she? Where's the baby?"

"It's okay, she's being looked after. Let's get you sorted out before you see her."

The curtains are drawn around my bed and once more I have no concept of time. Seb pokes his head out to attract the attention of a nurse.

"Good evening!"

The young nurse checks my notes and adjusts the flow of the drip, then hands me paracetamol in a small paper cup.

"Open up for me."

She inserts a thermometer in my mouth, takes it out and checks the reading.

"All good. You did so well! Baby Haddon was safely delivered."

"Where is she now?"

The nurse takes a seat next to the bed.

"We're just keeping an eye on her. She showed some distress during labour, so we're continuing to monitor her heart rate."

"Oh...will she need it for long?"

"We keep a close check on the first 24 hours after birth. As you know, she's arrived at almost 36 weeks gestation: we classify babies at that stage as late preterm."

My fears are mirrored in Seb's eyes, and he's the first to speak.

"What are the chances of her having any... problems?"

"At the moment, baby's breathing seems slightly shallower than we would like, so she's currently in the NICU, the Neonatal Intensive Care Unit."

All I hear is shallow breathing and NICU. My eyes well. The nurse takes my hand and her tone becomes more gentle.

"Please don't worry; it's perfectly normal for a baby born at this stage of development. We have to be aware of the possibility of respiratory distress syndrome in preterm babies. It's where they need a little help with breathing in the early days, perhaps because the lungs haven't fully developed. We're not sure whether this is the case for your baby - certainly, she's not requiring invasive assistance like a ventilator - but we're keeping a check on her oxygen levels and giving her a little extra as necessary."

I dry my eyes with a tissue Seb hands to me, slightly less alarmed. "Can I see her?"

"Of course. But you'll need a wheelchair to get about for the first couple of days. You lost almost 1.5 litres of blood. The transfusion should be complete in an hour or so. How about I fix you some tea and toast, and you go visit her when you're done?"

We thank her and she leaves for the kitchen. Seb sits down again, clasps his hands around my free one.

"I'm so sorry I wasn't here when she arrived... when you needed me. Thank God Harry was ..."

Tears pool in his eyes and his voice quavers. Seb doesn't cry often, so it makes a big impact. A lump swells in my throat.

"Don't apologise - you weren't to know she was going to come early. None of us had a clue." I shake my head. "If it wasn't for seeing the annex in that state, maybe she'd still be growing inside me now."

I think back to when and how labour began. *Was the presence in the house responsible for the onset of contractions?* I'll never know. But I do know the baby and I were in danger, whether from shock or something more sinister, and she was still not out of the woods. When I think about it now, the savage destruction of the cot, the brutal power behind it, my stomach tightens, wrenching the recovering muscles in my abdomen.

Seb squeezes my hand, seeing me wince with pain. "Are you okay?"

"Yes – just thinking about it."

Seb frowns as he wipes his face. "Harry told me what

happened. I can't believe it..." His eyes catch mine and he quickly corrects himself. "Sorry, bad choice of words. I do believe it – but it's just so incredible. To be honest, it's knocked me for six."

The nurse returns with wheelchair and buttered toast with marmite. Never before has toast tasted so delicious. I eat and drink quickly, eager to see my baby and put the concerns of the house to the back of my mind. The nurse returns to remove the drip, but I soon learn I have to be patient. Even sitting up and swinging my legs round the side of the bed takes all my strength and my head spins. I've never felt so weak and drained, like my batteries have run out and my muscles are made from jelly.

Seb eases me into the wheelchair and we're off down the corridor. I try to catch the faces of the other women and babies on the ward as I'm wheeled along, see if I recognise any from the hospital induction day, but most have their curtains drawn or are otherwise sleeping.

The NICU is on the floor below. A wheel catches in the opening of the lift, the wheelchair tilts forwards almost unloading me. I gasp but we both see the funny side, a welcome relief after the past 24 hours.

The lift slides open and we're confronted by the reception for the NICU. The atmosphere here is noticeably different: tense, quiet. Relatives sit in the small area next to the desk, looking anxious and drained. We give our surname to a brisk nurse who shows us to a room where there are four baby units. She points to the incubator in the corner by the window. She takes the time to show us how to access the unit, how to touch our baby without disturbing the wires. She promises to show us how to feed her and reassures me that I will be given help at every stage.

Once she leaves, we settle down next to our beautiful girl. I insert a hand through the window and stroke her tiny, perfect hand, the velvet of her cheek. Love instantly overflows for this little bundle, so vulnerable, attached to wires. More than anything, I wish for her to be well and free, but I also feel guilty for having this thought when there are babies who look far more needy and delicate in this room. I read similar thoughts crossing Seb's face as his hand creeps in next to mine.

"Hello again, sweetheart. You're doing so well. Won't be long now till you can come home with us."

Seb's finger traces her cheek, his hand unfeasibly large next to her petite face. "You're going to be strong, just like your mum, I can already tell," his voice cracks with emotion.

On the way back to the ward, we're buzzing with a mixture of powerful emotions: pride, responsibility, fear, love.

"I wish she didn't have to be in there," my voice partially muffled by the tissue wiping my face.

"I know, but hopefully it won't be for long. She's not a bad weight, Bea. 5.8 pounds, good for a 36-week delivery. The nurse measured her as 45cm. They told me that her slightly reddish skin and lack of hair is perfectly normal at this stage."

I nod, unsurprised that he had already investigated the stats.

"It will be hard but we've no reason to think she won't pass her checks. We just need to keep on top of her milestones, make sure we know what her peers should be doing every few months."

Once I'm back in the bed again, and we've pulled the curtains round for some privacy, Seb returns to sit near me. He strokes my fingers with his thumb, the look in his eyes earnest and serious. The positivity he showed only moments ago, when talking about our little angel, has drained from his face.

"I feel terrible for not having taken the situation at the house more seriously, earlier on." His face creases with shame and bafflement. "I found it so hard to comprehend. It doesn't bear thinking about, what could have happened if she was there... inside that cot."

251

His voice trails off, broken. I've never seen him less sure of himself, defeated.

"I don't know what to do. I don't want to burden you with it now, but there's no way I want any of us to stay in that house when there's a risk to your safety, her safety. But what can we do?"

His face is desperate, wretched, but instead of churning me up inside, it has the reverse effect. A part of me, some nerve or sinew that's been strung out and stretched almost to breaking point, starts to relax. It's taken this traumatic event to reunite us; it's still terrifying, but much less daunting, knowing I'm not facing it alone.

It's time to share everything that has happened and all that I know, even the parts I'd held back, waiting for more concrete evidence. I tell him my hunch that the presence only manifests to expectant women, and the dream that Harry and I shared. Obviously, this necessitated telling him of Harry's pregnancy, but I knew she wouldn't object in the circumstances. I tell Kath's story of the former tenant of our house, whose baby had died and how this led to the trauma and ultimate suicide of his wife. Finally, I fill him in our investigations at Heveningham Hall, which identified William Catchpole as the potential tenant and father of "N.C" and the further lines of enquiry suggested by Mrs Turbiton.

His face is creased with concentration as he takes it all in. "You've made a lot of progress, both of you, but where's this going? How's it going to help the situation at home?"

"I don't know. But I think we should dig deeper - try and find some closure for whatever it is that remains restless in our house. And we need to make sure Harry doesn't stay there alone."

He nods. "Explains why she met a friend from London for dinner tonight."

Another thought crosses my mind. An idea that would go some way to making our return to the farm more feasible, but may prove a step too far for Seb.

"You know, there's something else we could do, to try and make the house safe."

"What?"

I pause. "Exorcism."

He's expressionless for a moment and then exhales through his teeth. "If someone had told me I'd be contemplating that last year...even last month... I'd think they were insane. But why not? We can't uproot again: can't afford it, without a crippling loan. If we can free the house from whatever's there, surely that's the best outcome?"

I'm relieved he feels the same way.

"Leave it with me. I'll try and get it sorted before you come home." He looks at his watch. "It's half-nine. I'll be kicked out soon. After I've looked into exorcism, I'll explore the census information."

It's his turn to look apprehensive.

"It feels wrong saying it, after everything you've been through, but I think it makes sense for me to go back to work on Wednesday - postpone parental leave until you're both out of hospital. What do you think? Then I could be on hand to help at home, when I'm more likely to be useful."

I smile and nod.

He slips on his jacket, pulls up the zip. "On the way out, I'll chase up getting someone to show you how to express."

He leans in and kisses me tenderly. His voice drops to a whisper, his cheek still touching mine.

"You don't know how relieved I am you're both okay. I'm so proud of you both. Everything will be okay. It has to be."

CHAPTER 33

Bea

Time moves irregularly in hospital. Some hours drag forever, when you're waiting to speak to a doctor or anticipating visiting hours. Others pass in a blur: a constant cycle of expressing milk, feeding, changing nappies, being monitored, resting, taking medication. The day loses all of its normal rhythms.

Hospital is supposed to be the place for rest and recuperation, yet sleep is nigh on impossible. The combination of bright lights, constant buzz of voices and wheeled equipment is the antithesis of a peaceful environment.

But I can't fault the care and support I've had in my first few days of being a parent. Early yesterday I woke with painful, heavy breasts, like they had become water-balloons overnight. A breast-feeding support nurse showed me how to express milk by hand, teaching me how to gently massage the glands, turgid with milk, to soften and drain the liquid, while using my thumb and finger to pump out the milk. It felt ridiculous at first, like milking a cow, but soon I got the hang of it, particularly as the process had to be repeated eight times a day.

Now, at day three, she's learning how to feed from me

directly. I can't describe the intense stir of emotion I felt the first time she suckled. On the previous day, when we'd enjoyed skin to skin contact, her body tucked under the blanket, her smooth skin next to mine, the connection felt so tender and precious. But breastfeeding took us to a new level of intimacy. The first-time, tears rolled down my cheeks. A nurse came to help, thinking I was in pain, but with a laugh I reassured her all was well.

She's just finishing her early afternoon feed now. I've had to tickle her toes twice to stop her from dozing off mid-feed. When she seems to have had enough, her latch breaking as she slips into sleep, I carefully lift her back into her cot, the nurse supervising her tubes and wires once more.

The doctors are hopeful she can be moved to the new baby ward at the end of the week as both her weight and oxygen stats are good. To say Seb and I are relieved is an understatement. Of course, she'll still need to be carefully monitored in the future – hearing, eyesight, as well as developmental milestones – but we're close to crossing the first hurdle.

I make my way back to the mother and baby ward. A wheelchair may no longer be required, but my body has yet to fully recover. My legs are like lead. I feel like I have to squeeze the muscles in my abdomen to avoid parts of me slipping out and spilling on the floor.

With relief, I'm back in my chair and turn on my lap-top. While I wait for it to whirr into life, I think about today. I can't wait to speak to Seb to find out how the exorcism went. He lost no time in looking into it, contacting the local diocese and, through them, the Deliverance Team. If it was happening to someone else, I would have laughed. The idea of a team of experts specialising in cleansing and removal of spirits seems far-fetched and more fitting for the horror films I watched in my teens. But it's happening to us, and I'm grateful they can help. In fact, after Seb explained the circumstances and shared photographs of the damage to the cot and annex, they made our case a priority.

Yesterday, he researched the census entry for our house for 1861, the time when William Catchpole was in residence. Apparently at that time, he was aged twenty-two and his wife was the only other adult living there. Her name was Maud Catchpole - she was only twenty years old.

Maud. I play with the sound of it in my head. To me, it sounds melancholy, austere, a name etched in past centuries and I can't see it returning to fashion any time soon. I imagine the owner of the name wore a sack-coloured dress, practical but dull, a whitish cloth over her pinned back dark hair. Her hands were red and rough, her lips thin, her eyes dark and tinged with sorrow. I wonder how far her image differed to the one in my mind? Was her life hard? Did maternal instincts flow naturally for her or did she struggle? Many questions for which I'm unlikely to find answers. At least I may have more luck uncovering information about her untimely death.

I bring myself back to the present, click on my emails. There's a message from Harry dated yesterday, 22.15.

Hi Bea,

So pleased to hear you and the little one are doing well! Seb's just returned from the hospital. I've deliberately restrained myself from visiting, to give you and him some space, but I'd love to come and see you on Friday, if that suits? Can't wait to see her again too!

She knew how to make an entrance, didn't she?! The birth was certainly an eye-opener, and if I'm honest, a terrifying glimpse of what's ahead for me. I've always known you were amazing, but now...hats off to you.

Seb's been great about my pregnancy, making sure I'm not left alone in the house. Kath's been fantastic too - when Seb's not around and I'm not occupied with historical sleuthing, she's made her place open to me. I'm hoping that we'll all feel more comfortable after the exorcism (feels weird writing that word). Seb's done well to arrange it so quickly. We've agreed that it's best for me to be out of the house then, although part of me would be fascinated to see it.

Seb's being aware of my "condition" made me feel less apprehensive about telling Mum and Dad. I dropped the bombshell last night on the phone. They were taken aback, but I think the blow was softened by just having become grandparents! Naturally they showed concern about how it will impact on my career, the financial position etc. But it wasn't as mortifying as I thought it would be.

Anyway, I thought I'd update on what I've discovered so far, about William Catchpole and N.C.

As you know, Seb found out that William's Catchpole's wife was called Maud. With her name and district, I was able to trace details of her birth and death. She was born on 1st February 1841 and died on 30th October 1867. Her cause of death was given as "Self-inflicted harm, whilst of unsound mind". This seems to tie-in with Kath's story of the poor mother who jumped from the moving carriage on the way to the asylum. We can now give her a name, at least.

I checked out the graveyards at two local churches, to see if I could find where the Catchpoles are buried. I found no information at the first one I visited, St Peter's in Spexhall. To be honest, after spending a fruitless hour, wandering the graveyard and trying to decipher weather-worn gravestones, I doubted my chances of finding anything. But at St Margaret's in Heveningham I was in luck. After half an hour or so of wandering the churchyard, the local vicar came over to offer help – Reverend Simon Marks. He was a nice guy and he told me where the graves for the mid-Victorian period were likely to be located. Together we found William's grave, Bea! Without his help, I'm not sure I would have discovered it; the stone was small, by comparison to some of the others, the lines of letters and numbers partially eroded. It simply bore his name, William Alfred Catchpole, born 1st March 1837, died 9th November 1869. So, he *would have been only 32 years old. Young, but sadly not uncommon for Victorian times.*

I lift my head to work through the dates: Maud died 30th October 1867; his death was almost exactly two years later. *Close in time - could there be a connection?* Perhaps he never got over it.

I return to the screen, eager to learn more.

Brace yourself, Bea: there was another gravestone. Next to William's was one belonging to… Nathaniel Catchpole. His bore the words: "Beloved son, gone too soon, born 21st January 1867, died 26th July 1867. This must be NC! Less than six months old when he died: I can't imagine how awful it must have been for the family. Explains the impact it had on Maud… But that was it. Two graves, two headstones: no mention of Maud.

I told Rev. Simon Kath's story, which I believe relates to Maud. He was very knowledgeable and gave me a rundown on how attitudes changed towards suicide during the 19th century. Apparently, before 1823, they were treated as sinful and as such their bodies were denied burial in consecrated ground. Instead, they were often buried at crossroads, with a stake through them. Horrific!

He said that after 1823, a law was passed that meant suicide victims could be buried in churchyards, but only during the night and without a Christian service. He said he's only been a vicar at St Margaret's for six months and does not have detailed knowledge of the history of this particular church or the plot, but he thought it likely that Maud would have been buried next to her child, during the night, but without a head stone or a proper service. It seems such a tragic memorial of her life, even if she managed to be buried next to Nathaniel. Thank God the church and society has a more tolerant attitude towards mental health problems today.

The last piece of the jigsaw. Armed with Nathaniel's name and date of birth and death, I contacted the General Registry Office and obtained the reason of death given on his certificate: unknown. So, it seems that not only did the Catchpoles have to deal with the horror of losing their baby too early, they received no explanation for it. Perhaps it was Cot Death? It wouldn't have been recognised as a cause back then, but it could explain why a doctor found no physical explanation for his death.

Well, I'm exhausted so will hit the sack now. We're all crossing our fingers for tomorrow. Take care, give baby a kiss from me, and hopefully I'll see you on Friday,

Harry xxx

I look up from the lap-top, stunned. Thanks to the detective work of Seb, Harry and a helpful vicar, we have identities for the protagonists of Kath's tale: William, Maud and Nathaniel Catchpole, and more idea of how they came to pass.

When Kath first told me the story of the family, it resonated with me – tragic, dramatic, mysterious.   Reflecting on it now, hormones raging and heart brimming with love for my new-born, tears streak my cheeks and splash the keyboard.   Imagine losing your child so young: the pain, the anger, the emptiness Maud must have felt.   It's hardly surprising Nathaniel's unexplained death deeply affected her. Who wouldn't suffer in her position? And yet, rather than being treated with sympathy and support, she was destined for the asylum.

I've no way of knowing whether Maud's spirit lingers in my house or whether it relates to someone else. If it's hers, at least I can understand why she struggles to rest and perhaps seeks to make contact with those who could suffer a similar fate. *But is she trying to protect mothers and babies, or is she the source of the danger?* If the latter, I should feel anger towards her and the threat she posed to my family. Strangely, I don't; I feel only sadness for her. Based on instinct, not evidence, I think her intention is benign, but who knows?

My head spins with the implications and repercussions of these discoveries, all of which I'll have to shelve for when I get a moment with Seb alone. My parents are shortly to arrive and this is not something I want to share: the origins and causes of our haunted house may be one piece of news too much for them.

Mum and Dad were emotional when I phoned them after I'd come round. Dad's voice was thick. Mum flooded me with questions, comparing the baby's weight and delivery to when Harry and I were born. I wonder how it will be tonight, them seeing their grandchild for the first time.

Mum and Seb were the first to push through the doors, Dad trailing several seconds behind.

"You all came together?"

I'm sitting propped up in bed and they take it in turns stooping to kiss me before closing the curtains to give us some privacy. Mum and Dad stand awkwardly, not knowing where to sit given there were only two chairs either side of me. Dad signals for Mum to take one and wanders off in search of another.

"Yes. Your father drove us from Chelmsford and we met Seb at your house. I know you mentioned it needed modernising, but I hadn't quite appreciated how much."

I'm keen to steer the conversation away from the property.

"Yes, but we'll get there in time. Thank you both for the lovely new baby card."

She smiles and Dad returns with a plastic chair. "We wanted to give you this in person." She hands over a gift bag. Inside is an envelope and two packages, one of which I hand to Seb to open while I take the other. Seb reveals his first: a lovely outfit, a brown corduroy pinafore with stripey multicoloured top and matching tights.

"I left the tags on in case you didn't like it – and I've got the receipt."

"Don't be silly – it's lovely."

My package contains a very different item of clothing. I hold it up, and many folds of white unravel. It's a vintage christening gown: the top layer is a fine netting, studded with tiny embroidered flowers and finished at the bottom with lace. The sleeves are puffed and elasticated, a small curved collar at the neck with three tiny buttons.

"It was yours, when you were christened. We thought you might like to use it for …" She pauses. At first, I thought she was making the point that we had not yet named our daughter, but I see she is overwhelmed, blinking repeatedly to hold off the tears while she tries to finish her sentence. Dad, equally affected, reaches for her hand,

"It's a beautiful dress and a lovely idea, something Seb and I will talk about, thank you." My hands reach to open the envelope, the third gift, but my Dad stops me.

"That's just a cheque – we thought you might want to use it to buy a larger item for the baby – maybe a cot or pram."

"Thank you, we'll put it somewhere safe. A cot is a great idea," Seb and I exchange meaningful glances as I pass it to him.

"Now, would you like to visit the NICU to meet your grand-daughter?"

We make our way to the lift and across the floor to the NICU. No more than two people are permitted next to each cot, and I snap up the opportunity to have time alone with Seb.

"There she is, by the window in the corner," I point through the glass. "You two introduce yourselves – take your time, no rush. We'll wait in the reception."

A mixture of emotions sweeps over their faces, even Dad, who you might have expected to be desensitised by his profession. Initially there's fear, from the volume of equipment surrounding these tiny babies, then the glow of joy from setting eyes on their first grandchild for the first time.

I turn to Seb. "Let's go. I want to know everything that happened today."

We find a seat away from other parents in the NICU reception and keep our voices low.

Seb clears his throat, "Well, it was quite an experience."

"Who was there?"

"A man and woman from the Deliverance Team – both vicars – and Rev. Simon from St Margaret's and me. Harry met them initially, to explain what she had witnessed, but she left before they began. Obviously, they understood why you were absent, but I think they would have preferred to have talked to you, given you experienced most of it. Harry and I filled them in as best as we could."

"Did they seem surprised?"

"Not really. They took lots of notes – particularly the story about the woman who threw herself from a carriage on the way to the asylum and the loss of her child. I explained our investigations – how we believe the story connects to Maud."

"Did you show them where the wall was upstairs – the moving door, the crib, my journal?"

"Yes, and the photographs of the annex as you found it. I tidied it up a couple of days earlier, but they got the gist. I also showed them the damaged pieces of cot I'd kept. We took Nathaniel's crib upstairs and the exorcism was carried out in the spare room. We prayed several times. The female vicar leading it spoke to Maud directly: she said it was time for Maud to rest now, to be with the spirits of her son, Nathaniel, and of her husband, William, and to leave the living in peace."

"And what happened?"

"Nothing – so far as I could tell. I thought I could smell a faint herby smell after the service, but that might have been my imagination. They told me to get in touch if we continue to have problems."

I nod, letting it sink in. I was underwhelmed. It didn't seem enough. *Could it really be that simple?* I'd spent months in fear, came close to physical harm. *Would this be enough to rid us of the shadow over the house?* Only time would tell.

"Well, I feel better about coming home – I just hope it's worked." I check the time – Mum and Dad would be with us soon and I had something else I wanted to discuss in private. "I've been thinking about a possible name for her..."

"And?"

"I don't know, but I thought it might be nice to have some kind of recognition of Maud.."

Seb balks. "You're joking, right? There's no way I could handle Maud as a name. Not after everything that's happened. I don't even like it!"

"No, no I don't mean that. We both liked Audrey, when we were discussing names. The similarity in spelling... AUDrey... Maud... somehow it just feels right."

His eyebrows arch as he tilts his head and nods slowly.

"Audrey... Audrey: yes, I like it."

CHAPTER 34

Bea

"**H**ave you got it?"

"Yes, don't worry. It's already in the boot."

I lift Audrey in her car seat and he locks the front door behind me. The breeze is a surprise for Audrey, stirring from her scrunched up sleep, her body wriggling with this new sensation on her skin. Seb strokes her cheek gently and after emitting a few guttural grunts, she falls back to sleep. I never had any doubt that he'd make a fantastic dad, but watching this tenderness starts me weeping, again. He looks at me quizzically and I laugh. I can't seem to control my emotions at the moment; they veer one way then turn sharply in the opposite direction. Hormones have a lot to answer for. I'm hoping to find more stability after today.

Seb has done an amazing job with Nathaniel's crib. He arranged for a plaque to be inscribed and has hammered it onto the side, treating the wood with weatherproof varnish. At the bottom he drilled holes to make sure water could drain for the plants that will grow inside.

The condition of an aged crib, converted to plant container, is probably not at the forefront of most new parents' minds in the first few weeks after they leave hospital with a new-born baby. However, concerns for the safety of our child, once in the confines of our home, are numerous and extraordinary. No doubt we will worry about how well Audrey feeds, any sign of nappy rash and the difficulties she has settling at night. Her first fever, the times she gags on her milk, and every cry will unsettle us, just as they worry all new parents. But fear of the supernatural - unnerving sounds, haunting smells – unanticipated and sometimes violent consequences of a presence in our house – are not the normal concerns of an average new parent.

But perhaps we have no reason to be concerned anymore. The house certainly feels different since I've returned: brighter, lighter in atmosphere. I hope it's not just wishful thinking, the anticipation of success after the exorcism. It helps that Harry says she feels calmer here. Although she's returned to Mum and Dad's, she's visited us a few times since the exorcism and has noticed a difference. And, of course, if the problems were to return – scratching sounds, moving doors and smells, to name a few – Harry would be more receptive to them, given her pregnancy.

We're on our way to a memorial service for Maud, to be conducted by Rev. Simon at St Margaret's. I buckle up as Seb checks and re-checks the car seat is nestled properly in the cradle of the rear seat-belt. Before he starts the engine, I reach across to squeeze his knee.

He takes the gearstick, checks the rear-view mirror and rolls into reverse and then out of the car-park. I twist round, conscious I've not heard or seen Audrey for several minutes, a rare occurrence since she's been born. All I can see is the back of her car-seat, her face shielded from my view. My stomach tightens.

"Don't worry, I can see her face in the baby mirror. She's breathing and sleeping. All's well."

With this reassurance, I relax, allow myself to succumb to the hypnotic effect of motion and peace. I have to nap when I can these days. I remember the last time I fell asleep next to Seb driving. The journey from Greenwich to Suffolk in the winter. A different season, a new family – it feels like a lifetime ago. I think back to the struggles I had then, coming to terms with my pregnancy. I'm in a different place now, more confident about us as a family, me as a mother. I don't know all the answers yet, but I'm ready to find out. It all feels manageable. Perhaps that's one positive impact of what's happened here: once you've experienced true fear, a total inability to control things around you, you're better prepared to deal with situations you can at least partially control.

I stir as the car slows down. We turn into the church car park. Audrey senses the change in motion and starts to make the noises that precede a cry. She doesn't give us much of a chance. In the time it takes me to clamber into the back and release her from the car seat, and for Seb to rescue the changing bag from the boot, she's worked herself into a frenzy. I barely register Seb telling me he'll try to find the vicar; I can only focus on her and her need for milk.

Too late I realise my position is poorly supported. Audrey is latched on and sucking with determination, as though deprived of food for days. But her enthusiasm backfires: the milk emits too fast and she gags as it squirts in her face. Enraged by the experience, and, it seems, by my chuckling reaction, she cries again. I gently support her, nose to nipple, and she suctions on, her need for milk surpassing her indignation.

Just as she falls into a satiated doze, Seb returns to the car. Thankfully Rev. Simon lingers by the gate to the church. I haven't yet mastered the art of holding Audrey while jiggling boob back into place and refastening bra, without exposing vast amounts of flesh.

Seb stoops to my window. "Good to go?"

"Yes. If you put the pram together, I'll settle her inside and you can carry the crib. With a bit of luck, she may have had enough milk to sleep through."

As smoothly as I can, I transfer Audrey to the pram, wrapping the strap through her legs and across her tummy. It feels warm, but probably not enough for her, so I wrap an extra blanket around her tiny frame. She stirs, but hopefully the movement of the wheels over the pavement will soon lull her back to sleep.

"Good afternoon. Beatrice and Audrey, I'm guessing?" Rev. Simon introduces himself - a smiling, short, round-faced man, formally dressed. He shakes my hand firmly and peers into the pram.

"Pleased to meet you both and warmest congratulations. Shall we make our way to Maud's resting place?"

Rev. Simon leads the way. As I cross the graveyard, I'm struck by the significance of the occasion. I come here as a mother, overwhelmed with love for her new baby, to acknowledge the life and death of another mother, whose love no doubt burned just as bright for the child she bore and lost.

It feels like a blessed coincidence when Rev. Simon's pace slows and comes to a standstill beside a plot more bathed in sunlight than any other in the graveyard. It was exactly as I pictured in my mind: the simple curve of the headstones for William and Nathaniel, the surface weather-worn and partially covered with lichen and moss. Next to stone recognition of father and son, Seb lowers the beautifully restored crib, crammed with blooms of purple, gold and white spilling over the wooden sides. The grain of the oak is visible, the surface glossy and smooth. The initials "N.C" are still visible, but the side bears the brass plaque:

Maud Catchpole

1.2.1841 - 30.10.1867

Wife and Mother

Rest in Peace

"I know they wouldn't have used the short-form date... not in Victorian times... but we couldn't fit it in the longhand version," Seb says apologetically. "Chrysanthemums are supposed to represent motherhood, apparently"

I put my arm around his waist. He's gone to so much effort, for Maud and for me. "It's perfect. You've done a fantastic job. Thank you."

The words of the simple service wash over me as I focus on the picture I've painted of Maud in my mind, the pain of her loss beyond any I could imagine. Seb reaches for my hand as my cheeks dampen with tears of respect. But as Rev Simon makes the sign of the cross and we murmur Amen, I'm left not with sadness but a sense of peace. It glows inside, warm like the sun on our bowed heads.

We walk back to the car, silent but satisfied. Today, in this graveyard, marked on her precious son's crib, we've given Maud the remembrance she deserved.

To be recognised as a loving mother.

To be remembered next to her family, forever more.

EPILOGUE - MAUD

They came with their crosses and prayers, calling my name.

Their speeches and actions suggested I was the root of the danger. Fools! They were blind and unwitting of my work; my duty that had kept me tied to the farm. I waited. I watched. Only then did I intervene, seeking to protect the unborn and their mothers. Tirelessly I had fought to keep them safe from the evil within those walls.

Once they beckoned, those who sought to banish me, I was powerless. Their words broke my tether, released me from the farm, my home before and after the date of my passing. Unfettered, I roamed the landscape, lost without purpose, invisible yet present. My voice was the wind rippling through the leaves, my touch was the breath of breeze upon your skin, my fragrance the herb of protection.

It was later when the minister's words, uttered by the gravestone of my husband and son, drew me towards the celestial light raining down on my beloved's crib. Well-intentioned sentiments of sanctuary, of rest, of recognition. There I dissolved in the golden rays, peaceful, my time on Earth complete.

Vanquished from the farm yet reunited with my son, I bear the dwellers no grudge, but who will keep watch for them now?

AUTHOR'S NOTE

You may be wondering, as I often do when reading similar novels, how much of this story is based on real people and places. The answer is: more than you'd imagine and perhaps more than will make you feel comfortable.

When I was about eight or nine, my aunt and uncle moved to a cottage in Ubbeston, Suffolk, the house that inspired Oak Tree Farm. My aunt and uncle both had strange experiences while they lived there, associated with one of the bedrooms upstairs in particular, where they felt like they were being watched. I have deliberately avoided speaking to them about it for the purposes of writing this book as I wanted to work from the memories that made such an impression on me as a child. My recollection is that they discovered that the upstairs and downstairs measurements of their house didn't match, and when they drilled through the wall of the staircase, they found a tiny, boarded-off room, containing nothing but a black Victorian pram. They moved house as soon as they could afterwards.

I'd like to think that my memory is correct and that I haven't embellished what happened, given how it played on my mind then and still spooks me at the age of forty-seven. Even if my mind has played tricks, the hidden pram was a helpful stimulus for poor Nathaniel's concealed crib.

To be true to the local area, I have used real towns and landmarks in this story: Halesworth; St Mary's Church; All Saints of Wickham Market; Heveningham Hall; St Felix's asylum in Melton. However, the information about these places is not factually correct and I have relied on my imagination in describing them. The characters and story are also fictional, although I have carried out research to make them as believable as I can.

ACKNOWLEDGEMENTS

Thank you to everyone who has supported me in writing this book, in particular my first readers who gave invaluable feedback: Julie Waters, Zara Pink, The Novice Novelists writing group (Paul Walker, Mona Mobeen, Teresa Baker and Olivier Eastwell), Danny Maclean, Jagruti Patel, Iain Wheeler, Rosemary Hayes and Frances Cleaver. I'm grateful for your time and wise words.

Thank you to Elizabeth Barber and her writing group for reviving my childhood love of storytelling.

Special thanks to my amazing family – husband Mike, children Poppy and Barney, my mum and my sister Gemma – for your love, encouragement and belief.

Printed in Great Britain
by Amazon

40822529R00158